SHATTERED
Memories

THE
CHARLESTON
EARTHQUAKE
SERIES

1

DEBBIE LYNNE
COSTELLO

This book is dedicated to my husband, a man
who trusts God when trials come his way.
I love you. You are my hero.

And

To my four children, who innocently give me
fodder for stories.
I love you to the moon and back.

Shattered Memories
The Charleston Earthquake Series
by Debbie Lynne Costello

Published by Wakefield Press

ISBN: 978-0-9861820-2-0
E-Version ISBN: 978-0-9861820-3-7

All Scripture is taken from the King James Version of the Bible.

This book is a work of fiction. Names, characters, places, incidents, and dialogues are either products of the author's imagination or used fictitiously. Any resemblance to actual people, organizations, and/or events is purely coincidental and is unintentional by the author.

Edited by Lora Doncea www.editsbylora.com
Cover Design: The Killion Group, Inc.
www.TheKillionGroupInc.com

Acknowledgments

I want to thank Kathy Maher (Kathleen L. Maher) my critique partner who brainstormed with me, encouraged me when I needed it, polished this story until it shined, but most of all who prayed with me and for me. You will meet an old gentlemen in this story by the name of Gideon Sharpe. I fell in love with a young Gideon in one of Kathy's stories. Thank you for allowing me to use that wonderful character. Kathy guided me through Gideon's part in this book to keep him true to his character. A special thanks to MaryLu Tyndall, Laurie Alice Eakes, and Louise Gouge who have prayed for me and helped me in more ways than I could count. I couldn't have brought this book to fruition without each of you.

Thank you to Fran O'Donnell, curator at the Manuscripts and Archives Office at the Andover-Harvard Theological Library for giving me permission to use the 1886 picture of the church you see on the cover.

Above all I want to thank my Heavenly Father who has put the love of writing in my heart and given me the words to put to paper.

Chapter 1

Charleston, South Carolina, August 30th, 1886

"Why can't you have him arrested and demand our money back?" Olivia Macqueen frowned at her brother. It seemed a simple enough solution. She shuddered at the thought of once being engaged to the detestable man they now discussed.

Simon gave her a placating smile but his eyes didn't dance as they would if the smile were true. "It'd be bad for business."

Olivia shifted on the floral tapestry chair across from where Papa sat holding Mama's hand. "Why? He deserves that and worse."

Papa cleared his throat. "We could lose all confidence with our policyholders if they learned that one of our employees had embezzled funds."

Simon sneered. "You mean if they found out they weren't even real policyholders. This could ruin our family name *and* our business. I wish I'd never talked you into hiring Lloyd. Then he'd never have swindled us—" He stole a quick glance at Olivia, his eyes pleading forgiveness. "I'm sorry."

Olivia's throat went dry. Of late, it had been easy to forget what Lloyd Pratt had done to her. With the attention her brother's old friend, Drew, had been lavishing on her, Lloyd had faded to an unpleasant memory. "Nothing to forgive. He means nothing to me now. Besides, his unfaithfulness was actually a blessing in disguise. I'd hate to have married such a scoundrel. And I wouldn't have gotten to know Drew." However, breaking the engagement with Lloyd had angered him so much that he had taken his fury out on her, requiring her to seek medical attention.

"Drew?" Simon wiggled his brows, mischief playing behind his mock surprise. "When did you start calling Dr. Warwick by his Christian name?"

Heat rushed to Olivia's cheeks. Simon could be such a pest with his teasing. He knew very well she'd been calling Drew by his Christian name for some time. It was only around her father she'd avoided using it. Father had always felt the need to coddle her and Mother, more so after Lloyd had hurt her. No need for him to worry that she might have her heart broke again. "Do I really need to answer that, Simon?"

Simon chuckled, his eyes dancing. "I do believe my little sis is blushing. I think she's smitten with my dear friend."

Olivia pretended to glare at Simon. "I *believe* we have a more pressing matter at hand—seeing Mr. Lloyd Pratt gets his comeuppance."

Papa stood and paced the parlor floor, his hands clasped behind his back. He turned, creases appearing between his brows. The gray sprinkled throughout his dark brown hair softened his features and gave him a distinguished appearance. "Simon's right. We've got to handle this with utmost care. If word got out it *could* ruin us. And we don't know how many people he wrote fake policies for or what other ways he may have embezzled." He stopped and looked at his son. "How could we have missed this for a year?"

Simon brushed his fingers down his mustache. "It's my fault. I should have gone over the books with a fine-toothed comb. Any man who can't be trusted in one area can't be trusted in others as well."

"I suppose it would have been difficult to find missing

policies or false claims without knowing what you were looking for." Papa sighed and resumed his pacing,

"I should have suspected. After the cyclone of '85 there were questions. Remember we had several people claiming to have policies that we could never find? I should have investigated then rather than letting Lloyd handle it."

"He said it was just an error in the books and he'd taken care of it. We'd heard no more complaints. There was no reason to doubt his honesty at that point. What is done is done." Papa returned to his seat next to Mama. "Tomorrow, first thing, we need to find out which clients are without policies and get them posted."

Simon leaned forward, resting his arms on his thighs, hands dangling between his knees. "Do you know how much money that could take?"

"I don't care if it takes our last penny. I'll not have our good name in tatters." Papa shot the words back like the kick of a rifle.

Mama, who never involved herself with Papa's business affairs, picked up the fan suspended from her wrist and waved it in front of her face. Her dark blonde hair pulled back in a chignon set off her high cheekbones and her flawless skin. Olivia had been told often enough that Mama looked less like her mother and more like an older sister. Her beautiful face was now pinched with worry.

Olivia dragged her gaze away from her distraught mother and let it fall on her father. "I don't understand why we have to suffer for what that dreadful man did. Why can't we go to the authorities and ask them to keep the information private? Surely they would understand our dilemma."

Papa gave her a patronizing smile, and she knew if she'd been within arm's reach, he'd have patted her hand. "One thing I've learned in life, Olivia, is that if you tell someone your secret, it is no longer a secret."

"But Mr. Pratt should have to pay for this. It's not right that he walk away with no consequences and a large portion of our money."

Still leaning forward, Simon fisted his hands. "Oh, he'll pay all right and there will be consequences. I'll see to that. Did he think he'd never get caught? He's lucky that none of the people he stole policy money from have come to file a claim."

Papa stood and took Mama's hand, helping her up from the settee. "Enough of this for tonight. We're upsetting your mother." He gazed down into his wife's eyes with so much love that Olivia's heart hiccupped. Drew's face came into view. She imagined the two of them sharing that kind of intimate love. The thought of spending her life with the man she loved warmed her.

When her parents had left the room, Olivia leaned in toward her brother and whispered. "So, what are you going to do about this?"

Simon stretched and yawned. "Tomorrow I'm going to try to make sure every client has an active policy."

"You know very well that isn't what I mean."

He winked. "I plan to find the proof we need if it's the last thing I do."

Dr. Andrew Warwick left the hospital after checking on a patient and sauntered down Mazyck Street, unable to get his mind off Olivia, his best friend's sister. When they were young boys, he and Simon saw Olivia as a nuisance—someone they could annoy when bored. Then they grew up and Drew's medical studies occupied all his time. Simon took on responsibilities of his own, and they rarely spent time together.

But when Olivia showed up in his office last year

seeking medical attention, he could hardly believe this was the little sprite he'd delighted in tormenting as a boy. She'd grown into a beautiful woman.

Drew gave in to his impulse, passed Meeting Street and turned down Church Street, heading toward the Macqueen house. It had taken him almost the whole year to gain her trust, and he knew why. After looking at her injuries, her story of taking a bad spill hadn't rang true. He'd recognized the telltale signs of abuse even if she'd denied it.

Thinking about the late hour, he quickened his pace. He would continue past the house if the windows were dark. But if lights did shine, he'd visit under the pretense of seeing Simon as it was a bit late to visit a young lady. Having a good friend with a beautiful sister one loved was indeed an advantage.

The Macqueen's home came into view. Lights blazed from the windows, casting yellow beams onto the lawn. Taking the steps two at a time, Drew couldn't help but smile—the perfect way to end his night. He tapped lightly, and a few moments later the door opened. To his disappointment, Simon stood before him, a cocky grin on his face.

"Drew, how nice of you to come see me." Simon leaned his shoulder against the frame.

"After a long day at work, I thought your charming personality would brighten my evening." Drew grinned back and strained his neck to see beyond the slim body blocking his view.

"Looking for something?" Simon's eyes glittered with mischief.

The sound of swishing fabric emerged. "Simon Macqueen, have you no manners? Invite our guest in." His lovely Olivia looked as ferocious as an angry nurse when taking on an unruly patient.

"He's *my* guest. I may not want him in the house." Simon winked at him.

She pushed past her brother, giving him a playful slap on his arm, and smiled past him. "I'm sorry, Drew. My brother has the manners of a boar."

Drew sidled past his best friend. "Shall we put him out with the rest of the herd?"

The tinkle of her laughter floated on the air like sweet music.

"Just you try. I can still take you down." Simon's words followed the couple. "And let's not forget you two need a chaperone."

Drew snorted. "I'm certain you were the one yelling 'uncle' the last time we had this discussion."

Olivia intercepted. "Really, now. You'd think you two were still schoolboys, the way you carry on." She took a seat by the window and arranged her dress.

Simon elbowed Drew. "You heard my sister— behave yourself."

Drew took a seat across from her where he could easily take in Olivia's beauty and put an end to the bantering.

Simon was always full of himself. That was part of the fun of being around him when they were young. But right now, Simon's sister captured all of his attention.

Olivia rubbed her arm above her wrist. He couldn't help but wonder if it still pained her. Her hand slid down to her bracelet dangling on her wrist, and she fingered it. Why was she nervous tonight? His gut twisted. Would she say yes to his proposal? He'd planned a very special Friday evening when he'd ask for her hand in marriage.

He gave her a soothing smile. "I'm pleased you're still up. Seeing you has brightened my long day."

She lifted her head and locked eyes with Drew, the corners of her mouth lifting. "As you have mine." Her gaze shifted toward Simon, then back to Drew.

"I thought I was the one who had bright—"

Drew shot Simon a warning glare that stopped his good-natured friend midsentence. He wished he could be alone with Olivia, but that was not appropriate. Someone had to be a chaperone, but Simon was like a boisterous puppy.

"I'm looking forward to our special day Friday." That was an understatement. He'd been counting down the days eagerly. She didn't appear nervous now. His fear of her saying no was getting the best of him.

"As am I, Drew." Her lashes fluttered.

His heart stuttered. He loved to hear his name on her lips. He'd never tire of it. Spending the rest of his life with Olivia couldn't happen soon enough. She had to say yes when he asked her.

"Am I invited?" Simon teased.

"No." Olivia glared at her brother.

Sweet mercy, she was beautiful. Light brown tendrils escaped the hair pulled up into one of the latest fashions. Beautiful brows arched over almond-shaped blue-gray eyes—eyes that breached his heart and soul. He caught himself right before he let out a sigh.

Simon cleared his throat. "Are you going to just sit there gawking at my sister?"

Olivia's cheeks turned crimson, but she quickly turned to Drew. "Did you hear about the earthquakes that were felt in Summerville?"

Drew jumped in before Simon could remark. "I read an interview in the *News and Courier*. A Summerville resident was said to have heard a rumbling sound northeast of town, which was followed by an explosion that sounded like a cannon. But many are skeptical."

Animation lit her face. "Some are saying a boiler

probably blew at one of the numerous phosphate works, or someone was blowing up trees with dynamite."

"I suppose it's entirely possible that a tremor was felt. Time will tell." He leaned forward. "What do you think?" He already surmised what her answer would be.

"I think too many people felt it for it to be some sort of an explosion. Some say that even Charleston felt the tremors. That's too far for it to be anything other than an earthquake."

Simon grinned. "Well, it caused a buzz that will keep Charleston talking for a few days anyway. Maybe we'll get some more clients out of it."

Olivia gave her brother a look that Drew couldn't quite decipher. Simon only shrugged.

♥♥♥

The next evening after Drew's visit, Olivia sat in the parlor with her parents. She drew the needle up through the handkerchief she embroidered thinking about the camaraderie that her brother and Drew had shared the night before. "Simon sure flew out of here. You'd think he was late to see his lady love."

Mama peeked up from her needlework. "If the boy ever finds one. I'm ready for grandchildren."

"You can't rush love. I learned that." A shiver slivered down Olivia's spine at the thought of Lloyd. She'd questioned if she would ever fall in love again after what Lloyd had done to her. He'd definitely hurt her in more ways than she could count. The welcome thought of Drew quickly replaced the unpleasant memory. She smiled inwardly. She wouldn't mind giving her mother the first grandchild.

When she and Drew first started courting, doubt had harried her. As a little girl, dread would fill her when she saw him with her brother. The two of them together were as mean as cross-eyed snakes. Like the time they'd tied her shoes together while she napped in a chair, then stole her doll, woke her up and ran. When she jumped up to go after them, she fell flat on her face. The two laughed and disappeared with her doll. It took her the whole day to find where they'd hidden it.

Boys and tomfoolery must go hand in hand. Her brother now was a perfect gentleman, albeit a character— he'd never intentionally harm anyone. Surely Drew was the same. The two boys' pranks were just that, childish pranks. She hated the way doubt tried to nudge its way into her thoughts. She needed to keep reminding herself that Drew was a doctor and had taken an oath to help people. He was nothing like Lloyd even if she'd known Lloyd for years and never thought him capable of the things that he did.

"Your brother rushed out of here to finish up some late night business," Papa replied to her question.

"Did you get the policies written and posted?" Olivia inquired.

"We hope we were able to track them all down. Simon's gone to check on a few loose ends."

"Ouch!" Mama pricked her finger.

"Are you all right, dear?" Papa's tender voice inquired.

Mama nodded and dabbed her finger on a handkerchief.

Papa pulled out his pocket watch. "It's nine fifty."

Olivia folded the white handkerchief she'd been working on and placed it in the basket beside the settee. She stretched her arms as she stood. "I think I'll head to bed and curl up with *Pride and Prejudice.*" She waved her hand in front of her face to give herself some temporary relief from the heat. The sultry day hadn't been relieved by an evening breeze. The curtains hung limp as an unusual stillness filled the air.

She reached the archway and turned to say goodnight. A long low rumble drifted in through the window as if a heavily-laden horse-drawn wagon approached on the street. But within seconds, the low rumble turned into a terrifying roar. The floor rolled beneath her feet. She grasped the archway wall. The whole house swayed as if dancing to the horrendous thunder. The chimney buckled and bricks spit forward like a child tossing blocks to the floor. A scream caught in her throat. Papa threw himself over Mama, his eyes locked with Olivia's. Pain splintered through her head as her knees buckled beneath her.

Chapter 2

After returning home from the hospital, Drew made his way toward the great room in the back of the house where light spilt forth and his brothers' voices carried down the hall. Their tenors were so similar it was difficult to tell them apart, much like their looks. They often passed for twins. William's eyes, however, were deep brown where Christian's were blue, and William's brown hair was a shade darker than Christian's. But there the differences ended. They both had a strong square jaw with a cleft in their chin. Their eyes told the story of their mood. With a smile, he remembered how Mother used to say they could fight just looking at each other.

Drew paused and glanced behind him. He heard what sounded like a heavy train barreling down the tracks, heading his way. But there were no tracks on this side of town. The rumble grew louder as if the train would break through the walls of his home.

Continuing toward his brother's voices, he paused as vibrations crept up his legs from the floor. The walls swayed around him. Pictures fell from their hooks. Glass crashed in distant rooms. As if an invisible hand had taken a pencil, a line drew itself from the far end of the ceiling until it stopped at the opposite wall.

Drew yelled, trying to make his voice heard above the horrendous sound. "William! Christian!" He tried to dash to the room but was flung to the floor instead. He met his brothers as they crawled from the room. "Get outside."

Christian, his youngest brother, stood but was hurled back to the floor as it groaned beneath them.

William, the older of the two, glanced up at the ceiling.

"Mother, Father—"

"Go." Drew gave his brother a push toward the back door. "I'll go get them." He pulled himself up and clung to the wall.

"I'm not leaving you in here." William stood, holding his ground.

"Don't argue. Out!" He supposed it was the anger inflicting his voice that made William submit to his authority because his brother suddenly pivoted and stumbled for the door. Christian made it to the threshold and looked back, his hand on the knob. He jerked the door open.

Using the wall for stability, Drew spun around and hurried to the stairs where he found Father grasping the rail while half-carrying Mother down. The shuddering of the house stopped as quickly as it started, and Father straightened and lightened his grip on his wife.

Drew heaved a sigh of relief. "You two all right?"

"We're fine. Where is everyone?" Father's hand rested on Mother's back as he guided her down the last two steps.

"William and Christian are out back. I came looking for—" Before he could finish, the groaning returned with an angry vengeance, sending the floor rippling beneath their feet as if the wood were an ocean wave. Church bells rang in the distance, announcing the quake's return.

"Where's Jo?" Drew had to yell above the clamor.

Mother shook her head, her eyes wide with fear.

"I'll find her." He turned to his father. "Get Mother outside." With that, he wrapped his hands on the banister and took the stairs two at a time, wondering if they would collapse beneath him.

Rushing to JoAnna's room, he entered, a lamp and water carafe smashed on the floor. "Jo!" His gaze swept the room. Gas lights flickered.

She wasn't there. He ran down the hall sticking his head in each room and calling her name. Plaster fell from the ceiling and toppled to the floor. The house groaned its complaint.

Drew charged down the steps, bumping the wall as the stairs lifted and fell beneath his feet. He grabbed the railing to keep from tumbling to the bottom. *Lord, let me find Jo.* It felt as if the air had been sucked from his lungs, but he had to get to his sister. The drawing room stood empty. A crash sounded, drawing his eyes to the wall that held his ancestor's emerald knife in a framed glass case. The knife and case hanging on the wall had fallen on the old family wedding book case, shattering both and sending splintered glass to the floor. He turned and ran room to room, sticking his head in and calling for her as he went.

The house stilled as he reached the kitchen. He stopped. Distant cries and screams flooded through the open windows. Was it over or only another lull? His gaze darted around the room. Then he saw her—lifeless, on the floor.

"Jo." He ran and fell to his knees beside her. Blood dripped from an open wound on her head. She moaned. Without checking for other injuries, he scooped her into his arms and dashed to safety before the whole house gave way.

Outside, Mother let out a cry and rushed forward. "Is she…"

"I think she fell and hit her head on the stove. She seems to be coming around."

"I'm fine." Jo lifted her head. "What about everyone else?"

"Everyone's safe." Drew strode to a white iron bench that sat near the large magnolia tree in their back yard and set her down. He turned to his father. "I have to check on

Olivia."

His father nodded. "I think there will be a lot of people who need us tonight. As soon as I see that Jo has no other injuries I'll be heading out."

"Do you mind if I take the surrey rather than my curricle? If Olivia or one of her family is injured—"

Father threw up his hand. "Say no more. Go, she may need you."

Christian and William followed him to the stables which were surprisingly intact. They readied both carriage and wagon. Drew snatched an oil lamp from a hook and matches off a small shelf then tucked them under the seat. Christian heard the moan first. "Listen."

Olivia opened her eyes and couldn't move. The heavy wooden frame of the doorway had collapsed on her. She tried to turn her head, but that, too, was trapped. Burning fear raced through her veins. The ground had quieted. How long had she lain here? Were Mama and Papa injured? What of Simon and Drew? The faces of the people she loved and cared for flashed through her memory. *Dear Lord, spare us all.*

"Papa." Dust choked out her words. She tried to swallow. "Papa." He should have heard her.

She tried to gain leverage and push her body from beneath the rubble. The weight was too much.

"Papa. Mama." Her cheek pressed against the smooth wood of the floor.

She heard it before she felt it. The same terrorizing roar she'd heard before. Screams filled the air. She wasn't the only one who knew what was coming. The trembling of the ground started as if it, too, were afraid of what was to come. And come it did. Within seconds the ground shook so violently, she was certain the whole world could feel it.

"Papa! Mama!" She screamed their names with all she had in her. As the rumbling noise increased, the sounds of her home falling all around her accompanied the quake. Olivia gave into a sob. She was going to die.

♥♥♥

William and Drew stilled. The ominous rumble returned, starting as a low growl. No one had to say anything. Christian ran to the horses still stabled and threw open the doors. William and Drew pulled the harnessed horses and their burdens out. The earth quaked beneath them, roaring like a lion ready to devour. For a split second, Drew wondered if the ground would open up and swallow them.

A distant cry pierced the air.

"Lord, have mercy on us." Mother collapsed against Father.

The horses stomped and tried to rear. Drew tightened his hold. William soothed the teams with cajoling.

The houses lined along the street seemed to bow and curtsey to one another as the land rippled beneath them. Drew hopped on the driver's seat. These tremors could continue indefinitely.

"I'm going with you." William handed the reins of the other team off to Christian before clambering up.

Christian opened his mouth as if he'd argue.

"Father will need someone to go with him." It would only make sense that Christian, not yet a doctor, go with their father.

Christian gave a clipped nod. Drew snapped the reins, sending the harried horses into a run. The ground sunk below the carriage wheels, sending the horses out of synchronization. Drew pulled back and the horses halted.

"Maybe we should wait till the ground stills." William's hands clutched the seat.

"I don't think I'm going to get them to do anything as long as these quakes keep coming." Drew leaped down and spoke softly to the terrified animals, whose legs nearly knocked together in fright.

The quaking stopped as he crooned to the horses. With the ground quiet once again, Drew climbed back on the seat, and they slowly made their way down the moonlit streets, weaving around the throngs of people who'd moved to the center of the thoroughfare for safety. He thanked the Almighty for their well-being while rushing down the road where cries of anguish reached his ears. As they neared the corner, the sobs grew louder.

"Help me. Please. Someone help me. Oh, God, don't let my husband die."

Drew yanked the horses to a stop, and he and William dashed to a distraught woman by a collapsed house.

William pulled the woman away from a man pinned beneath bricks and mortar. He set her gently on the ground in a safe place. "Ma'am, stay here. My brother and I will get your husband to safety."

Drew dropped to his knees and threw the bricks and debris off the victim, thankful for the moon's light. The man moaned, his head thrashing side to side. William appeared and together they freed him.

"Can you hear me?" Drew leaned in near the man.

"Y-yes."

"We're doctors. Where do you hurt?"

The man gasped as he tried to sit up and collapsed back on the ground. "My leg. I-I can't move my leg."

Drew moved his hands down the leg. No bone protruded from his skin, but the femur was likely crushed. "Do you have pain elsewhere?"

The man gritted his teeth. "No. The leg is enough."

Wails carried on the evening's still air. Women's

voices. One of them could very well be Olivia's. He turned to the woman.

"His leg needs to be set. If you can find someone to take him to the hospital…" He suddenly realized he had no idea how the hospital had fared in the quake. "I must keep going. There are others who may need assistance."

"No." The woman rushed to her husband who clasped her hand.

"I will be fine. It's only a broken leg." He gritted his teeth. "There are others out there that may not have been so fortunate."

Drew could hear the pain in the man's strained voice and admired him for his sacrifice. "If I can, I'll come back this way and see if you are still in need of help. But I can't tell you how long that will be."

The man nodded and Drew and William retreated to their carriage. Even as the carriage rumbled over the streets strewn with debris, Drew could still hear the agonizing cries of the injured. What other horrors would they find down the road? Drew's stomach knotted and swirled as his thoughts rushed to Olivia. Sick with worry wouldn't do. He was a doctor—he couldn't be weak now. Not when half of Charleston required his help. Not when Olivia might need him. The thought gave him resolve.

The roads were nearly impassible with the brick and mortar that had spilled onto them. He feared they might have to unhitch the horses and finish the distance on horseback.

Most of the people had moved to the streets where no buildings were nearby or to the parks where they were safe from falling stones and bricks. They milled around in groups, some singing in an attempt to calm the terror set upon the people of their city while others talked quietly as they hugged and consoled each other.

The singing from the park faded as he reached King Street. The people before him in the street screamed and pointed as some new terror filled them. Drew glanced behind him to see the lurid glow of a city ablaze, looking as if heaven itself flamed.

A strong voice broke through the noise. "Repent. Repent, you reprobates. This is God's judgment come down upon us. Fall to your knees you miserable sinners and pray. Pray we don't become as Sodom and Gomorrah."

"We are all going to die!" A woman hugged her children to her.

"'Tis the Lord's return. There's nothing to fear if ye know Him," cried another.

People fell to their knees and begged God's mercy, while others openly repented. It was as if he witnessed Charleston's greatest revival.

Drew shook his head, wishing he could comfort these people and assure them that this wasn't God's judgement. "Now isn't the time to be adding to these people's fears. There's enough panic without preaching damnation."

William nodded. "I agree. He should be attempting to maintain calmness and assuring them that everything will be okay."

Not wanting to waste any time, Drew nudged the team forward. After several more times on and off the carriage helping the distressed, and after telling himself he'd not stop again until he was at Olivia's door, the silhouette of a man hefting large pieces of wood off of a collapsed building yelling for his loved ones tore at Drew's resolve. Maneuvering the carriage off to the side of the street, he and William rushed to the frantic man.

It was odd, how little he and his brother had spoken since they embarked on their mission to reach Olivia. The gravity of the devastation seemed to have stolen all their words. Drew sensed that William understood the urgency he felt to reach Olivia, and at each stop his brother stole a glance in his direction.

Putting his mind to the task of finding the missing family, Drew heaved a large piece of the cornice from the wreckage—and saw a child's shoe. Fear for the little girl's life stabbed him and he tossed off the remaining boards, uncovering a cubby hole where only God's angels could have kept the child safe. She whimpered as he gently pulled her from her prison and handed her to her father. He hugged her to him and let out a sob.

"Drew?" William looked at him over the destroyed home.

Drew stumbled over the mangled wood and hull of what was once a home. He made out the form of a body. He leaned closer and saw a woman crushed by a thick joist. He lowered his head and listened to her chest as he felt for a pulse. He shook his head. She hadn't survived.

"I know. We need to get her out…for him." William nodded to the man who'd set his child on the grass and squatted down before her.

They pulled the woman's still body out and carefully placed her on the grass. Drew made his way over and put his hand on the man's shoulder. "How many of your family were trapped in here?"

"Three. My wife, our little girl, and our baby boy."

A mewling broke through the surrounding noise. Drew swung around to see William coming their way with what looked to be a cradle.

"Is he all right?" The man stumbled toward William.

"Doesn't appear to have a scratch on him." William handed the wooden cradle to the father, and the little girl reached in to touch her baby brother.

"God has been merciful. Perhaps my wife will be

uninjured as well." His voice trembled as he spoke.

Drew caught William's gaze. That meant he'd not seen them pull his wife from their home.

Putting his arm around the man, Drew guided him to the still form of his wife. "I'm sorry. It was too late when we found her."

"No. You don't know." He fell to the ground and scooped up her lifeless form, drawing her to him. "You're not a doctor. You don't know." He ground out the words as he struggled to his feet with his wife in his arms.

He hated to rob the man of his hope, but he had a little girl and a baby that needed his attention. "But I am a doctor, we both are. I'm sorry to have to tell you, but your wife has passed."

A cry tore from the man's throat like a wounded animal. "You're wrong." He clutched his wife to him as if he could breathe life back into her.

William cleared his throat. "I'm afraid my brother is right. We're sorry."

On his knees, the man rocked to and fro. "You can't leave me, love. I can't do this without you." Another sob escaped.

"You have two small children over there that need you more than anything right now." William's words pried the man's gaze away from the limp form and urged him to look at his children.

"I need her." His eyes pleaded understanding.

"They need *you*." William nodded toward the children.

"Go to them. We'll find something to cover your wife with." Drew glanced around for a piece of fabric and caught sight of a drape.

Once they had covered the young mother, they headed once again for Olivia's. This time, after what he'd just seen, Drew determined nothing would stop him.

Chapter 3

Dust filled the eerily still air. The people had fled from the streets to the nearest squares for safety. The only ones who remained were the injured and those tending them. Another tremor had shaken them, and Drew was ready to crawl out of his skin to discover Olivia's fate. Panic had risen within him with each destroyed house they passed and with each injured or dead person that had been pulled from the ruins of a once-beautiful Charleston. Time and again they had to stop to move debris from the road so they could pass. Each time he contemplated unhitching the carriage, but he worried he would need it.

As soon as they arrived at Olivia's home, Drew's heart seized in his chest. The house had completely collapsed. There was no peak, no roof, and no walls. The house had literally been shaken to pieces. The top floor had crashed down to the ground, leaving nothing but wooden sticks standing. Tossing the reins to William, Drew leapt from his seat and sprinted toward the wreckage.

"Olivia? *Olivia!*" Drew yelled. The panic he'd felt only minutes earlier turned to terror. Gazing at the demolished structure, another frightening thought clutched his chest. "Simon!" Oh God, not both of them. "Simon! Olivia! Can you hear me?"

He closed his eyes and envisioned the layout of the house. They would most likely have been in their rooms readying for bed or in the parlor. He opened his eyes, and was reminded that the upstairs was now down. There was no door to open, just mounds of wood to climb up and over. Maneuvering his way over bricks and broken wood, glass shattered beneath his feet. It was a balancing act trying to remain upright as he worked his way through the rooms of the house. Finally making it to where the family met each time he'd been over in the evening, he carefully tossed aside anything loose, frantically searching for any signs of the family. Even with his eyes adjusted to the darkness, it was difficult to make sense of the wreckage.

Stopping to stretch his aching back, he stuck a sore knuckle in his mouth without thinking and tasted the metallic mixture of blood, dirt, and plaster. The pain in his back only compounded the tightness in his chest as his heart constricted with urgency and fear. He had to find Olivia and Simon. Lord have mercy, he couldn't lose either of them— or both. Drew dug frantically, William nearby. Time ticked by while every minute could be the difference between life and death. His gut twisted.

Pulling off a large chunk of bricks, his hand hit flesh. "I found someone!"

William hustled over. Together, they freed the body—a man. Drew held his breath as he attempted to see which of the two men of the house they'd released from this prison. Dust covered the man and with the moon diminished by a rogue cloud it was hard to make out details. He leaned forward. No breath came forth. A lump formed in Drew's throat. He brushed the white powder from the man's face, his hand skimming over a clean shaven face. He let out a cry of anguished relief—Olivia's father.

Guilt fought for dominance over his relief that it was not his best friend, Simon, dead in his arms. Mr. Macqueen was a good man and didn't deserve this fate, either. He shook his head, speechless at the loss. They lifted the father and Drew caught sight of a smaller figure beneath. After setting him on the grass, Drew hurried back to what had once been a settee, and to the other victim. He knelt down before the woman whose size and hair color could very well have been either mother or daughter, and felt for a heartbeat and breath.

Drew's chest cinched as he scooped her up in his arms. No breath came from her, either. He'd hoped that since she was sheltered beneath Mr. Macqueen's body her life had been spared. "I can't tell if it's Olivia." His voice caught.

William followed him back over to where they'd laid Olivia's father. He placed the body next to Mr. Macqueen's.

"I think it's his wife." William lifted her hand and placed it on her stomach. "She's wearing a wedding ring."

Relief surged through him, again. "Is it wrong to be grateful it isn't Olivia?"

"I think God understands." William's voice held no judgment, only calm steadiness.

Up until this moment, even as he'd worried about Olivia and Simon, he'd never truly entertained the idea that they were dead. Screams and cries could still be heard in the distance, a reminder that many families were facing the same fate. The odor of sulfur permeated the air and was joined by the faint smell of smoke. Filling the sky, a fire's orange glow backlit the bleak scene.

He continued to excavate the fallen structure, searching and praying he'd find his friends alive. If only they had some daylight to see better. He went through the demolished house, but the destruction was so massive—he had no way of knowing if he'd missed them.

Drew didn't know how much time had passed, but his exhaustion told him it had been many hours. Several more tremors had come. The last one had felt as severe as some of the first. With so many tremors continuing to shake the ground it was hard to say if he had a home to return to or if it looked much like this.

William straightened and pressed his hands in the small

of his back. "Drew, we need help. It's late, we can't see well enough with the little light we have, we're tired…let's go back and see how things are on the home front."

So his brother's thoughts were wandering to their own home, too. He knew William was right. They'd tried to sift through all they could, but it was too much for the two of them in the dark. Yet how could he leave Olivia if she was here? A woman, alone—what terrors was she experiencing? That is, if she still lived. "But she needs me…It's like I'm giving up." He threw a large beam full of nails out of the way. Life wouldn't be worth living without her. Surely she was alive. He could feel it inside of him.

William stumbled over the debris and put his hand on Drew's arm. "I know how much both of them mean to you, but if we wear ourselves out, tomorrow when the sun rises we'll be too tired to work. Come." He nudged Drew forward. "We'll get up early and be here at dawn. Maybe we can get some extra hands to help."

Drew nodded but couldn't bring himself to say the words that he was quitting. He tested his weight as he set each foot down, making his way out of the house and toward the carriage. They cut through the room where they'd found Mr. and Mrs. Macqueen.

"We should find something to cover them." Drew looked in the direction where they'd placed the husband and wife.

"I pulled sheets and draperies from here. I just don't know where I threw them." William held up his lantern and his gaze swept over the destruction.

Deciding to walk along the exterior of the home, Drew took a step toward what was once the doorway.

He stopped. "Did you hear that?"

"No. What was it?"

"I'm not sure. I thought I heard something." Drew

cocked his head in hopes of hearing it again. Did he want to hear something so badly that his mind registered something that wasn't even there?

William shrugged. "Probably some wood or plaster falling through as we walk."

"Maybe." But even as he stepped away and wood and glass cracked under his weight, and even as his feet met the soft cushion of grass, he couldn't stop from sending a glance back to the spot. Olivia was there somewhere waiting for someone to find her.

"We'll come back first thing."

Drew walked to what was once a large picture window and started tugging free the cloth window dressing. Giving it a jerk, shards of glass tinkled to the ground, a few splinters biting into his thumb. He ignored the pain and freed the material. He covered the two bodies of his friends' parents. It was time to go home.

William hopped up into the carriage. "I'll drive."

Drew shot one more look over his shoulder. He couldn't really make out any detail, just that the house was no more. His gaze was drawn to one spot and his stomach knotted. Putting his foot on the step, he couldn't heft himself up to the seat. It was as if an invisible force held him where he was—love.

"Something wrong?" William gathered the reins in his hands.

"I'll be right back." Drew grabbed the lantern, spun, and dashed back to the structure. Making his way back to the spot that haunted him, he knelt down and started moving boards, plaster and broken household items.

William called to him, but he ignored his brother.

He didn't even know what he'd heard or if he'd really heard anything. But something in him told him not to quit. A sense of urgency seized him. He dug faster. He pulled a

thick piece of finished wood back, probably part of the
archway.

And then he saw her.

A cry escaped his throat. "Olivia."

He cleared the rubble from her. One arm lay over her
head as if she'd tried to shield herself. Her body lay twisted
in an unnatural position. The rush of blood echoed in his
ears. His heart raced, beating enough for both of them.
Bending down, he tipped his head and laid it to her chest.
The steady patter of her heart sent a dizzying wave of relief
through him.

William squatted by his side and began freeing the
lower half of her body.

"She's alive." Drew cradled her in his arms, his throat
choking with a sob.

His brother threw off the last piece of debris. "Let's get
her in the carriage."

Drew hugged her to him as he carried her to the
carriage. He handed her off to William and climbed aboard.
Once he took his seat, William gingerly placed her back in
his arms.

His brother urged the team on, pulling the carriage
toward home. That is, if they still had a home. Again he
was reminded that their house could look much like the
Macqueen's did. But thankfully all of his family had made
it to safety. At least the last time he saw them.

He gazed down at Olivia. Unable to see the beautiful
features that he loved so much, he ran the back of his finger
over her skin. He leaned in, his lips nearly touching her ear
and whispered. "You have to survive. Do you hear me? I
have plans for us."

"Want me to go right to the hospital?"

"No, go to the house. Father is probably helping people
there, since the hospitals are most likely overflowing." His

father was the best doctor in Charleston in Drew's eyes. He would help Olivia as soon as they arrived.

Drew ran his hand gently over her hair. His hand grazed a large lump at her temple—most likely the cause of her unconsciousness. He pushed negative thoughts away. She'd be good as new in no time…she had to be. But where was Simon?

"Where is your brother, Olivia? Was he at home? Did we miss him in the ruins?" If only she could answer him. Relief filled his heart that he'd found her, and yet his stomach knotted at not knowing what injuries she'd sustained and not finding Simon. Should they have stayed longer and searched for him?

The carriage stopped a few minutes later and Drew looked up to see the fate of his family home. Oil lamps and candles lit the yard. Makeshift beds and pallets covered their lawn. But behind it all, his house still stood.

Drew stepped off the carriage, still carrying Olivia, and made his way forward, his eyes searching for his father. He spotted him squatted down attending to a young boy and hurried toward him.

"Father, can you look at Olivia?"

His father straightened and turned to him. "Your mother has made a few more pallets for incoming injured. Lay her over here." He pointed to a blanket on the ground.

Drew cautiously laid her down, missing the feel of her warmth as his arms released her. "She's been unconscious since I found her. There's a large lump on her left temple. We found her under a lot of heavy material in her house."

Father gently probed the nodule. Then his hands glided around the rest of her head, neck, and down to her arms. He stood and rubbed his chin between his finger and thumb. "From what I can tell, there are no broken bones, just a sprain. Internal injuries are hard to diagnose when the

patient can't respond to questions or pain, as you know."
His brows furrowed. "All we can do is wait and pray."

Drew glanced around at the ground littered with
bodies. "I'd thought to take her to the hospital. She'd get
round-the-clock care there."

"The hospitals are gone…all of them. Why did you
think we are tending to people here?"

Drew shook his head. "I didn't really put any thought
into it. My mind is elsewhere." His gaze shifted to where
Olivia lay.

Father laid a hand on his back. "We'll pray she pulls
through. What about the rest of her family? Do you know
anything?"

"Her parents didn't make it." Drew took in a deep
breath. "We couldn't find Simon. We plan to go back
tomorrow and search some more. But we don't know if he
was at home at the time of the earthquake." His mind
flittered back to mere hours before when he and Simon
playfully goaded each other.

"Hopefully Olivia will come to before morning and can
give you some answers."

Drew knew what his father was thinking. If Olivia
remained unconsciousness for days, each day that passed
made her survival less likely. "She's going to be fine."

Father smiled, but there was pain in his eyes. Drew felt
as if his air supply had been cut off. Father had his doubts.

"I need to get back to seeing patients. You up to
helping, Son?"

Drew spent the next several hours cleaning and
covering wounds, setting broken bones as best he could,
and checking new injuries as the people arrived. He, his
father, and two brothers worked tirelessly, trying to keep up
with the flood of patients. Every fifteen or twenty minutes
Drew would return to check on Olivia, but she remained

unconscious.

♥♥♥

Five days had passed. *Five.* And still Olivia hadn't moved. Drew hovered over her bedside, checking her vitals once again, murmuring prayers for her miraculous recovery. Christian had managed to go out and find a builder while he, William, and Father tended to patients. JoAnna had gone to stay with an elderly widowed friend who'd been sick. Mother was busy trying to do the job of four nurses.

Mr. Hunt, the builder, had come and inspected the house and declared it safe to return to. Although there was missing plaster throughout the house, cracks in the walls and ceilings, and loose bricks in the chimney all needing repair, those things could wait while much-damaged houses were rebuilt.

Once it was deemed safe, they moved all patients into the house. It eased Drew's mind some to have Olivia out of the elements and under their roof—but still she languished.

He could hardly stand to look at his father for the pity he saw in his eyes. Sometimes being a doctor had its drawbacks. He knew what his father was thinking. She was slowly wasting away. When in a coma, the patient lost the ability to swallow and cough. Those voluntary reflexes were gone. They couldn't give her anything more than water and a thin broth. And even with that, each time he poured it down her throat, he risked aspiration and pneumonia.

He knew Father was right. Every day was a miracle. He couldn't get enough water in her to keep dehydration away. His prayers seemed to fall on deaf ears. At times when he looked into her ashen, hollow face, he wondered if perhaps what the people of Charleston and Summersville were saying was true. This was God's punishment on an immoral society.

But knowing Olivia was a godly woman, as well as seeing children and babies as they died from this tragedy, he knew it was a lie being fed to him and others. He refused to entertain such thoughts.

Drew's mind wandered back to his biggest test of faith so far. Mother had come to him as he finished setting a broken arm.

"Excuse me, Drew. I have a patient for you to see when you're done here."

Seeing to a young girl, he tied a sling around her neck and gingerly slid her arm into it. He gave the mother careful instructions before following his mother to the new patient.

"What's the injury?" He asked as they stepped into the room set aside for male patients.

"I didn't see the wound, but from the blood on his trousers, I'd say a pretty bad cut." Mother continued on past the cots to a small room. "I put him in here."

Drew pushed open the door of the small room they used for treating patients before moving them into the bed areas. His patient sat in the chair.

It took everything he had to honor his Hippocratic Oath and not do an about face and walk out.

"Lucky me, I get to see you." Lloyd Pratt smirked.

"The hospital is receiving patients at their new location." He glared, hoping the man would leave.

"I would have gone there, but I couldn't walk that far."

Drew considered offering him their carriage. "What happened? It's a few days late for it to have happened during the earthquake."

Lloyd folded his arms in front of him. "I was helping a friend carry some things from his house and cut myself on a piece of broken glass."

Drew knew the man never helped anyone but himself.

The sooner he got Lloyd Pratt out of their home the better. He sighed and steeled himself to help him.

After stitching the large gash in Lloyd's thigh, he stepped out of the room and nearly ran in to Father.

"Drew, how much fluid have you gotten in Olivia?"

Drew pulled the door shut, hoping that Lloyd hadn't heard his father. But when Pratt made a production of hobbling out of the room, Drew knew he had. Suddenly the man collapsed. Drew saw through the man's theatrics, but Father insisted Lloyd stay overnight to make sure he hadn't lost too much blood. Drew gritted his teeth and helped Father raise Lloyd up, leading him to an empty pallet.

Drew knew he was up to something. Lloyd had repeatedly tried to see Olivia the past year against her wishes. The fact that Drew courted her didn't seem to matter to Lloyd. Drew kept an eye on him throughout the day, but the man didn't move—he just watched everything with hawk eyes. When evening fell, Drew made himself a pallet on the floor near the door of the women's room to make sure the scoundrel came nowhere near the room or Olivia.

He awoke the next morning as the sun peeked over the horizon, casting a brilliant line of dark orange into an amber sky. It was as though the Almighty was making all things new—from the fractured city, to the wounded all around him, to his own splintered heart. He rubbed the sleep from his eyes and cast his gaze over to where Olivia lay. Perhaps this was the sign she would miraculously awaken and assure him all would be well.

Was it his wishful imagination or had she stirred? Her position looked slightly different. He rushed over to her bedside and knelt beside her as he clasped her frail hand between his.

She twitched.

His heart stumbled. Moving one hand to her cheek, he leaned in. "Livvy, darling, can you hear me?" Lord, how his heart ached for this woman. As close as he'd come to losing her only reminded him how precious she was to him—more precious than the diamond ring he still carried in his pocket.

He patted his jacket pocket, feeling for the engagement ring. Somehow, keeping it close to his heart kept her close and gave him hope that she'd recover.

Her lashes flickered but didn't open. How he missed those blue-gray eyes that reminded him of the Atlantic after a storm. He rubbed the back of his finger over her cheek and imagined her smile trained on him, her infectious laugh floating on the air like music. How his worry would ease if only she would give him a sign. But she laid still as stone. Had he imagined the movement? "Love, can you hear me?"

Her eyes cracked then sprang open. She looked like a frightened rabbit as she blinked and focused on him. She yanked her hand from his. "Who—who are you?"

Chapter 4

Drew's heart swelled with hope of her recovery. "Rub your eyes and get the sleep out." He gently brushed the hair away from her face.

Eyes wide, Olivia flinched, looking ready to bolt.

He smiled, trying to ease her apprehension. She probably struggled to gather her thoughts. "Good to have you back, love." He grasped her thin hand, and lifting it to his lips he kissed it.

She tugged her hand back and clasped the other over it. Her gaze darted around the room. "Please...who are you and how did I get here?" Her gravelly voice bared witness to her condition.

Drew reached beside where she lay and picked up the carafe to fill her glass. He coaxed her to drink as he held the water to her lips. She must be dazed and not realize what she was saying. "You've had me worried out of my mind, love. You're at my parent's home. We've made it into a temporary hospital."

"Why-why do you keep calling me that?" She edged toward the far side of the cot and winced.

"Livvy, it's me." He waved his hand in front of her face to see if she could see it. She flinched and looked back at him. Thankfully she didn't have vision problems. But uneasiness filled him. "Don't you recognize me?"

She shook her head and grasped the sheet, pulling it up to her chin, her bottom lip trembling.

His heart cinched. Didn't she remember him? He loved her. She loved him. How could she not remember? "It's me, Drew."

She seemed to study his face. "Drew Warwick?" Her

hands loosened their grasp on the sheet, sending a flood of pink through her white knuckles.

Joy surged through him. He grinned. "The one and only. Do you know how much I've missed you?"

"Can I have another drink? I'm extremely thirsty." Her eyes went to the water in his hands and she gave him a puzzled look. "Why did you miss me?"

He brought the glass to her lips and tipped it. A trickle of water glistened down her chin. She'd lost so much weight that the once-fine bone structure of her lovely face now looked hollow and sharp. "You've been unconscious for over a week. I was beginning to wonder if you'd come out of it."

Beautiful blue-gray eyes stared up at him from her gaunt face. "What happened? Why am I here?"

"We had an earthquake. I've never seen the likes of it. Even the cyclone of last year can't compare to the devastation that this quake caused. Charleston is barely recognizable. The Lord was with me because with only the light of a lantern I found you under debris from your house."

"My house? What of Mama and Papa and Simon? Where are they?" She tried to sit up, but her face twisted in pain.

He couldn't tell her that she'd lost her parents and Simon was still missing. Not yet—it would be a shock to her delicate system. She needed time to digest what he'd already told her. "You just rest. Very few people are staying in their homes. We're still experiencing tremors—several a day. The acting mayor, William Huger, is assessing the damage now and plans to have housing up for all who need it. Right now, it's near impossible to find anyone."

A tear slipped out of the corner of her eye, making a trail across her temple and disappearing into her hair.

Drew reached out and with the back of his finger wiped it away. "Don't cry, love. We'll get through this."

"You shouldn't call me that. Lloyd wouldn't like it." Her eyes widened. "Have you seen him? Have you seen my fiancé?"

"Your fiancé?" Drew looked on in dismay as realization dawned on him.

She had no memory of their year-long courtship.

♥♥♥

Olivia stared at her brother's best friend. He looked as if…well, she wasn't really sure what he looked like. At first he looked as if she had spoken in a foreign language and didn't understand a word she said. Now he looked shocked. She cleared her throat. "It's been so long since I've seen you. You must not know. I'm engaged to marry Lloyd Pratt." She tried to smile.

"Lloyd Pratt?" He suddenly sounded hoarse.

"Yes. Do you know him?"

"I do. I'm aware of who he is, though I don't know him well." His Adam's apple bobbed as if he tried to swallow something down. "But did you just say you're *engaged* to him?"

Why did he wince? Suddenly she was worried for him. "Are you all right? You don't look well."

Her mind raced to a troubling conclusion. *Oh Lord, please no.* "Lloyd…he's not…not dead is he?" Dryness returned to her throat. She grasped the water he still held in his hand and sloshed it as she pulled it to her mouth. Her hands trembled. Water fell on the sheets, dotting the white fabric with light gray drops. She gulped the water and forced herself to meet his gaze when he told her.

"Lloyd Pratt is alive." His brows furrowed.

If she didn't know better, she'd say he looked angry. But that was silly to think that such a question would anger him. He'd said himself he didn't know Lloyd well. His strange reaction didn't matter. What was important was that Lloyd was alive. "Thank the good Lord."

"Indeed." His gaze met hers.

"Do you know how I might reach him? I'd like to see him."

For some reason, he looked like a scolded puppy. He pushed himself up and glanced around. "I have to check on a few patients. Then I'll see what I can do."

Olivia gazed around for the first time. She must be in the Warwick's house, and it appeared they were all attending to men and women on cots and pallets in the two rooms. The sleeping area she and other women were housed in looked to be the great room without the furniture. Pallets and beds were arranged in short rows around the room. Some were empty. Drew said she was unconscious for over a week. It was unbelievable.

As she lay on her cot, Olivia searched for signs around the home that an earthquake did, in fact, take place. As if to confirm her thoughts, the floor began to rumble. Her cot trembled like one would jiggle a small child's bed. Gasps filled the air. A small boy cried out for his mother. She scanned the room. Cream-colored walls had large gaping holes from fallen plaster. Several cracks in the ceiling merged into one large fissure, giving way to the thought the whole upper floor could come crashing down.

Her gaze sought out Drew. He re-dressed a young man's arm wound, seeming to have no concern for the crack above them. As if he could feel her watching him, he glanced up and smiled. Her racing heart stilled and she returned his smile.

Drew approached with a small stool. He plopped it down beside her cot and eased down onto it. "Did that frighten you?"

"A little."

"I thought it might. We've been feeling those daily. Other than some loose plaster coming down it doesn't seem to be causing any structural harm."

"It shakes like that every day?" Her stomach did a small flip.

"Yes, but we're safe. Like I said, the tremors aren't doing any more damage. I guess the ground is just trying to find its place to settle back in. When you're well and able to get up and around, I'll take you out and let you see what has become of our beautiful Charleston."

She glanced above her. "You're sure the ceiling isn't going to tumble down?"

"We had it looked over thoroughly before we moved the injured in here. As long as we don't get another big one, I think we're safe."

"Is that possible? Another huge earthquake?"

He patted her hand. "Only God knows the answer to that. But from what little I've heard, they don't expect any more."

She pulled her hand away, knowing her fiancé would never approve. "How can I find Lloyd?"

He pulled his hand back and rested his forearms on his thighs as he leaned forward. "About Lloyd..." He took a deep breath.

Her head spun. He was about to tell her Lloyd was dead. Her heart sank as fear speared through her chest.

"You aren't engaged to Lloyd anymore."

A lump rose in her throat. "You said he wasn't dead." Needles pricked the back of her eyes.

"He's not. He's alive and well. Too well if you ask me." The last of his words he'd said under his breath, but she'd caught them.

"What's that supposed to mean?"

"He isn't honorable." He shrugged as his eyes locked on hers.

"How dare you. Don't forget that's my fiancé you're speaking so poorly of, and I do take offense to it." How could Drew—no, she'd not think of him as Drew anymore, they weren't children and he certainly wasn't a person she'd want to be close with. But how could he say such a terrible thing about Lloyd? Any man with an ounce of principle would never attempt to taint another man's character.

The muscle in his jaw went taut as he stared at her. He swallowed. "You and Lloyd are not engaged. You haven't been for a year now."

"Why would you say that? Of course we are."

"Olivia, I'm not trying to frighten you or make you angry. I think when you were hit on the head and lost consciousness you've forgotten a few things. I'm sure it'll all come back to you."

"I'm having no issues with my memory. I remember how mean you were to me when I was a child." She snapped the words out like a leather whip.

He recoiled, so she'd proven to him that her mind was working just fine. And apparently his was too, because he obviously knew exactly what she was talking about. Silence followed, but he seemed to be gathering his thoughts.

"I've told you how sorry I was for that. It was just boyish fun teasing you. It was never meant to be mean." Tenderness touched his eyes while wrinkles of concern deepened on his forehead.

She tried to move and winced. Pain shot from her ankle up her leg and down into her foot. Trying to adjust her body without moving her leg, she attempted to find a more comfortable position. "You never told me you were sorry."

"I di—" The corner of his lips lifted in a smile then

dropped. "You don't remember."

What was his problem? Her memory was fine. "Oh, I see. So whenever I don't agree with you, it's going to be because of my memory."

He cocked his head and raised his brows. "What's the last thing you remember?"

Why did he test her, and what did she remember? What did she do the day she was injured? He'd said he'd found her in her house. No recollection of the earthquake came forth. Surely she would have been aware it hit, unless it happened while she slept. Yes. That must be how it happened.

His voice broke through her thoughts. "Do you remember the cyclone of '85?"

"Of course. Everyone remembers that if they went through it. And those not here need only walk down the streets or see the damaged or destroyed wharves to know."

"But they were all repaired. Yes?" His gaze held hers.

Hadn't the Great Cyclone blown through recently? It seemed as if it had. But it all blurred together. She could remember the relentless winds, the water that had surged over the battery wall—flooding the city, and the quiet that had followed the storm…only to have the winds return from the opposite direction and cause even more damage. In the aftermath, the streets were piled so high with debris one couldn't get through them on carriages. Mayor Courtenay had immediately begun the clean-up efforts, but whether they had finished yet wouldn't come to mind. How long had it been since the storm? Her stomach twisted as she tried to put the jumbled thoughts together. The pieces of the puzzle refused to go into place. She let out a huff. "Mr. Warwick—"

"Dr. Warwick, but you can call me Drew."

"I do remember hearing you'd gone on to Medical

School. So you are a practicing doctor now I see." The knot in her midsection eased with the memory. A piece of her life fell into place. "Well, Dr. Warwick, I can't seem to recall if the clean-up was finished. I'm tired and my mind seems to be…tired, also." She certainly wasn't going to say confused.

He nodded. "Do you remember coming to see me in my office about an injury you'd sustained?"

"I think you're mistaken. I've never seen you as a doctor. I didn't even know you were one." Why was he doing this? It must be another of his childish jokes. He obviously hadn't grown up yet.

"I saw you after you broke your engagement off with Lloyd."

"You keep saying that." She narrowed her eyes. "And why did we break off our engagement?"

"You never said." He shifted in his chair, but his gaze never left her. The seriousness of his expression almost made her believe him. Almost.

"Just as I suspected. I never said because it never happened. I don't find this funny at all. I'm not a little girl anymore that you can pull the wool over my eyes."

He grasped her hand. "Livvy, try and remember. You and I have been courting for almost a year. Our first date was at the theater. Remember? We got caught in that dreadful downpour afterwards and we were both soaking wet despite the umbrellas?"

Frantically, she shook her head. "No. That isn't true." She jerked her hand back.

"Yes, it is. I took you home and you wouldn't let me leave until the storm passed. You brought me some of Simon's clothes to change into. We sat and drank hot cocoa, waiting for the rain to subside."

"No. You're lying." Olivia clamped her hands over her

ears. Why was he doing this to her? Tears poured from her eyes much like the relentless rain Dr. Warwick had just described. And yet when he called her that name...*Livvy*...there was something that stirred within her.

"I wouldn't lie to you. I care too much. You have to remember." He gasped. "Oh Lord, please let her remember."

A bristly cold tremor went down her spine. Stinging pricked the back of her eyes, and she swallowed the lump rising in her throat. She wanted to get up and run away. She wanted her parents. *She wanted Papa.* Papa always protected her—if only someone could tell her where her parents were. She was alone. The lump began to swell in her throat again and a tear escaped, trickling down her cheek. But Dr. Warwick said Lloyd was alive. "Where's Lloyd? I want Lloyd." Her voice burst out louder than she'd meant.

The older Dr. Warwick rushed toward them. Drew stood and walked toward the gentleman, meeting his father a few cots over. They made their way to the other side of the room out of hearing range. The two conferred for a moment. The father turned and walked away.

Resignation filled Drew's face as he moved toward her, his brown vest covering a white cotton shirt tucked into his trousers. Why did she think of him as Drew? It seemed so...so natural. She blinked. It must be from childhood memories or when he told her his name.

He gazed down at her. His jaw tightened. "I'll bring you Lloyd Pratt."

Chapter 5

Drew raked the patients with his gaze searching for Lloyd. A large archway opened the rooms into each other. Where had the rat disappeared to? And how on earth had he slipped by him without notice? Fine watchdog he was. Drew stalked toward the door that led to the piazza. If Lloyd had been in the house when Olivia had yelled his name he'd have come running like a pig to the slop bucket.

Trusting his father in this matter took all his strength. He didn't agree with him, but not because his advice wasn't on the mark. Father's expertise was invaluable, but the truth was hard to swallow when he was a man in love. To let her believe she was engaged to Lloyd took every ounce of his will power. He'd been tempted to follow his own path, but if he went against Father's advice and Olivia never regained her memory, he'd never be able to live with himself. Instead of forcing the truth on her, he'd let her discover it for herself. Lloyd Pratt would show his true colors. He'd just pray it wouldn't take long and he wouldn't hurt her like last time.

He shook his head. Pratt would take full advantage of the situation if he wasn't reined in. And Drew was the only man to pull back on the reins. Who knew how long it would take Olivia to see what kind of man Pratt was? He had to figure out how to keep that man from taking advantage of Olivia without her suspecting his interference.

What did she ever see in Pratt to begin with? He must be a master at deception to have taken her in. Before he allowed Lloyd to see Olivia, he'd set him straight and make it clear on where both of them truly stood.

The screen door hinges squeaked and the wood panels

crunched against the wooden lap siding. Several patients, sitting in chairs, who'd chosen to stay rather than go to the newly-moved hospital, jerked their heads around. Lloyd lifted his head from where he lounged in a rocker, a complacent look on his face.

Drew continued his trek toward the steps not stopping as he spoke. "Lloyd, we need to talk."

His nemesis got up and sauntered over to where Drew waited under a large sweetgum tree, out of the hearing range of the other piazza occupants.

Lloyd leaned his shoulder against the tree, taking his weight off his injured leg. Maybe the appendage did pain the man. He'd still get no sympathy from Drew.

A smug look splayed over Lloyd's face. "You want something?"

Drew sucked in a deep, steadying breath, hoping it would calm his nerves. It didn't. "Olivia's awake."

Pushing away from the tree, Lloyd winced as his weight came down on his right leg. His smugness disappeared and was replaced with true concern. "How is she?" His black brows rose.

Drew took a moment to observe the man who now held the advantage over him though he didn't know it. Lloyd's hair was black as the soot from recent fires and cut shorter than most wore their hair—almost as if to stand out or rebel. A short beard and mustache covered his dark skin from days of no shaving. And his eyes were as dark as William's. He supposed a woman could find the man attractive. Not something he particularly wanted to admit.

"She is doing as well as can be expected, considering."

"You mean because she's been unconscious?"

Telling Lloyd the truth was going to be the hardest thing he'd ever done. He'd find out soon enough. It was best to let Lloyd know that he would be watching over her.

"That and…and the fact that she has lost part of her memory."

Lloyd shoved his hands in his trouser pockets. "How much has she lost? Just the earthquake?"

"She's lost over a year of her life." Drew watched as the truth dawned on Lloyd and calculation began behind his scheming eyes.

A grin split his lips. He cocked his head. "So we're still engaged."

Heat like a searing coal shot through Drew's veins. "No. You are not *still* engaged. She'll know the wedding must have been called off. If it hadn't, you two would have already been married."

His lips dropped to a frown. He shrugged. "So we postponed it. Happens all the time."

Drew clenched his fists that hung down by his side, wishing he could plow them into this good-for-nothing's jaw. "Her memory *will* come back. So don't start lying to her. She'll hate you for it."

Lloyd shifted his weight onto his left leg and crossed his arms in front of him. "I'm sure you tried to tell her otherwise. What? She didn't believe you? Oh, wait. She would hardly know you, would she?" He sniggered.

Drew flexed his hands still at his side, running the one line of the Hippocratic Oath through his head. *I will prescribe regimens for the good of my patients according to my ability and my judgment and never do harm to anyone.* He prayed the Lord to grant him self-control to keep that last part. "She remembers me." Just not as a grown man. The thought made his chest cinch. "In the meantime, don't think I'll allow you to get away with mendacity. I won't let you fill her with falsehoods and half-truths."

"Don't think I'm going to let *you* tell me what to do. Remember *I* was engaged to her."

Reaching out, Drew grasped Lloyd's upper arm in a firm grip and glared at him. "Don't hurt her. If you do, you'll pay for each tear that falls. You understand?" He tightened his grasp.

Lloyd jerked his arm away. "Don't threaten me *doctor boy*. I'll meet you on a field any time you want."

Drew let him limp away. A duel? Those had all but gone out. He'd not heard of one since the Cash-Shannon duel in Camden. He may have no use for Lloyd, however, he'd never be able to pull the trigger. His conscience wouldn't allow it. Shrugging off the cold thought of consequences of such tomfoolery, Drew yelled out one more order. "Don't tell Olivia that her parents are dead. We don't know what that'll do to her."

Lloyd halted and glanced over his shoulder. "What about her brother?"

"She knows he's missing, but in the destruction and confusion of the aftermath, that isn't unheard of." Drew tried to keep up the faith that Simon would one day walk in, but he knew that just like Olivia's coma, each day that passed made the outcome less promising.

"Simon's dead." Lloyd swung his head back around and bounded up the stairs as if he'd suddenly been healed.

♥♥♥

Lloyd grinned. Sure looked as if fate had smiled on him again. First the earthquake stopping any inquiry and putting the only people who could send him to prison in their graves, and now Olivia had forgotten the whole sordid past. What luck. Yes indeed, fate had smiled on him. Well, he didn't really know if Simon was dead, but it was pure joy seeing the look on Drew's face when he gave him the news. And if Simon was alive, he was pretty sure that could be taken care of.

Hurrying into the house before the buffoon could stop

him, Lloyd slammed the door behind him. He chuckled. Drew and Simon were such good friends. Drew probably still stood in the same spot, shocked by the news. He glanced out the screen to see Drew reeling. How glorious that he had been able to be the bearer of such an unpleasant message. For almost a year he had to observe as Drew manipulated his way into Olivia's life. Well, it looked like those days had come to an end.

Olivia was his once again. His love for her still consumed him with fevered thoughts and angry, sleepless nights. Although there were times when he wondered if she were to give him everything he wanted if he'd still feel his driving need to have her. He'd only been protecting her from himself when he took on a paramour.

The memory of Olivia huddled in a corner after he'd lost his temper flashed through his mind. She'd asked for it by breaking their engagement. He shrugged off the soft sentiments attempting to turn him weak. Everything was changing and he had a whole new chance at life. If she thought they were still engaged, and with her family all dead and gone—or soon to be, they could marry immediately. Excitement coursed through his body as his gaze fell to her lying on the cot.

"Olivia, sweeting, I've been worried sick about you." Lloyd hobbled to her bed, remembering how she cared for injured birds and stray cats, nurturing them back to health. Every bit of sympathy helped. He'd gladly play her wounded pet.

♥♥♥

When the familiar intonation of Lloyd's voice reached her, Olivia twisted around to see her fiancé. "Lloyd. Oh, Lloyd. I've missed you so. I've been so scared and alone."

"I'm here now, sweeting." He opened his arms to her.

Olivia pushed herself up and grimaced. Her body still

felt bruised, but it was her ankle that gave her the most trouble. Pushing against the bed to sit up sent a stab of pain up her calf. She wasn't sure if it was from the pain in her ankle or the pure joy of having a loved one near, but tears streamed down her cheeks as she collapsed into his arms.

He sat on the cot and drew her to his chest, strong muscular arms encircling her. She was safe. He'd take care of her. She sniffed and wiped the tears from her cheeks. Curling tighter to him, she sought his warmth. Not for the heat, but for the comfort. She could get through this now that Lloyd was here with her.

Remembering his limp, she touched his leg. "You've been hurt."

His muscles flexed beneath her head in a shrug. "Nothing too serious. Holding you makes me forget all the pain."

Leaning back to gaze into his eyes, she caressed his cheek. Prickly whiskers grazed the palm of her hand. Her stomach swirled being back in the security of his arms. When she'd woken alone and no one seemed to know where Simon, Mama and Papa were, she had to admit she'd been filled with trepidation. But when Dr. Warwick kept telling her they were courting and she was no longer engaged to Lloyd, fear had burned up her throat. Now that Lloyd was here everything would be fine. He'd take care of her and help her find her family.

She glanced at her hand still stroking his cheek and startled. Her ring! Where was her ring?

"Is something wrong?" He turned his head and pressed his lips against her hand.

She should tell him. Her stomach twisted. She must have lost it during the earthquake. If the house was in the ruins that Dr. Warwick said, she might never find her ring. *Simon would be glad she lost it.* Her gut gave another twist.

Where did that thought come from? "I-I'm just trying to understand all that's happened. I've lost everything."

He took her hand from his cheek and squeezed it in his. "We should marry right away. I didn't lose my house. You'd have a place to go."

He was so thoughtful. Willing to sacrifice his last days of being single— But shouldn't they be married now? "What's today's date?"

"I've rather lost track of time. Somewhere around the tenth."

"Of?"

"September. I'm sorry I forgot you don't remember." He kissed her forehead.

Olivia frowned and tried to make sense of the date. "1885?" Dr. Warwick had said she'd lost a year. He hadn't thought it through very well if he didn't think she'd ask.

"I wish I could tell you yes, sweeting, but the year is 1886."

Olivia glanced up to see Dr. Warwick watching them, his face etched in pain. She stole her gaze away, trying to push off the hollow sadness his look carved through her. "But shouldn't we already be married?"

He shifted. "It had to be delayed."

"I don't understand. Did something happen?" She met his gaze.

He glanced away and for a moment she thought he might get up. Inside she pleaded for him to look at her, but he continued to stare off across the room where the doctor stood. His body became rigid. "I didn't feel I had enough money to give you all you deserved, so I postponed the wedding against your wishes. You understand now don't you, darling? I couldn't bring you into less than you had—it wouldn't have been fair to you. It's been torture having to continue courting and not to have you as my wife, but your comfort had to come first. I hope you aren't angry with me."

Her heart wrenched inside of her. He had to be the most thoughtful man. How could she be upset with him? She smiled. "I couldn't be angry with you."

He turned back to her, returning her smile. "Then there's nothing to keep us apart anymore. I'm now a wealthy man. We can marry tomorrow if you wish."

Her smile faded. Confusion still filled her—all of her thoughts and memories were more like a puzzle. What she remembered somehow seemed blurred by what she'd forgotten. It was hard to put all the pieces of her life together when a year was gone. How did one just pick up and continue on? "I couldn't marry until we find my family. They'd want to be there for such an important day."

He pushed back and grasped her shoulders, looking deep into her eyes. "What if they've died? You'd be alone then."

"I don't want to think about such a thing. Dr. Warwick said that many people are living in tents and temporary structures. He said our house is destroyed. If that be the case, my parents could be anywhere. They could be searching for me. That's why I need to get out of here."

"You didn't answer my question. What if they *have* all died?"

A shiver slid down her spine sending chill bumps to her arms and legs. He spoke as if he knew something. "There would have to be a proper mourning time."

He quirked his brow. "In times like this, mourning traditions can be overlooked."

Indignation rose within her at his callousness. "I'd never dishonor my parents in that way. I'd live in a hovel first. They are wonderful parents and when that time comes, they will get my full honor and respect."

His shoulders fell. "It's possible they have gone out of town and found a place to stay. It could be hard to find them. You can't wait forever. Especially with the situation as it is."

"My parents wouldn't leave me here not knowing my fate."

"They could have been forced."

"It would take that, but they'd come back." Her stomach knotted. Lloyd was supposed to make her feel protected and cared for, but instead she found herself wanting to run. An invisible force pulled her gaze back to where the doctor still stood watching like a sentinel. Why did that give her comfort? She should be appalled by his behavior. She met his gaze. Her stomach lurched and she sucked in a steadying breath.

"What?" Lloyd swung his head around, his eyes zeroing in on Dr. Warwick. "He *should* make you gasp. You can't trust him. He seems to have developed a perverted infatuation with you while you were unconscious."

Chapter 6

If evil could be felt, Drew felt it now. And the worst part about it was he could do nothing about it. The malicious look that Lloyd Pratt gave him made the hair on the back of his neck stand up. But that was why he planted his feet where he did. He wouldn't trust the man if he swore on a saint's hallow. He was like a chameleon— around Olivia he changed his color. But he was still a blackguard that bled red.

After the initial shock of Pratt bellowing out that Simon was dead, he recognized the lie. Lloyd had no way of knowing what happened to Simon. It wasn't as if they were on speaking terms. And he knew that his friend wasn't in the destruction of his home. Drew had taken his brothers and some friends and moved every board, wall, and beam. Simon wasn't there. And deep down, when he prayed, he had peace that his best friend lived. He wasn't sure what was keeping him from his family, but whatever it was, it was a good reason.

Shifting his gaze from Lloyd to the woman he loved, Drew wondered if he could continue the pretense he played while he waited for her to regain her memory. His chest cinched. The danger she could face put his senses on alert. Lloyd needed to be watched when he spent time with Olivia.

Drew lifted his chin. As a matter of fact, Lloyd seemed well enough to be released. That would take care of the dilemma temporarily. But what to do when Olivia was well enough to leave? He'd somehow have to make sure she didn't leave.

Lloyd's glare tugged Drew's gaze back to the problem.

A sneer lifted his upper lip before he turned and pressed them to Olivia's cheek.

He stalked toward him, bumping against the cot. "Excuse me. Visiting hours are over."

Lloyd snorted. "I'm not a visitor. I'm a patient."

"Not anymore. I'm releasing you. After seeing how easily you could bound up those steps outside, I've determined you are well enough to leave. If you feel you need more assistance, you can go to the Agricultural Society Hall. I understand all patients from City Hospital and Roper Hospital have been moved there and the doctors are providing full medical services to the community."

"I told you not to trust him. He's just trying to get me out of here so he can take advantage of you." Lloyd growled to Olivia.

"I'm trying to protect her." As soon as the words left his mouth, Drew knew he shouldn't have said them. Olivia looked frightened and confused, her eyes jumping back and forth between the two men, but not landing fully on either.

Lloyd stood and tugged on Olivia's arm. "You can come with me."

Drew intercepted. "No. She isn't well yet and hasn't been released. She can't go anywhere at this time."

Olivia whimpered as Lloyd jerked her to her feet. She swayed on her one foot, while she held her other off the floor. Drew pushed around Lloyd and scooped her up, settling her back on her bed. With eyes as round as a fifty-cent piece, she slid her tongue over her cracked lips. He didn't know how she'd managed to stay upright with nothing but a small bit of water and broth dribbled down her throat for the past week.

He pinned the imbecile with a glare. "For pity sake, are you trying to kill her? She's just woken up from a week's coma, not to mention her ankle is severely sprained. And you think she can simply get up and walk?"

She pressed her head down into the pillow and pulled the sheet up to her chin, hands quivering. The whites of her doe eyes revealed a growing panic. He lifted his hand to run down her cheek, but she pulled away. His heart felt like it was put in a vice. Frustration welling inside of him, he shoved his hand through his hair. How could one night, one earthquake, one tragedy, change his life so drastically?

There wasn't a time in his life when he felt so helpless. He needed to be in control of the situation. One thing he could do was see Lloyd Pratt to the door. "You can follow me. I'll have our driver take you wherever you need to go."

Lloyd sniffed. "How kind of you."

Drew wound his way between cots and out the back door. When he'd seen Lloyd off, he hurried back to Olivia. Her body trembled. Lord have mercy, surely she didn't have a fever. "Are you cold?"

She shook her head so slightly he almost missed it.

"Can I feel your head to see if you have a fever?"

"I'm not running one."

"Can I check to put my mind at ease?"

"Y-yes." Her shivering grew stronger.

Drew laid his hand on her forehead then her cheeks. It felt so good to feel her skin beneath his hand. He pulled his hand back and smiled. "You're right. No fever. And you're not cold?"

She shook her head again. That left fear or shock, and she didn't appear to have other symptoms of the latter. If only she'd let him wrap his arms around her—protect her. His hands itched to run through her hair, to feel her breath on his skin. But none of that would do. It'd bring her anything but comfort.

But there was someone who wouldn't frighten her. Someone who made everyone feel loved and cared for. He grinned. Why hadn't he thought of that sooner? "I'll be right back."

Dashing into the parlor, he found his mother sorting out a new batch of supplies Christian had brought home. "Mother, could you come sit with Olivia? She needs someone she can trust."

"Of course, dear." Mother patted the cotton gauzes and straightened. "I'm so thankful the dear girl finally woke up."

Drew threw his arm over his mother's shoulder. "There are some things you need to know. Olivia doesn't remember the last year of her life."

"Oh my." Mother's hand came to her throat. "Is it permanent?"

"We don't know. I hope not. But that's what I need to talk to you about. She doesn't remember me other than I was her brother's childhood friend, and of course those memories aren't too good. She won't remember you. And she doesn't know that her parents are dead and we don't know where Simon is. Father thinks that it's best if we don't try to make her to recall. Just let her learn things as she's ready."

"I understand, dear. I won't say anything."

He gave her a squeeze. "One more thing, she thinks she's still engaged to Lloyd Pratt."

Mother gasped and turned. Her hand came up and cupped his chin. "Oh, Drew. I'm so sorry. This must be breaking your heart."

"It is. But if you can calm her, Mother, it'll help ease my worry."

Drew let his mother go on to Olivia and he made his way to another patient. Adelaide lay on a cot writhing in pain and Christian sat by her side holding her hand, stroking it. The irony of the situation didn't escape him.

What were the chances that two brothers would each be caring for the woman they loved? Adelaide's blonde curls matted against her forehead as she thrashed her head from side to side. Drew put his hand on Christian's shoulder and gave a gentle squeeze. "No improvement?"

Christian shook his head. "I feel so helpless."

"I know." Drew gazed into his brother's eyes and gave him a sad smile. "It doesn't seem fair, does it?"

♥♥♥

Olivia drew in deep breaths in an attempt to calm herself. When Lloyd and the doctor had stood toe-to-toe staring each other down with those menacing looks, fear rose up inside her. Her throat went dry just thinking about it. The trembling wouldn't stop. She gulped in another lungful of air, but nothing seemed to help. The jumbled thoughts and memories danced around in her head, making it impossible to put the pieces together—not that all the pieces were there. But if she could understand what had happened in her past, maybe she would be able to put it all together.

The soft sweet voice of Mrs. Warwick drew her attention as the woman spoke to one of the other patients. Olivia glanced around at the empty beds. Once again she wondered how many had been used. Were they all full at one time? If so many beds were full in this one house, how many people had been injured, and were her parents and Simon safe and well or were they too lying on a cot somewhere wondering where she was?

Picking up a small wooden stool as she passed by it, Mrs. Warwick continued Olivia's way. Taking a seat next to her, she smiled. "How are you, my dear?"

"I'm doing better." She waited to see if there was a reason the matron came to speak with her.

"I'm Mrs. Warwick. The elder doctor's wife and the

mother of these handsome doctors you see working around here. And if you ever see a red-headed young lady wandering about, that would be my youngest daughter, JoAnna. She's helping an elderly friend right now." A twinkle lit her eyes and Olivia immediately liked her.

"I thought you might be the doctors' mother. Drew favors you." And he did with those dark brown eyes that at a distance looked black. But there was something else that niggled at the back of her mind. She just couldn't pull it to the front. She knew they were family. She'd never doubted that from the moment she saw them together. Perhaps it was from childhood when Simon and Drew were best friends. She could have met the family at some point.

"So I'm told." A smile lifted her lips and spread over her face. "I'm told William does too. Although, it's a funny thing, Drew and William are said to look like me, yet Christian and William are told they look like twins. When they were younger, people couldn't tell them apart unless they were side by side even though William's hair was much darker. Why do you suppose that is?" She patted Olivia's hand. "Oh, you don't have to answer that. Is there anything I can do for you? Get you something to eat? Brush your hair? Bring a bath?"

Mrs. Warwick was as sweet as her voice. Joy radiated from every part of her, making her more beautiful than she already was. Her loosely bound chestnut hair held highlights of silver. Deep set, dark brown eyes sparkled with kindness.

"All those things sound lovely."

"Let's start with some food. I'll order you up a light meal." She disappeared and within minutes returned with a brush in one hand and several pillows in the other. Gently helping Olivia sit up, she propped the pillows behind her back.

"There, much better. Now I can work on these snarls while Mrs. Benninger fixes you some vegetable soup and bread."

Mrs. Warwick ran the brush through Olivia's hair, carefully working out the matted mess. Olivia relaxed for the first time since she'd woken. Closing her eyes, the gentle tugs and massage of the brush lulled her into a sense of security. Her heart warmed and memories of her mother combing her hair floated through her mind.

"You have beautiful hair, Olivia. So like your mother's."

Olivia smiled. It was as if Mrs. Warwick knew she thought of her mother. "Do you know Mama?"

"Of course, dear." She stopped brushing. "I mean to say we've seen each other at different functions and events."

Olivia nodded. "Mama loves to stay busy."

"As do I. No sense wasting the days the Good Lord has given us. There's always work to be done for His kingdom." She stroked the back of Olivia's hair. "A nice braid, how would you like that? It should allow you to lay on it without discomfort while keeping your hair in order."

"Anything to keep my hair from looking like I imagine it did."

"First we'll get you some privacy and then get you bathed and your hair washed."

"I must look a fright."

"Nonsense. You're a lovely young lady. A few hairs out of place can't change that."

Olivia let out a breathy giggle. Drew, who was bending over a patient as he changed his dressing, swung his gaze her way. Heat filled her neck and face. She pulled her eyes away. "It is hardly a few. You're just being kind."

She snorted and Olivia giggled again hearing it come

from such a proper lady. Her gaze immediately went to Drew, who watched her in turn. A smile touched his lips. Once more an inferno crept up her neck. She smiled back and glanced down. Why did that embarrass her and what was more troubling, why did she think of him as Drew when she was engaged to another man?

♥♥♥

The smile that had lit up Olivia's face had sent a surge of joy through Drew. For a second he saw a glimpse of the woman he knew. Though she looked thin and frail, the smile that played on her lips gave him new hope. Sending Lloyd packing was the best move he'd made all week.

He glanced back in the corner where Olivia's bed sat. Mother busied herself trying to fasten sheets to the wall. He weaved through the cots, making note that some could be taken up. "Can I help, Mother?"

"I'm trying to give us some privacy so Olivia can clean up. Could you help me?" She handed him the corner of a sheet.

"Why don't you fill the tub and I'll carry her to the bathing room. I'm sure she'll be much more comfortable there." As would he. Otherwise how could he keep his mind on work? He glanced around at the men lingering on their cots in the other room. He wouldn't have to worry about their minds wandering either.

Bathing was something they had all taken for granted until the earthquake hit. Until last week they'd been without running water because it had taken days for Charleston Waterworks Company to make basic repairs to their main lines. Drew smiled. Always a silver lining. Olivia would be able to enjoy a nice bath and he'd be able to concentrate on work.

It had been tough ministering to their patient's needs with no water easily accessible. But the company pressurized the mains long enough for people to fill their water tanks, and Father heard that the water system would be up and running any day.

Mother scurried off, promising to return as soon as the bath was drawn. He should leave, too. But his feet wouldn't carry him away. "How's the ankle?"

"Sore. But mostly when I move it."

"Do you mind if I take a look at it?" He wished she'd look at him. He wanted to see her beautiful blue-gray eyes.

She stole a fleeting glimpse his way and pulled the sheet tighter around her. "I'm sure it's going to be fine."

One minute she was smiling at him and blushing, the next she was skittish as a mouse. What was going on in that head of hers? "If you need anything, I'll be around. Just call me...Drew...remember?"

She glanced up at him as she nodded. "Do you think Lloyd will be all right? His leg won't get infected, will it?"

Drew's muscles turned to iron. He ground his back teeth, reminding himself that she truly believed the scoundrel still loved her and that she loved him. "If he does what he was told, he should have no more than a scar to show for his injury."

She nodded again. "That's good. Thank you for taking such good care of him."

I'd do anything for you. But in truth, it was Father that had insisted Lloyd stay on. If he'd have had his way, Lloyd would have been treated and sent home the first day. Not exactly following through on the Hippocratic Oath he took. "As I said, if you need me, I'll be around."

Drew moved away as quickly as he could. He feared his chest had been laid open and exposed to her when she spoke with so much concern over Lloyd. The more that she mentioned her ex-fiancé, the more Drew found himself loathing the man, though he knew hate was akin to murder.

It was wrong, but he couldn't seem to stop. Thankfully Lloyd was gone. Now if he'd only stay away. But the gleam in the man's eye as Drew escorted him out told him otherwise.

A half hour later, Mother hailed him from across the room as she attempted to get Olivia into a sitting position. Father cut him off midway.

"Where is Mr. Pratt?" Father's tone was clipped.

"I discharged him." Drew couldn't look him in the eye. Not one patient had been released without a conference of at least two of them.

"Did William or Christian agree?"

"I didn't ask. It was more than obvious he misled us to keep himself around Olivia."

"We had an agreement, son. No one, not even I would allow someone to walk out those doors without at least two of us concurring."

Drew couldn't tell if his father was angry or disappointed. He glanced over where mother helped Olivia. "Father, I'll answer the rest of your questions in just a moment. I need to take Olivia to the bathing room."

He turned to leave, but Father stopped him. "I'll take her. You stay right here."

"She was nearly my engaged. I'm capable of taking her."

Father glared at him. "But she isn't and she doesn't remember anything except being in love with another man. A man you sent home." He poked his finger in Drew's chest. "That young woman over there is frightened and alone. And you sent away the only person who brought her comfort. And why? Because you are more concerned about yourself and how jealous you are than about her well-being. I love that young lady like one of my own daughters, and I won't see you jeopardize her health to ease your mind. Now go find William, he needed help with a patient. I'll see to Olivia."

Chapter 7

Lloyd paced across the study floor. Drew was a problem. With Olivia's parents gone and hopefully Simon too, things could be going his way. . Olivia might never remember the past year, or her memory could return in ten years or tomorrow—that's what Doctor Richardson had told him when Lloyd had paid him a visit to find out the possibilities. He certainly wouldn't trust any of the Warwick doctors' information. The less Olivia saw of Drew, the less chance she'd ever recall they were courting.

He walked over to his desk and tugged the top right drawer open. Gaping down at the black metal, he ran his fingers over the barrel before picking up the Colt. He stroked the firearm, enjoying the feel of it in his hand. He liked the way the double-action revolver made him feel powerful.

Drew Warwick had made the past year of his life miserable. He'd stolen another man's fiancée and showed no shame in doing so. The man needed to pay for his transgressions. If he'd only left Olivia alone, she'd have come back. She loved him. They were going to marry. But Warwick had to stick his nose in their affairs and turn her against him.

He laughed. Well it looked like fate had smiled on the better man. He put the Colt revolver back in the drawer and slowly pushed it shut, watching as the gun disappeared from his sight. No, he'd not kill him if he didn't have to. Let Warwick suffer like he did. Let him watch day after day as Olivia returned to her rightful beau—as they attended the races, balls, and the theater together. Let the doctor endure the same kind of pain he did. And let him watch as they became husband and wife. He chuckled. Maybe they should send him an invitation to the wedding.

Lloyd sauntered to the oval mirror hanging above the half table and straightened his tie. He turned his head both ways, glancing at his profile. Looking his best was important if he wanted to keep Olivia's attention. It was time to get her away from Drew Warwick. She'd been awake for a week—plenty of time to recover.

♥♥♥

Olivia hobbled and half hopped to the chair nearest her bed. A whole week had passed since she woke and her ankle remained sore. Rolling her ankle to ease out the stiffness, she winced. Gracious, she needed to get back on her feet and find her family. She missed them terribly. Even though Lloyd had come by every day to see her, it hadn't filled the loneliness that descended on her at times. And she couldn't fault the Warwick family. They certainly had made her feel at home.

Only a few cots remained scattered around the house. Funny, how one could be surrounded by people and still feel lonely. It had to be the emptiness she felt when she thought about Mama, Papa, and Simon. Her heart ached when her mind returned to them. They must be wondering where she was. They were probably every bit as sick with worry as she was or even more. They had most likely remained together.

She was the only one alone. Tears pricked the back of her eyes. She was tired of not getting answers from Drew or Lloyd. That was the only thing those two seemed to agree on—that in the chaos of the city it was near impossible to find her family. She pushed herself up from the chair and swallowed the growing lump in her throat. Well! She'd prove them both wrong.

Gingerly, she put her weight on her sore foot. She

could bear the discomfort. She hobbled to the corner where several canes rested in a rack and plucked one out. A little tall, but it'd do in a pinch. Pushing out the door and onto the piazza, she headed straight for the stairs. She attempted to brush the wrinkles out of her gown as she took the first step. Between her throbbing ankle, her weakened state, and not paying attention to what she was doing, she felt herself falling. Her cane swung unmercifully and her hand clawed the air for anything solid, but came up empty.

Scrunching her eyes shut, she braced for the impact. Instead of hard concrete, her body met the soft but firm body of…she opened her eyes. "Doctor Drew."

He smiled.

A warm tingling seeped into her body—starting where her body touched his. "I mean Dr. Warwick. Oh my. I thought I was falling, and well, actually I was falling, but I thought I'd be hitting the pavement and instead I hit your— well, I would have plunged to the ground if you hadn't caught me. I didn't mean to call you—it's just that I was so—"

His grin grew until his eyes sparkled.

Lord, have mercy please. She was rambling. She gathered her thoughts together. "Thank you for rescuing me."

Mischievous eyes peered down at her. "I'm happy to oblige any time."

Her tummy did a little flip. He was a handsome man. She pulled her gaze away, but stopped at the sight of a red bump rising on his temple. "What happened to your head?"

"I was attacked by a cane." He winked at her.

She reached up and gently touched the offending knot. "I am so sorry. I guess I wasn't paying attention. I somehow lost my balance and I must have swung the—"

He pressed his finger softly against her lip. It didn't

matter, because when she looked into his face and saw the adoration, her heart hiccupped and her mind went blank anyway.

With his arms encompassing her, he stood there gazing at her as if she was the most precious thing in the world.

"Get your hands off my fiancée." Lloyd stomped up to them, stopping inches away.

Drew never turned in Lloyd's direction and didn't loosen his hold on her or attempt to set her down. "Where were you going?"

"That would be none of your business." Lloyd's tone swelled with disdain.

"It's all right, Lloyd." She tried to sooth his ruffled feathers.

"No. It isn't. He has his hands on you in places…" Lloyd's eyes followed the line of Drew's arms holding her. "In places they have no business being. You're my fiancée."

Drew's hold tightened and a small muscle in his jaw twitched.

She didn't want a scene. And it was all her fault. What was she doing staring up at Dre—Dr. Warwick? Instead of insisting he put her down, she'd melted into his embrace. Of course Lloyd would be upset. Wouldn't she feel the same way if she walked up on him in another woman's arms? Guilt tore at her insides at the same time a vision flickered of Lloyd in another woman's arms. "You can put me down now. I won't fall." She turned to Lloyd. "Dr. Warwick caught me as I was about to tumble down the steps. I'm not too steady on my feet. My ankle gave way as I attempted to descend."

Dr. Warwick took the steps up two at a time and gently deposited her in a rocking chair on the piazza. "Now, where were you off to?" He took the cane from her hand and leaned it against the empty chair beside her.

"To my home. I wanted to start searching for my parents and Simon." She shifted in the chair trying to untuck some of the fabric that bunched beneath her.

"No." Dr. Warwick folded his arms, squaring his feet. "First of all, your ankle isn't strong enough, which you have just proven. And secondly *you* are not strong enough. Your body needs more time to recover." Concern etched each word.

Lloyd squatted down in front of her and took her hand. "Dearest, as much as I hate to agree with the doctor, he's right. You shouldn't be trying to walk around like this. I want you well to walk down the aisle as soon as possible." He lifted her hand to his lips. "If you want to go out I'll take you. I can carry you to my carriage and take you out to where your house was."

Where her house *was*? The thought of seeing the place she'd grown up in shambles nearly brought tears to her eyes. She hadn't thought about what she'd see when she got there. She wasn't ready to face that. She would much rather have Mama and Papa by her side when that day came—but how sweet of Lloyd to be willing to go to the trouble of taking her. He would make a good husband. He smiled and dimples deepened at the corners of his mouth. She'd always loved that about him.

Her stomach twisted. What was wrong with her? One minute she felt safe in the arms of Dr. Warwick, the next she was lost in the smile of her fiancé. If only she could understand why her emotions were so conflicted.

"Olivia, are you unwell?" Lloyd squeezed her hand.

"I'm sorry. My thoughts are so jumbled at times I can't get them together."

"Precisely why you are not ready to leave here." The doctor hadn't moved from his position and towered over her and Lloyd.

But Lloyd didn't seem to care or notice. He focused his troubled gaze on her. "I'll take good care of you, dearest, if you want to go out. I'll not let anything happen to you."

"You're not taking her anywhere. Not until she is cleared to leave by two of the doctors here." His fisted hands went to his hips.

Now the doctor was being impossible. She was a grown woman and could leave when she wished. Not to mention Lloyd was her fiancé. If anyone should have a say, it should be him. She didn't want to disappoint Lloyd or make him feel she agreed with the doctor. But before she could say anything, Lloyd stood up and spun around, coming face to face with Dr. Warwick. "I've had about enough of you."

When Lloyd's face turned mottled red and his hands clenched into fists, fear coursed through her veins. Her heart raced as tiny beads of sweat gathered on her forehead. "It's all right, Lloyd." She swallowed the rising alarm. "Truly. I'm suddenly not feeling up to going out.

♥♥♥

Drew was ready to take this out on the lawn. How could a true healer want to hurt someone so badly? Maybe this wasn't really his calling after all because he'd never wanted to put his fist into someone's face as badly as he wanted to right now.

Olivia's plea to Lloyd had run off the brute like water off a greased pig. Why couldn't Olivia see what kind of person he was? If she'd just remember why she'd ended their engagement a year ago, this whole fiasco would be over and she'd send him packing.

What he saw tore him up as he glanced over Lloyd's shoulder. She'd pressed her body so hard against the caned back rocker he was sure there would be an indentation.

White-knuckled hands grasped the chair arms. But it was her eyes that did him in. A look of pure fright. And he'd seen it before. A year ago and for many months thereafter. Until he'd gained her trust after a monster had shattered her trust of any man. Would she remember if he pushed things?

Another glance and he knew he couldn't do it to her. Not even for her love. He couldn't hurt her. He hated to back down to the mongrel, to look like he was intimidated, but he had to protect Olivia, even if it meant walking away. He spun on his heel and marched into the house, leaving her outside and alone with *him*.

Drew strolled through the house. Over half the beds had been vacated and taken away, giving ample walking room once again. The house began to look like his home again instead of a hospital. He stopped in the drawing room. The cracks in the walls and ceiling remained as a reminder of the tragedy, but things had been put back into a semblance of order. Walking over to his family's ancestral wedding book, he paused and skimmed his hand over the deteriorating cover. He picked up the knife once owned by Lady Brithwin, a many times great grandmother and ran his thumb over the emerald eyes of the finely engraved hawk on the handle. He'd have to see to the replacing of the cases for both items.

He left the room, passing through the dining area and into the kitchen where he caught a glimpse of his mother tucked back in the closet pulling out canned goods.

"Just the woman I want to speak to." He pulled the door open wider and leaned against it.

She glanced up from her stooped position. "What can I do for you?" Gathering several more cans and placing them in a woven basket, she stood.

"Will I be taking you away from urgent business if I ask you to go out and sit with Olivia on the piazza?"

"Not at all. I was just gathering food for some of our neighbors who lost everything."

"That's very kind of you, Mother, but you know there are soup kitchens set up all over the city. And canned foods are one of the few things that will still be good even if their houses are not livable. Of course, that is if they can get to them." He picked up the basket and carried it out to the long wooden table used for preparing foods in the kitchen.

"I know, dear, but I must do something for them." Three lines bunched together between her brows.

"Perhaps one of your peach pies or rice pudding would be a treat for them."

"What an excellent idea. I don't know why I didn't think of that. I'll do that right after I sit with Olivia. Maybe she'd like to come in with me and visit in the kitchen while Chloe and I bake."

"Sounds like a wonderful idea. And I'm sure she'd love to. If you need my help getting her to the kitchen, come find me." Olivia would never agree to his help unless Mother insisted and wouldn't take no for an answer. He could hope. The corner of his mouth twitched into half a smile.

Mother walked away. Drew slipped back into the men's sick room where Father looked up from examining their most challenging patient. They hadn't thought the man would live after he'd been crushed so severely. When the hospital moved to Agricultural Society Hall they had made arrangements to move him, however, his wife insisted he stay, feeling he would get much more personal care here.

He and his father and brothers had all agreed that regardless where the man stayed, only intervention from God would save him, so they let him remain and did what they could. Prayers prevailed and the man had regained consciousness three days ago. His recovery would be long and the man would walk with a limp if he walked at all, but he would live.

With no words spoken, Father went back to examining his patient. Things had been tense between him and his father since Drew had sent Lloyd home. His father's words haunted him daily. *"That young woman over there is frightened and alone. And you sent the only person who brought her comfort away. And why? Because you are more concerned about yourself and how jealous you are than about her well-being."*

But he did care about Olivia. That was why he didn't want her alone with Lloyd. He didn't trust the man. Father knew full well when she'd first come to him a year ago what injuries she'd sustained, as well as who had rendered them. He'd discussed the case with Father long before he'd ever started courting her. Why couldn't his father see that he was only trying to make sure Lloyd never had the opportunity to harm her again?

He loved Olivia more than life itself. Continuing on without her by his side was unimaginable. His hand went to his shirt pocket and he felt for the ring he kept there. He was going to marry her and build her a two-story house with a piazza that wrapped all the way around both floors. He needed her. And he needed her to remember. How Lloyd could pick up with her knowing she couldn't recall her past was not only reprehensible but unimaginably selfish.

Drew's worry was that as long as Lloyd lied to Olivia and kept up his pretense, she'd be content to remain where she was—after all, her last memories were of being happily engaged. Unless Lloyd showed his true colors. Naturally, he'd not do that until he managed to get her to marry him. And then. . .

Drew scrubbed his face with the palms of his hands.

Even if he could win her over, could he marry her when a part of her believed she still loved Lloyd? Could he settle for half her heart? What kind of character would she think he had? No. The only answer was she had to remember the past. She had to. *It was the only way.* As a doctor, he felt sure the longer that Lloyd hung around wooing her, and the longer she went without remembering, the less chance he'd get his Olivia back.

Chapter 8

Determined to do something besides sit in a chair or lay on her bed, Olivia straightened the medical supplies on the wooden lamp table in the small parlor looking for the liniment she needed. Leaning heavily on the cane, she smiled. Perhaps she could become a nurse since she'd enjoyed helping out the last few days. Most of the beds were now gone, but people stopped by daily to be tended. With the massive efforts to clean up the city, there seemed to be a fair amount of minor injuries occurring. Enough to keep at least one doctor home at all times, but today all three were there.

"Dr. Warwick, what did you say the ointment was I needed to use?" Olivia spoke the words to herself.

"Which Dr. Warwick, dear?" Mrs. Warwick's kind eyes peered back at her.

"Oh. I thought I was alone. But I was speaking of your husband, ma'am. It's confusing with so many doctors in a house."

The kind woman chuckled. "Why don't you call my boys by their given names?"

"It wouldn't be proper." Olivia bit her bottom lip. It *would* make things much simpler. And how many times did she think of Drew by his Christian name? Something she couldn't quite figure out.

Two of the objects of discussion walked into the room deep in conversation. Mrs. Warwick winked at Olivia. A sparkle lit her eyes.

"Boys?" Their mother called them and both men stopped speaking and looked up.

Olivia held back a grin. The two men standing in the

room—both at least six foot tall—looked anything but boys.

"Yes, ma'am." Drew spoke first.

"We have a dilemma. With so many Dr. Warwicks in the house, poor Olivia must explain each time I need to know which doctor she speaks of. Would it trouble either of you if she called you by your Christian names?" Her eyes danced with glee.

A grin spread across Drew's face. She loved the way his eyes smiled equally with his lips. Drew dipped his head. "I would be honored."

I would be honored. The words splashed up from a murky depth, casting ripples through her mind like a memory. She tried to reach out and grasp it, but it disappeared before her mind could reel it in. The simple sentence brought with it a warm feeling and happiness…even joy. She searched to seize the answer, but it was gone.

"I wouldn't want people to think—"

"You're like family now. You can call us by our first names." William, the more serious of the brothers, glanced at his watch before slipping it in his pocket.

"Thank you, William." Calling him that did feel more comfortable than she'd thought it would.

"And what about me?" Drew cocked his head. The smile in his eyes melded to an intensity of question.

"Thank you…Drew." Her stomach did the little flip it had done before when seeing him. Lloyd was her engaged—she mustn't let this doctor set her heart to wavering. She owed fidelity to Lloyd. He deserved her loyalty after he'd been so patient to wait yet another year for her. A year she couldn't even remember.

Drew raised his brows. "Is there anything I can help you with?"

"Your father a me to put salve on Mr. Dellinger's infected cut, however i 't seem to recall what it was I should use. I think it was oa k something. Does that sound familiar?"

Both men chuckled. Drew stepped over and pulled out a small glass jar. "You wouldn't by chance be referring to black drawing salve would you?"

"Yes. That's it. Thank you." At a glance, Olivia caught Mrs. Warwick and William slinking out of the room. Her heart sped up.

"Do you need help applying it?" His eyes locked on hers, a smile still on his lips.

"I think I can manage." Her voice betrayed her and quivered.

His gaze softened. "How are you doing? Really doing?"

She took the jar from his hands and her skin brushed his, sending her pulse into stutters. She ran her finger over the white metal lid in an attempt to calm her heart. "My ankle is much better. I can even put a goodly amount of weight on it. That is as long as I have the cane for balance. I'm afraid I'd take another tumble should I forget to steady myself." She bit her bottom lip to keep herself from rambling on like a ninny.

"I can see your ankle is improving by the way you shuffle around here helping everyone out. But what I want to know is how are *you* doing?"

She tried to swallow away the onslaught of sorrow waiting to betray her smile. Every day she tried not to think, just busy herself with whatever she could around the Warwick's home, whether it be hospital related or snapping beans in the kitchen. Anything to keep the ache inside her from showing. But the insightful doctor saw right through her.

She missed her family so badly it pained her. And as the days passed, she worried more and more about them. All of the Warwick men had been going to the hospital on different days to help out, and each of them had assured her they hadn't seen her parents or Simon.

But what if one of them were lying in a house just like she'd been, and what if they were wondering whether she was alive or dead, just like she wondered about them? The barrier broke and her tears spilt down her cheeks.

Warm arms surrounded her and she let go of all she'd held inside. Missing her family, the loss of a year, the fear of the unknown, the uncertainty of who she could trust all came out. His hand stroked the back of her head while the other held her upright. The pressure of his lips pressed against her hair. It wasn't right. She should push away. But the comfort she drew from his embrace tied her to him.

When every tear had been spent, she lifted her head. His shirt was wet with her weeping. "I'm sorry." She hiccupped. "I've gone and gotten your shirt soaked."

He gazed down. Compassion like she'd never seen overflowed from him. He looked as if her pain pierced him as well. "You can wet my shirt with your tears anytime. It's just a shirt." He lifted her chin with his finger and for a moment she thought he would lower his lips to hers. "You're more important than anything I own."

She attempted to step back, to put distance between them and to wipe the remaining streams from her face, but his strong arms didn't release her. "Still, I shouldn't have." She could see the understanding in his eyes along with the hurt.

"You still remember nothing of the past year?"

The screen door slammed shut. Drew released her as she pushed away. Losing her balance, she reached out and grasped hold of his arm.

A beautiful young woman with red hair stood in the archway.

Drew seemed to feel as uncomfortable being caught holding her as she was. "Olivia, I'd like you to meet my youngest sister, JoAnna."

Olivia let go of Drew's arm to face her. "It's a pleasure to finally meet you."

The young girl smiled, but concern etched her face. "Hello."

Olivia wondered if something had happened to the woman JoAnna had been caring for. She quickly swiped the tears from her cheeks.

"Did I come at a bad time?" JoAnna moved to the open archway.

"No, no. I'm simply overcome with missing my family and worrying over how they are getting along."

JoAnna, who looked to be several years her junior, rushed over to her and put her arm around her. "You poor thing. And I can see my big brother was taking advantage of your vulnerable feelings." She grinned up at her brother who promptly gave the sweet woman a frown.

The change in his mood sent a twinge of fear through her.

"Come, let's you and I go sit on the piazza. Fresh air is always good to clear the mind." JoAnna guided her toward the door.

Olivia glanced over her shoulder to see Drew brooding and watching them as they left the room. A chill slid down her spine. He didn't look happy with his sister. Was Lloyd right and Drew trying to take advantage of her loss of memory? His sister seemed to think so.

Yet, in the moment he'd made her feel protected...safe. But didn't the fierce look in his eyes also send a wave of fear? If only she could remember.

"Thank you for being so kind." Olivia hobbled out, leaning on JoAnna for support, having left her cane resting against the table in the sickroom.

JoAnna helped her sit and then took the seat next to her. "I'm sorry I've been gone so much."

Olivia cocked her head and examined the young woman. What an odd thing to say to a stranger. "I heard you've been busy."

She sighed and pushed herself back on the bench. "It's a fairly boring job. She's well now, but the poor woman is terrified every time we get a tremor. And the tremors are the most excitement I get."

Olivia smiled. What did one say to someone they didn't know and who walked in on a rather embarrassing situation? She'd like to ask her about her brother, but to ask a sister to betray family didn't seem right. If any of the Warwicks would tell her the truth she had the feeling it would be JoAnna. But she didn't want to cause Drew to be any angrier with his sister.

JoAnna seemed at a loss for words, also. She stared down at her hands. Olivia took in the scene across the road. The whole front wall of the brick home had crumbled to the ground leaving the inside of each room exposed. The sight reminded her of a dollhouse with its open rooms. JoAnna shifted beside her, drawing her attention back to the pretty redhead.

"Are you and your brothers close?"

"I suppose. They all like to think they're my father. I believe I shall never marry, for any man who looks at me twice has not only to win my father over, which I might mention would be the easiest of the bunch as he does wish to see me marry, but also must be brave enough to put up with my three overbearingly possessive brothers."

"They can't be all that bad." Olivia gave her a teasing

smile.

"Oh yes they can. You saw the look on Drew's face. Imagine being a man and wanting to court me and having to stare down three of those faces."

♥♥♥

Drew made his way down East Bay Street to the wharf to see if the supplies of bandages, splints, and laudanum had arrived from Wilmington. Thank the Good Lord phone and telegraph services had been restored in only three days and word had gotten out to the rest of the country. He couldn't imagine having no contact with the outside world. Not with all the destruction and chaos. How had people managed in disasters and emergencies without the technology of telephones and telegraphs?

Once the rest of the states learned of their plight, there'd been an outpouring of help. *The Courier and News* people had braved the earthquake and tremors, continuing to put out the news with little interruption, thus keeping Charleston up to date on the rest of the country as well as their own progress.

It was hard to imagine Charleston ever looking the same again—so much brick and rubble still littered the streets and walking areas. Businesses and homes were nothing but heaps of debris. Whole store fronts and other buildings were gone. The ones that had managed to survive had large cracks along the exterior walls. And still the tremors came, threatening to bring them down.

Would people ever be able to go to sleep at night feeling safe? Many still slept in tents and makeshift wooden sheds, which had been put up on lawns and in parks. Drew had read the newly-returned mayor wanted the population back in their houses and planned to have house inspections done to give the people confidence to return to their homes and a semblance of normalcy.

Charleston was strong. It would survive. They rebuilt in '61 after the fire raged from the Cooper River across one third of the city to the Ashley River. They bounced back from the war and the bombardment of their city when it was left not much more than a hull of buildings. They put Charleston back together after the Great Cyclone of '85 and they would do it again. This old city would endure. It would come back as beautiful as ever.

Drew sighed. If only he had as much confidence in his relationship with Olivia. The woman was never far from his mind. One minute he felt he made progress, like when he held her in his arms and she called him Dr. Drew, a name she used in teasing him, and the next moment he lost ground. He was at war with her ex-fiancé and it appeared he was losing the battle for her hand.

Fury still lanced a hot path through his heart when he thought about how the man had no claim to her, yet because of a natural disaster and an injury, Olivia believed herself engaged to him. It seemed so unfair. Oh, he knew the saying, *no one ever said life was fair*. He'd heard it since he was a child, but somehow right now life was the least fair it had ever been. Living for the Lord didn't appear to matter sometimes, either. It certainly wasn't getting him anywhere with Olivia. Granted he didn't serve God to get what he wanted. But it sure would be nice if God would answer his prayers. Weight descended on his heart. He wasn't being fair to God.

He shouldn't take his frustrations with Lloyd out on his relationship with the Lord. And because of that relationship, he knew he shouldn't, but Drew would like to thrash Lloyd for the lies and deceit—for trying to get her to marry him as soon as possible. It seemed every day Pratt turned up the pressure for her to marry him. Of course the man would, because he was aware that every day brought new possibility that she would remember the truth.

And yet, Drew knew that with every passing day there was a possibility that she'd never remember the truth—that they were in love.

If Lloyd would quit coming daily to see her, maybe Drew could make progress. But that wasn't going to happen. Drew could see what the man was up to. Each day he'd press his suit a little more.

Arriving at the wharf, Drew learned the ship had been delayed and he'd have to come back the following day. Retracing his steps, he passed by one of the local saloons. Loud music and song came from the establishment.

For an instant he hesitated and had the urge to go in and join the men. Drown his sorrows and forget the pain. Pretend that Olivia was still his. But he'd only wake on the morrow with the same ache in his chest and a new one in his head. He picked up his pace, suddenly wanting to get back and see how Olivia fared.

His father didn't watch Lloyd closely enough. He seemed to think that as long as Pratt was in their house there was nothing to worry about, but he didn't understand the lies that Pratt would feed her. And if he did, then he wasn't aware how much Olivia believed them. It seemed as if Father thought Drew overreacted and, of course, Mother went along with anything Father said.

And with both of his brothers off on their own adventures, that left Olivia unprotected. Drew grunted. He shouldn't have agreed to spend the whole day at the office

He'd been gone since early morning. They'd opened the office back up on King Street, and he'd spent the day seeing patients. Most were minor complaints with the exception of Mr. Morgan who'd been injured the first night of the earthquake and refused to seek medical attention. Drew feared the man would lose his leg because of his stubbornness. Morgan was a stubborn old coot, however, and Drew couldn't help but like him. He found it impossible to stay mad at the man for neglecting his injury.

Drew took in the strangers he passed and let work fade from his mind. A pair of Dragoons rode horseback down the street. Crime had been miniscule according to the paper, and considering they'd originally lost forty-some prisoners from jail, that seemed a small miracle. The escaped inmates were probably too busy trying to survive to get involved in criminal activities.

And it didn't hurt that even with the large Charleston police force, the police chief had put out the call for volunteers to serve fifteen-day terms. The Dragoons passed him, and he gave a nod of his head, recognizing the dark-haired one as a patient who continued to have trouble with his hip due to a war wound.

The two middle-aged men sat tall in their saddles. The Dragoons and the German Hussars that now patrolled the streets keeping them safe from looters were proud war veterans of the War of Secession and belonged to Charleston's blue-blooded families. He'd been mightily tempted to volunteer now that the influx of severely injured patients had dropped drastically.

Ordinarily he loved his job, but when he looked around at all that needed to be done around the city, he longed to be of greater help. Keeping the population safe sounded like a fine idea to him. And if it hadn't been for Olivia staying on at their home and Lloyd stopping by regularly, he probably would have taken a temporary leave of work. Father and his brothers could certainly take care of what patients they had. But he shuddered to think what his father would say had he pursued the impulse.

He needn't worry because he wasn't going anywhere until Olivia had regained her memory.

Hoofbeats drowned out his thoughts. A horse and rider pulled up beside him, matching his pace. Drew glanced over, but didn't slow. He was too anxious to return home.

The Dragoon he'd recognized moments earlier gazed down at him. "Good day, doc."

The ground rumbled beneath Drew's feet as another of the daily aftershocks that continued to plague Charleston hit. Another reason to get home—Olivia trembled every time one hit. "Can I do something for you, Captain Sharpe?"

"You still seeing the Macqueen woman?"

Drew stopped and narrowed his eyes. "Why do you ask?"

"Our families go way back, and as a token gesture of that friendship, I wanted to make you aware of something I observed."

"I appreciate that."

"Right after the earthquake hit," he scratched his salt and pepper goatee and paused that slow tidewater Virginia drawl of his, "Not sure if it was three or four days after the earthquake. Could have been five . . ." He gazed up at the sky as if the puffy clouds would give him the answer.

"Days don't matter. What do you wish to tell me?" Drew attempted to hurry him along, but winced at his own rudeness.

"I was passing by the Macqueen's home, and I saw that Pratt fellow who was once engaged to her digging through their belongings. At first I thought he was searching for victims, but when I yelled to him thinking I'd help him look, he took off a runnin'. Fell on some broken glass and limped away." He winced as he told of the incident.

"Did you see if he had anything as he fled?"

"Not that I noticed. Sorry. Like I said, I'd been thinking he was looking for people. But then as the days passed, I thought it strange that he'd run when I called out to him."

"Did you notice what area of the house he was searching in? Right, left, front, back?"

The Captain stroked his cropped goatee again. "It was the right, midway back."

"Thank you. Thank you very much." Drew shook his hand.

"Glad I could help." Captain Gideon Sharpe tipped his hat, pulled the reins to his right and turned his thoroughbred around, heading back in the direction he'd come from.

Drew glanced back and yelled over his shoulder. "I owe you, Captain Sharpe."

Drew smiled. So Lloyd Pratt has a secret.

Chapter 9

The sound of the train rumbled down the tracks. There were no tracks by her house and yet it grew closer and closer. Her heart raced in her chest. It was going to hit their house. She stood in the parlor archway. Papa and Mama sat on the settee laughing.

"Don't you hear it?" Olivia had to scream out the words so they could be heard above the ground-shaking growl. They both looked up at her.

Father smiled. "It's only thunder, dear. Go on to bed."

Mama laughed.

"No. The train has broken loose. Feel the ground." The floor lifted beneath her feet as if the train had gone underground like a great iron earthworm, unsettling her.

Her parents laughed and then their expressions turned to horror. Olivia swung around, expecting to see the train smashing through the wall. No train came. She glanced back to her parents. Now they were outside sitting on the same settee in the middle of a beautiful meadow and surrounded by men. Men that frightened her.

A voice cried out from beyond. "This is your doing, Olivia. This is your punishment."

She shook her head as the men lifted brick-laden hands.

"No. No!"

They smiled and evil seeped from their bodies. They pulled their arms back like slingshots ready to fire. She tried to move, but her legs were held down with weights.

"Stop!" She tried to lunge forward and ward off blows with her hands.

They released their bricks. Papa threw himself over

Mama. He gave her one last look. Sadness filled his eyes.

Olivia screamed and bolted upright. She gasped for breath. It was pitch black. Where was she?

"Olivia?" It was Drew's voice. His hand touched her shoulder. "Are you all right?"

She gulped down a breath and swung her feet off the cot. "Yes."

"What happened?" His comforting hand caressed her shoulder.

"A dream." Her voice cracked. "A very bad dream."

Drew knelt down beside her. She couldn't see him, but heard the rustle of his clothes, and the scent of woodland spice—his scent—filled her nose. A memory flashed before her, a warm fire, hot chocolate, and serenity. She took several deep breaths and found her pulse slowing, the fear melting away like the wax on a burning candle.

His other hand came up and he massaged her shoulders. Another memory flickered of the popping logs in the hearth while cold rain hit the windows from outside. The tension disappeared and she longed to rest her head on his shoulder.

"Do you want to talk about the dream?" His breath tickled her ear.

"It was Mama and Papa. A train was coming, but it wasn't a train. It sounded like one. And then they were in a field and some evil men stoned them with bricks and they said it was my punishment." She let out a sob. "It was so real."

Tender arms encompassed her and her wish came true. She laid her head on his shoulder and tears flowed. He rubbed her back and quietly whispered sweet words of encouragement. She sniffed, trying to get a hold of herself.

The stairs creaked, but she didn't open her eyes. She was safe. Drew would take care of her.

"Is everything all right?"

Olivia opened her eyes. JoAnna stood on the stairs holding a candle, throwing light into the room.

"Go back to bed. Olivia just had a bad dream." Drew's voice was quiet but firm.

"I'm not leaving you down here with her, alone. It could ruin her reputation." JoAnna glided down the rest of the steps, her white cotton gown flowing behind her.

Olivia pushed back. What was she doing in a man's arms in the dark and in her night rail? And while engaged to another man. Lord have mercy on her, she must be losing her mind. "I'm sorry, Drew. I don't know what I was thinking. You must think me forward to throw myself on you." She reached around and pulled the sheet over her shoulders and stared at his knee resting on the floor. "I should leave. I've shamed myself."

He tilted her chin up with the lightest touch of his finger. "You've done no such thing. And don't you even mention leaving." Tenderness overflowed in his voice.

She sniffed. Her bottom lip quivered. "I'm fine now. Thank you. I'd just like to go back to sleep."

Drew stood. JoAnna moved in next to him, the candle illuminating her brother's face as well as her own.

Worry carved lines across his forehead and between his eyes. Confusion knotted Oliva's stomach. How could both Lloyd and Drew look on her with so much compassion and caring when one of them was not telling the truth? She swung her legs back up on the cot and threw the light coverlet over her. "Goodnight. Thank you both for caring." Laying her head down on the pillow, she watched them leave the room.

"JoAnna, you have a knack for sticking your nose where it doesn't belong." Drew's stern voice floated on the still evening air.

"I was just protecting her reputation. Something *you* should have thought about, big brother."

"Keep your voice down, JoAnna. And might I remind you …"

Olivia strained to hear what Drew was about to say, but the only thing that followed was the creaking of the wooden steps.

She settled into her bed, blackness surrounding her. The picture imprinted on her mind of her parents and the rumbling train returned. Perhaps that wasn't just a dream. It could have been a memory sneaking back into her mind. It seemed too real not to have taken place. But what about the voice and the evil men lifting bricks? That couldn't have happened. The thought was ridiculous. Could part of her dream be real and part a figment of her imagination?

An aching in her chest overwhelmed her, leaving her heart heavy. Her stomach twisted like a sailor's knot. Her gut told her the dream wasn't just a dream. Something in it seemed like a memory. Not being able to pull up a year of past experiences was the most frustrating thing she ever endured. If only she could know for sure that this was or wasn't a dream. She didn't want it to be real. The uncertainty was better than the confirmation that they were dead. At least there was hope in that. But if she did remember, then Mama and Papa were gone. She'd never see them again.

Life would never be the same. And what of Simon? If her parents had died, then Simon was most likely gone, too. How long had it been since the earthquake? Somewhere near two weeks. If either her parents or Simon were alive, they'd have found her. Papa and Simon both would have pounded down every door in the city looking for her. A tear slipped out of the corner of her eye. She'd been foolish to hold on to such a weak hope. And why had she done that?

Drew. Didn't he try to convince her that her parents were probably in one of the tents in the city? Hadn't he promised her he'd keep watch at the hospital for them? He'd let her know if he saw them. He knew. He had to know. And Lloyd was just as guilty. Neither of them told her the truth. But Lloyd did offer to take her out looking. He'd said that he'd carry her to his carriage and drive her around town. It was Drew who'd refused to let her go, saying she wasn't well enough.

Lloyd was right. Drew just wanted to keep her here. And look at him tonight. What was he doing downstairs anyway? How did he get to her so quickly? A shiver crept up her spine. Did he sit and watch her while she slept? Lloyd had said Drew had developed some sort of perverted infatuation with her while she was unconscious. If that were true, he could merely be trying to gain her trust so that he could move in for what he was really after. She was in the Warwick's home and alone.

She had no one to trust.

Tomorrow when she got up, she would demand some answers. If he wouldn't tell her the truth about her family, then she would find out who kept track of the deaths. Someone certainly did. If she had to go to the morgue and to every cemetery in Charleston she'd do it until she knew the truth about her family.

If they had passed on, she would have to find comfort in knowing they were with the Lord. And if Drew lied to her, she'd pack her bags and leave. Well, she had no bags to pack. She had nothing—including a place to go.

But one thought dangled before her, tempting her like a piece of fruit on the tip of a tree branch. If she agreed to marry Lloyd, she'd have a home.

Olivia threw her arm over her eyes to block out the

beam of sunlight shining in her face. The night had proven to be long. She had lain awake until early morning birdsong filled the air before finally drifting off. She wasn't ready to wake up or to face what the day held.

Dishes clattered from the far end of the house and the smell of fried bacon called to her. She flopped to her side and opened her eyes. Drew sat in a chair directly across from her, watching her.

She blinked, hoping he'd disappear, but he didn't. Had he sat there all night? A creeping feeling crawled over her skin. She hoped she was wrong, but until she gained her bearings, she wasn't ready to talk to him. Not yet. She needed to gather her thoughts. And she was hungry.

"Good morning, Sunshine."

She frowned at his familiarity.

"Hmmm. Looks like someone woke up on the wrong side of the bed." He chuckled at his own little joke.

"I didn't sleep well."

His smile disappeared. "Are you ill?" Again the concern filtered through his voice. Could a man with perverse interest be so convincingly kind? Surely not.

How could the man disarm her so? She'd made up her mind last night about him. And now here he was wiggling his way back into her good graces. "No. I just couldn't sleep."

"Was it your dream?"

She sighed and closed her eyes.

"I'm sorry. You don't have to answer that." His chair creaked.

She opened her eyes to find him standing. "No. It's I who am sorry. I'm a bit grumpy this morning. But I'd rather eat breakfast right now than talk about it."

"I'll leave and allow you to get dressed."

He exited the room and Olivia sat up, throwing the

thick coverlet back. She bowed her head and prayed for her family and for the city of Charleston as she did every morning. Reaching under her bed, she pulled out a black leather Bible that Mrs. Warwick had given her and opened it. She'd read a chapter before getting dressed and eating breakfast. She said a silent prayer asking God to speak to her and comfort her heart through His word.

Reading John 16, she paused and reread verse 24. *"Hitherto have ye asked nothing in my name: ask, and ye shall receive, that your joy may be full."* Did God tell her she need only ask and her parents would be alive and well, that Simon would be alive? Her heart leapt, and she read the words again, "ask, and ye shall receive, that your joy may be full."

She smiled with hope that her family did live. Her happiness would be full. She closed the Bible and tucked it back under the bed. No wonder she'd had that terrible dream. Satan tried to discourage her from searching by trying to make her think she saw her parents die. But now she knew it for the lie it was. Today, she'd find Mama, Papa, and Simon.

♥♥♥

When Drew heard the *pitter patter thunk* of Olivia and her cane coming down the hall, he hurried to the table and pulled out her chair. The smell of cooked bacon and onion made his stomach growl. "I'm glad you're hungry. I had Mrs. Benninger fix you up an omelet."

She took her seat and cocked her head. "Sounds like if I can't finish it, you'll be able to."

He chuckled. "I'm not so sure about that. I had her make me two."

Mrs. Benninger came in and placed a plate before both him and Olivia. The ebony-skinned woman was in her sixties and had been cooking for three generations of his family. She'd been bought by his grandparents back in the 1840's when she was just in her teenage years. Upon the emancipation of slaves, she became their paid cook. When Grandfather had died, she'd come to work for his parents. She was the best cook in the county, and like a grandmother to him. Drew smiled.

"What you grinning like an old tooth comb for?" Mrs. Benninger thrust one meaty fist on her hip and scowled at him.

"Just wondering if you'll come be my cook when I get married." He glanced over at Olivia.

"Pshaw, boy. I ain't leavin' your Mother and Father until me or they's in the grave."

Drew winked at Olivia before turning his attention back to their cook. "I promise to pay you better."

"Money isn't everything. Your mother, she's the sweetest person I ever did know. Now why would I want to leave her?" She poured Olivia a cup of coffee and held the pot in her hand as if she was waiting on his answer before he'd get any.

"My wife will be every bit the kind person my mother is, maybe more." Out of the corner of his eye he glimpsed Olivia lower her head.

Mrs. Benninger's eyes softened as her gaze went to Olivia. "I don't doubt that at all. Nope. Not at all."

She poured his coffee, but Drew didn't say any more. He'd already made Olivia uncomfortable.

He had just finished asking the blessing on the food when his father stepped into the room and plopped the newspaper on the table.

"Hope you asked the blessing on mine, too." Father took his seat at the table.

Mrs. Benninger waddled over to the buffet and brought a cup to Father. "What would you like for breakfast, sir?"

She filled it and waited.

"An omelet sounds good." He took a sip of his black coffee as she left the room. "What are your plans today, Drew?"

Drew took a bite of his food as he watched his father. Since he'd realized Lloyd must have been looking for something at the Macqueen's, he'd been waiting for Saturday to come so he could ride over and take a look for himself. Enough time had passed that he doubted he'd find anything, but one never knew. "Thought I'd get out for a while today."

His father nodded. "Now that things are slowing down around here, I believe I'm going to take your mother for a ride in the country."

"I'm sure that would do her some good. She's worked harder than we have these last few weeks."

"Yes she has, and I thought it was time to get back to our Saturday rides. She needs to relax and stop her worrying—much like two other young people I know." He glanced between Olivia and Drew.

Olivia remained overly quiet through the rest of breakfast. She seemed lost in her thoughts. Thoughts that—unless recent—weren't of him. His chest cinched. Her progress seemed so slow, other than the healing of her ankle, which was coming along fine.

He pushed his chair back and stood. "I hope you and Mother have a good day. I've got to go back down to the wharf and see if the ship has arrived with our supplies."

What to do about Olivia? William had gotten up early and left, as had Christian. He didn't want to leave her with no Warwick men in the house for fear Lloyd would show up. If he took Olivia with him…Drew couldn't bear the thoughts of what that might lead to.

He'd looked through every medical book he had, trying

to find the answer to her memory loss, but there was no given cure. His hope in speeding along her recovery was to show her what they once had and pray she'd remember their past. But, at the same time, if she accompanied him, how could he search her home without her asking questions?

Her immediate protection was what was important. "Olivia, would you like to drive over to your house? Perhaps try to salvage some items? I'd be happy to escort you. That is, if you don't mind taking a quick trip down Bay Street to collect the medical supplies before we return."

A smile lit up her face, and he wished he'd offered the simple gesture days ago.

"That would be wonderful." She eased herself up from the table. "I'll be but a moment." She hurried off with cane in hand.

Drew took the last swallow of his coffee and set the cup down. "Were you planning on taking the surrey?"

His father dabbed his mouth with the napkin as he scooted his chair back. "I can take our other carriage if you need it, son."

"I was thinking that it might be easier getting her things in and out of."

"Then by all means, take it."

Drew grinned. "You can always use my curricle."

His father grinned back. "I might just do that. Add a little fun to our ride."

Drew had the team hooked up to the carriage, a large empty trunk loaded, and waited for Olivia when JoAnna appeared on the lawn.

"Olivia tells me you're heading over to her place today."

He eyed her. "That's right." He knew his little sister too well. He knew what she was up to.

"Mind if I tag along?"

"Yes, as a matter of fact I do."

She crossed her arms in front of her. "Are you still mad at me?"

"Mad? No. I'm just smart enough to know not to bring you along if I ever want to win Olivia's heart back." He raised a brow.

"What did I do? I can't think of one thing—"

"Exactly. You don't think. You blurt out whatever comes to your mind. Ordinarily that's fine, because most people aren't struggling with memory loss. But when you say foolish things like I'm trying to take advantage of Olivia, she doesn't know what to believe because she can't remember me in her past."

"Oh." Her defensive tone changed to contrite. "I never thought about that."

Drew held back a smile. He did love this little sister of his. She just had some more growing up to do. He supposed the blame for that could be laid on all of them. She'd been the youngest and they'd coddled her. "I know."

She stuck out her bottom lip. "I'm sorry. I'll go explain to her that I was just teasing."

She turned to leave and Drew gingerly wrapped his hand around her arm, stopping her.

"No, leave things be. I'll take care of my own love life. But be more careful in the future about what you say— especially if it's about me."

"I will, I promise."

"Thank you."

"Does that mean I can come?" Hope filled her voice.

"I'm afraid not. Moreover, I believe Father is going to have you stay here with the last few patients while he takes Mother for a ride."

JoAnna stomped her foot. "I'm not a doctor. How am I

supposed to care for sick people?"

Drew sighed. JoAnna tried his patience at times. "There isn't a sick person in there. All you have to do is wait on them should they need something."

"I'm not a servant."

"You are today." He chuckled.

"But I want to go with you and Olivia. I've been cooped up taking care of Mother's friend since the earthquake. Now that her daughter's here, I finally can get out and do something. But Father wants me to stay here taking care of more people." She unfolded her arms and clasped her hands in front of her. "It isn't fair."

"Listen to yourself, JoAnna. You're whining about not leaving the house when there are thousands of people in Charleston who would give anything if they had a home to go to. Mother has worked herself so hard she's lost weight, and Father wants to get her out of the house so she can relax. Christian and William are still gone morning 'til night working around this city. And I'll add, for your sake, they aren't out having fun at balls and theater, they're working. This is my first day where duty hasn't called, and I'm taking Olivia to see her house. Keep in mind all she has lost before you start complaining to me."

"I'm not complaining. I just want to go with you." She gave him that smile she always did when she tried to get her way.

He ruffled her hair. Something that annoyed her. "You're complaining and the answer is still no."

On the piazza, Olivia made her way to the steps. The simple blue cotton dress he recognized as his sister's nearly swallowed her. Had she not lost so much weight, it would have fit fine. JoAnna and Olivia had been close to the same size.

Drew dashed over to where she stood on the piazza and

presented her his arm. "Allow me to help, but keep that wicked cane away from me." He winked at her.

A beautiful rosy-red seeped into her cheeks. He loved how she blushed—something she always hated about herself.

She slipped her arm through his. "Thank you. And I will try to keep my cane under control." She paused at the top step and smiled at JoAnna. "Are you coming along with us?"

"I wish I was. But dear brother here won't let me tag along."

Drew frowned. What had he just told that girl? Did she ever listen to a word he said? "JoAnna."

She blew out a puff of breath that fluttered her bangs. "Oh, very well." She sighed. "The truth is someone needs to be here and care for the patients should they need anything."

"See that wasn't too hard, was it?" Drew reached over and pinched her cheek as they reached the grass.

She slapped his hand. "It doesn't mean I wouldn't rather go."

"We don't always get what we want." He was living proof of that right now.

Once down the steps, Olivia grasped the skirt of her dress as he helped her board the carriage. "I wish you could have come, too." She gave JoAnna an understanding smile.

"See—"

Drew cleared his throat and shot his sister a glare. She huffed and went in the house. Shaking his head, he settled on the leather padded seat next to Olivia and snapped the reins. "JoAnna's sweet, but she's young."

"She's very kindhearted. She's been lending me everything I need since I woke at your family's home."

"She has her moments." He slowed the horses and

steered them around some debris on the edge of the road. "Are you prepared for what you're about to see?"

Olivia leaned back and laced her hands together in her lap. "I believe as much as possible. You see, I was reading my Bible…well it's your mother's Bible. She lent it to me, you see."

He could listen to her ramble forever. It was amazing that even with her memory loss, she was still his same Olivia—always wanting to make sure what she said wasn't misunderstood. He loved her so much it made his chest ache thinking she might not ever be his again.

She took a breath and continued on. "I had thought that… well, more like I had come to the conclusion that because no one would tell me anything about my family that you were hiding their deaths from me. But when I opened my Bible," she aimed a glance his way. "Your mother's Bible, this morning I read John 16. And then I realized I was wrong. My parents are alive and so is Simon."

Drew tightened the reins without thinking, which jolted the horses and nearly threw the two of them headfirst into the street.

Chapter 10

"Whoa, whoa, slow down." Drew placed his hand on Olivia's arm. He felt every bit as confused as the horses who seemed to think the command was for them and not Olivia. "What do you mean you read John 16 and now you know your family is alive?"

Excitement spread over her face. "It's true. I know it is. I prayed and then I read the Bible. God's Word gave me the answer."

A sick feeling twirled in Drew's gut. "What does John 16 say?"

She rested her hand over his. "I have the promise memorized now. '*Hitherto have ye asked nothing in my name: ask, and ye shall receive, that your joy may be full.*' Don't you see, Drew? God is comforting me until I find my parents. I just need to ask, that's all."

Drew felt like he'd swallowed a mouthful of styptic powder. He could see no good end to this. Now he'd have to tell her the truth and posthaste. He couldn't let her continue to believe her parents were alive. It would be too devastating for her when she learned the truth, and she might never forgive him.

"I think you're jumping to conclusions here. We can *make* the Bible tell us whatever we want. It doesn't mean it's true in that circumstance. I'm not saying God can't or won't speak to you through His Word, I'm just trying to say..."

She stuck her finger an inch from his nose and pulled back her shoulders. "Now you listen here, I'm not going to let you ruin my joy. I will find my family. I don't want to talk about it anymore."

Drew groaned. Stopping the surrey in front of the house he found her at a mere three weeks earlier, he set the brake and hurried around to keep her from trying to alight on her own.

But instead, she sat there dazed with tears streaming down her face, staring in shock at the destruction of her home. Drew stepped to her side and took a firm hold of her elbow to ensure she not fall.

"Olivia, I'm sorry."

She sat speechless for several long moments. Finally, she swept away the tears and exhaled loudly. "Of course—they were rescued like I was." She looked down and allowed him to help her from the carriage.

Drew frowned as she grabbed her cane and pushed forward. "Olivia, I—"

"Don't apologize any more. I'm sorry for being so emotional."

"What?" She obviously still held to the belief that her family was alive. He couldn't convince her. He sighed his frustration before answering her. "My dear, who wouldn't be emotional seeing their home in this condition?"

"I'm glad you don't think so, but you might want to wait and pass judgment after you get to know me better." She gave him a timid smile.

He forced a smile and had to look ahead for fear he would pull her into his arms and kiss that look that he loved so much.

♥♥♥

Olivia cocked her head to get a better look at Drew. He suddenly seemed rather jumpy. The man sure struck a handsome figure with his rich brown trousers, white shirt and tan coat that pulled at his shoulders and narrowed down to a trim waist. And he had to be the epitome of gracious after she stuck her finger in his face and scolded him like a little boy and still he denied her extreme emotional vacillation. She went from scolding to tears in a matter of minutes.

Drew shoved his hand through his hair. She gasped and her heart stuttered. He was frustrated. She *knew* that. She *recognized* that gesture and she found herself wanting to coax the frustration out. It was as if she knew how to do it. But how could she?

What was going on with her? At times she felt a connection with Drew and it frightened her. He didn't scare her, but the idea that there was so much of her life she didn't remember terrified her.

Something wasn't right. Two men both claimed she belonged to them, which meant one or both of them lied. But she remembered her engagement to Lloyd. It seemed like it was only yesterday. And all she could remember of Drew was when they were children and he was full of mischievous behavior. She came near despising the boy at times. The only thing that kept her from it was in all of his naughtiness and antagonizing her, he was never truly mean like the other boys.

He never teased her about being fat. And one day on her way home from school, the boys were singing *Livvy, Livvy, too fat for the privy, went in circles till she got dizzy.* Drew happened upon them as they taunted her. He chased them all away threatening to tie their tongues in a knot if he ever heard them say another mean thing to her.

He was her hero from that day on because those boys never said a mean thing to her again. That is, until he and Simon stuck a lizard in her bed. And even though her memories of him weren't the best, she felt safe with him. Maybe because he was a doctor.

"Are you all right?" He swung in front of her and gently took hold of her shoulders.

"You seem to be asking me that a lot." She tried to laugh it off to keep the tears from flowing.

"It's because you've been through *a lot*."

"I'm fine. I promise."

How could he look at her with so much compassion? Or was that passion? Her breath caught and her tongue slid over her bottom lip. His eyes fixed on her lips. She swallowed. He looked as if he were going to kiss her. And she wanted him to. Oh, heavens. What was she thinking? This would not do.

"Maybe I could find some of my dresses and bring them back with me if there were any that survived." Her voice squeaked.

He took a step back and glanced toward what was once her home. "I'll help you look. Is there anything else you'd like to look for?"

"My engagement ring. I know it's probably impossible to find in this devastation, but I thought I'd look around the area where you found me."

His hand went to his chest, over the pocket.

"I haven't told Lloyd I lost it yet. So if you don't mind keeping that between us." She needed to make it clear that she wasn't asking him to lie. "That is, as long as he doesn't ask you."

"I don't think you have to worry about that. Lloyd and I aren't exactly on friendly terms."

Staring over the remains of her home, tears threatened again, but Olivia refused to allow them to flow. "There is so much wood and brick and debris. Now that I'm here, it seems like an impossible task to find anything."

"Point me in the direction of where we should be searching and I'll try to get rid of enough of it to where you can look for your clothes. We'll find your dresses. After all, I found you." He smiled at her.

The piles of rubble were frightening. Her family could have been crushed under it. No. The Bible said her joy would be full and that couldn't happen without her family. "You've been through all this once, right? L-looking for Simon and my parents?"

He reached out as if to cup her face, but instead let his hand fall to his side. "I've dug through the rubble until my hands bled. But I wasn't paying attention to articles. I was just...We can search for your clothes as well as anything else you'd like to try and salvage."

Relief swept through her. "Where should we start?"

"Where your room was."

She bit her lip. "If...if I can find it."

"Do you mind leading the way?" Drew pulled off his jacket and tossed it over the back of a broken chair that had been hurled into the yard.

Guiding the way, Olivia maneuvered around the perimeter of what was formerly her grand brick home. Once to the rear side of her home, she slowed. Her room had been on the second floor in the back corner of the house. Now there was no second floor. She could only gesture to the collapsed wreckage.

Drew gently eased her to the ground, then he got to work.

It didn't take nearly as long as she had expected to find her gowns. Drew had climbed over bricks and under fallen wooden beams and then dug down, tossing all manner of debris aside, until he pulled out the first dress.

Olivia's hand went to her chest. "You found one."

"I think I found the pot of gold." He grinned. "Or maybe I should say the pot of gowns."

"How does it look?" It comforted her to think she'd have her own clothes to wear again.

He flipped the dress over giving it a thorough

examination. "A little dusty, but no tears."

He laid it aside and pulled out several more from the same spot. Throwing them over his arm, he carried the gowns to her.

Taking them from him, their hands brushed and tingles soared up her arm. "I can't tell you how much I appreciate this, Drew."

"I'm glad I can be of assistance."

"I'll fold these and put them in the trunk you brought." She stood up and took a couple of steps. "I'm so glad you thought to bring it."

He began rolling up the sleeve of his white shirt now covered in dirt. "Do you need anything else from here?"

Heat filled her face and neck. She did want some of her personal items. But she'd die if she had to tell him that. "Nothing for you to get. I'll pack these clothes in the trunk and come do a little digging myself. There are some other things I need, but you wouldn't be interested. Well, you might be interested, however, I wouldn't want you to see—" She sighed. "I'll come look."

"I don't mind. Besides, I don't want you climbing through here. You can barely walk without that cane and you're just now gaining your strength back."

"I'm fine. I want to do it myself."

"Well, want to or not, I'm not going to allow you to." He thrust his fists on his hips.

"I'm a grown woman, Drew Warwick, and I can do as I please." She turned and hobbled back around the house as she made her way to the carriage. But once there, she realized she'd have to climb onto the surrey to put her dresses in the trunk.

"Need some help?" Drew's breath grazed the back of her neck, sending a warm cascade of thrill down her spine.

She jumped, not realizing he'd foreseen her need and

followed her. "Please." She handed him the gowns. "Those need to go in the trunk."

Heading back to her bedroom area, Olivia walked as quickly as possible, heavily leaning on the cane for support.

"Olivia Beth Macqueen. If you take one step into that house, I'll turn you over my knee."

She gasped. "You wouldn't dare." Just who did he think he was? Her father?

Drew raised a brow. "Do you want to try me?"

"Go away, Drew. I can see to the rest on my own." She could hear his footfalls gaining on her and she tried to hurry.

He chuckled. "You don't think you can outrun me do you? I'm not letting you crawl into that mess—it's much too dangerous. I won't take a chance on you being injured."

"Oh, for heaven's sake. I'm quite well, and I don't believe you anyway. You wouldn't lay a finger on me." And somehow, deep down, she knew that was the truth.

"Maybe not. But I won't hesitate to throw you over my shoulder and deposit you back on the surrey seat." He held his body rigid, determination etched into his face.

"But I need my undergarments and I'll not have you—" how did he get her to say that? She clenched her back teeth, refusing to blush, and gave him a defiant stare.

The corners of his mouth twitched as if suppressing a smile. "I have a mother and two sisters. I won't be shocked by anything I see."

"Two sisters?"

He chuckled. "I have an older sister who is married and lives in Beaufort."

This was not funny at all, even if he did have two sisters. "But I wear these. Why…why you might as well see me without my dress on. No. That's not what I mean. I mean it would be like seeing me half dressed. Oh! That isn't what I mean either." She glared at him. Why did he make her ramble so? She knew he was doing everything he could to hold in his laughter. "It just isn't right. I'm not your sister or your mother."

"No, you're not, and I thank the Good Lord for that." His eyes seemed to be consuming her. "But I'm still not going to allow you to go in there. If you want them, I'll get them."

"What would my fiancé say?"

His humor evaporated, and his fierce scowl caused her to suck in her breath. He swung around and marched toward the back of her house. The idea of going in and helping lost its appeal. Instead, Olivia walked the perimeter of the house until she reached what was once the entrance.

Closing her eyes, she envisioned her home as it was. Papa, Mama, Simon, and she were in the parlor. She embraced the memory of their evening ritual and longed to return to it. But the look on Simon's face reminded her of what she'd just seen on Drew. He wasn't happy. She tried to clear the fog from her mind, but instead her stomach twisted as she tried to remember. She looked to Papa who was pacing the floor with hands behind his back, but she couldn't see his face.

"Olivia." Drew touched her shoulder. "Are you feeling ill?"

Her eyes flew open. "I'm trying to remember. But the memories stay slightly out of my grasp."

♥♥♥

If he'd have known she was trying to remember, he'd have left her be. He thought she might have been upset with him for ignoring her after she'd mentioned her *fiancé*. It was safer to ask her if she felt unwell than to ask if she was mad. He'd learned that from his sisters—the response was always much more pleasant.

But it cheered him that she tried to recall her past. He just hoped that if she did remember, that nothing he'd done recently would cause him to fall short in her eyes.

His heart pounded. Whether she remembered or not, she would eventually find out the truth about her parents, and then she'd learn he'd been the one to find them. She may never forgive him if he waited. *Oh Lord, give me wisdom.*

"Something bad happened." Olivia's eyes were closed again.

Yes, and because of it, he'd lost the thing most precious to him. "It's been a hard time for the whole community. But Charleston always prevails."

"That's not what I mean." She shook her head. "I feel like something happened in this room. We were all together, Mama, Papa, Simon, and I. Simon was angry. Papa was upset, but I can't see his face."

"Was I there?" He held his breath, hoping.

She frowned at him. "Of course not. Why would you be there? It was family."

He let out a hiss that sounded like a bellows releasing air. He hoped her memory was of her and Lloyd's breakup a year ago. "Do you remember anything about the conversation?"

"I'm trying, but it just isn't coming to me." A watery glaze covered her eyes.

The desire to pull her to him almost overwhelmed him, but he wouldn't force himself on her. She would have to choose him. He'd not have half her heart. It was all or nothing, and he'd not settle for the latter. He gently caressed her shoulder, hoping to encourage her. "It'll be fine. One day all of your lost memories will return."

She looked up, hope filling her eyes. "They will? Does everyone who loses their memory always get it back?"

"Not always." He attempted to keep his voice gentle, but still her shoulders fell and the hope he'd saw moments earlier disappeared. "But yours will."

"How do you know that?"

"Because I'm not going to give up until you do remember." How could he? It would be like giving up half of himself. He couldn't live without her. And now that her parents were gone and still no sign of Simon, she was alone. Alone and at the mercy of a scoundrel.

"I hope you're right. Because I can't explain how frustrating it is to be missing a year of my life. To have phrases, smells, and sights trigger memories, but to have those recollections snatched away before I can grasp onto them and know where they fit in the puzzle of my missing time is more than I can endure." She quickly wiped away a tear that had fallen.

An invisible band tightened on his chest. Gritting his teeth to help him stay his willpower and not pull her into his arms, Drew wrapped his hand around the back of her neck and began to softly massage her tense muscles. He leaned his head next to hers. "Have faith," he whispered.

She sniffed. "I'm trying, but it's hard."

He gave her what he hoped was an understanding smile. Because he *did* know how hard it was to keep believing. "I found a chest of drawers and put two drawers over by the carriage for you to look through and see if what you need is in there. Would you like me to look for anything else, Livvy?"

"I don't know. I had such grand hopes when I came here that I'd find my ring and get the things that I wanted. And I thought I'd see my parents. I just thought they'd be here. That they'd come by and find me standing by our home."

"Do you know who might be looking out for your

family business right now?"

"I'm sure wherever Papa is, he is making sure business goes on as normal."

"What if he couldn't see to it or Simon? Who would then?" Drew held his breath, hoping she didn't inquire why he was asking.

"Papa has a friend at the bank that sometimes helps him out. He told Mama before that Mr. Helms at the bank would run the business should Mama ever need him to. He's taken care of the business in the past when Papa took us up to New York City."

"I see. So if your father couldn't get to work for some reason, Mr. Helms would take over?"

She scrunched her brows. "I suppose so. Why?"

"Livvy, we need to talk." But not yet. He'd do it on the way back or maybe even once he got her home. He took her arm and guided her back to the drawers full of clothing that he had pulled out. "See if you need me to find anything else."

He hurried away before she could ask what he wanted to talk about and before he told her the truth. He needed to look in the area that Lloyd had been searching, and he'd try and retrieve anything else Olivia wanted. Midway down on the right, he slowed and began scanning the area for signs where Lloyd had been digging. What caught his eye weren't signs of excavating, but broken glass with drops of dried blood. He examined the spot and went to an area that looked as if someone had intentionally stacked the debris in a structured pile.

Glancing over his shoulder, he made sure Olivia was still occupied with her clothing. Throwing aside the rubble, he attempted to make sense of what room he was in. The upper floor collapsing down to the main floor made the going slow and difficult.

But the more wood he threw aside, the more he could see. When he pushed a large piece of wall off the pile, he uncovered a desk. One leg on the desk had broken so the desk teetered down six or eight inches when weight was placed on it, but other than that, the piece of maple furniture looked to be in remarkable condition.

So what was Lloyd looking for? Money? Deeds? Important papers? He needed time to go through the whole desk, drawer by drawer and paper by paper, to find out what the scoundrel searched for.

Olivia's voice penetrated his thoughts. "Drew, I think this is all I need. Did you find something?"

He pulled on the piece of wall that had hidden the desk. Groaning and with burning muscles, he heaved the large piece back to its earlier position. He glanced over the area and wasn't satisfied. The desk wasn't hidden well enough.

"I'm coming." He stepped around the glass, making sure he didn't make the same mistake as Lloyd.

She waited until he stood before her then asked, "What were you looking at up there?"

"I found your father's desk. I thought to return later to gather the papers from it in case of anything of importance, but now that I've uncovered it, I fear to leave it. After we put your clothing into the trunk, I'll use the drawers to fill with papers." He looked around wondering what was still beneath the rubble. "I'll return later to find anything else of value left behind."

"That's so thoughtful of you, Drew. And I know my father is really going to appreciate it."

"Let's get you off your feet." He lifted her up and onto the seat, feeling sad for what he knew and she didn't. He'd need to get to the bank as soon as he could and speak to Mr. Helms.

He handed her up the two drawers.

"Would you please turn around while I take care of my belongings?"

Drew turned his back to her and waited until he heard the snapping of the metal clasps on the trunk. She handed him the empty drawers and he hurried back to her father's desk.

Once he'd emptied the seven smaller desk drawers into the two larger clothing drawers, he hefted them up and slid them under the seat. Then he settled himself onto the driver's seat beside Olivia. He'd barely nudged the team forward when Olivia turned to him.

"What did you wish to talk with me about? Was it my parents?"

Chapter 11

Olivia sat with her shoulders back and her hands in her lap. She'd tucked the cane under the seat and a good portion of her clothes were in the trunk behind her. It was turning out to be a better day than it had started. Seeing her home no longer stood tall and proud on her street was hard. She tapped her fingers together waiting for Drew to answer her question. He'd said he wished to talk to her, but then never brought up the subject.

They'd had several hours together alone—plenty of time to talk. She drew in a deep breath and sighed. He glanced over at her and tightened his hands on the reins.

"Are you upset with me?" She didn't look his way, but kept her eyes on the road. He did seem to throw a fit of temper when she'd mentioned her fiancé. So maybe it wasn't her parents he wanted to talk about.

"Not at all. Why would I be upset with you?"

"It's just that you said we needed to talk, and now when I ask you about it, you don't look very happy."

"I promise you, Livvy, I'm not angry with you." His smile was sad and tugged at her heart. "Let me unload your things and then we'll go out on the piazza and talk."

They reached the Warwick's place and after setting the break, Drew helped her down and handed her the cane. "I'll help you up to the house."

"I can make it on my own." The drawn look of melancholy on his face worried her. She reached out and laid her hand on his bare arm, sending her stomach into a flurry. "You go ahead and get the trunk unloaded. I'll take my time."

She walked carefully to the house and listened as Drew

pulled the carriage around to the back. What had happened that put him in this mood? He seemed more than sad, almost brokenhearted.

Watching the ground and then the steps with every lift of her foot, she made it to the piazza with no problems.

Exhausted from the full morning's adventure, she collapsed onto the bench, secretly hoping Drew would sit beside her. She closed her eyes and leaned her head back. It'd be good to wear her clothes again. Drew was so thoughtful to take her home and allow her to get her things. She smiled, thinking about how embarrassed she'd been when he'd wanted to get her unmentionables. But he'd been a perfect gentleman about it and never said a word after finding them, just took them to the carriage.

"I hope that smile's for me." The voice wasn't the deep tenor of the man she daydreamed about.

She popped her eyes open. "Lloyd. I didn't realize you were here."

He strutted over to her and took the seat she'd hoped Drew would sit in. "Of course you didn't. You were out gallivanting with Warwick. What kind of woman goes running around town with a man when she's engaged to another? You've probably ruined your reputation."

Olivia jerked to attention. "I-I was doing no such thing. Drew took me to gather some of my things from our home."

"Drew. So now you're on a first name basis with this cad? I'm not leaving you here another day. You're coming home with me." He grasped her arm and started to stand.

"I couldn't get up and go anywhere if I wanted to, Lloyd. I've no energy. And you needn't be so upset about Drew. I call all the Warwick men by their Christian names, with the exception of the father. It's too confusing any other way."

"I'm sure that's what *he* convinced you of. The man is

nothing but a liar and a manipulator. I want you away from him. My house is as safe as the day it was built and there's plenty of room for you."

His face turned mottled shades of red. She scooted closer to the arm of the bench and away from Lloyd, as unease filled her. "And that would save my reputation? Leaving a house of medicine and caregivers to live with a single man?" The words sent a shiver down her spine.

He squatted down in front of her, his cologne of lavender filling the air. "We can marry now. Why wait? I've been telling you we need to. Now you have a reason why we should."

"I'm not marrying until I find my family."

"You might as well come to the realization that they are probably dead."

Olivia gasped. "How could you say such a thing?"

He shrugged. "Because it's true."

"If you were right, which I highly doubt since none of the Warwicks have seen any of my family come through the hospital or heard any news, I would be in mourning for months and couldn't marry."

"I wouldn't trust a word any of those men told you. Especially Drew. He's on a mission to win you over and he'll lie, cheat, and steal to get what he wants."

Leaning away, she pressed so hard against the bench arm that it dug into her hip. "You hardly know him. How can you say that?"

He snorted. "I know his kind. They're all the same. Just come with me and I'll find a safe place for you to stay."

The soft click of the screen door opening didn't register until Olivia heard Drew's voice.

"How many times do I have to tell you that she's not going anywhere?" A muscle in Drew's jaw flexed.

"You've become tiresome, Warwick. Go away." Lloyd

shooed him like an annoying insect.

"You forget where you are, sir." Drew squared his feet.

"Come on, Olivia. Let's go." Lloyd sprung to his feet and tugged on her hand.

"Please, Lloyd. Just go." She couldn't look at him. She was so confused. He frightened her and Drew brought her comfort, yet she was engaged to Lloyd. She almost wished that what Drew had told her when she first awoke was true, but he'd not said anymore about their courting which led her to believe her memory was correct after all, and she was engaged to Lloyd.

Lloyd glared at her. "I wonder if you'd feel the same way if you knew he's been lying to you."

Olivia glanced between the two. "What do you mean?"

"Go ahead, Warwick. Tell her. Tell her how you found her parents dead and pulled them out of their home."

She gasped and shook her head. "That's not true. You're the one that's lying, Lloyd."

He sneered at her. "Ask him if you don't believe me."

Lloyd was trying to turn her against Drew and she wasn't going to allow him to do that. She trusted Drew. He'd been nothing but good to her. "If that's the case, Lloyd, then why didn't *you* tell me?"

He shifted his feet. "I didn't believe him, that's why."

"But you do now?" She lifted her chin.

"I don't know. But he either lied to you or to me."

Lloyd sounded so sincere. She turned her eyes to Drew who'd gone white. Her stomach churned. She didn't want to ask him because she knew what he was going to say. "Is…is that true, Drew? Are my parents," she swallowed garnering the courage to say the word, "dead?"

"It isn't like he's making it sound." Drew took a step toward her.

"Stop. That isn't what I asked. Are my parents dead?"

Her eyes burned, waiting for the answer she didn't want.

"Yes." His shoulders sagged. "I found them before I found you, but it was too late. They had already gone on to Glory."

Lloyd snickered. "Nice way to put it. But it still doesn't change the fact that you lied to her."

"Livvy—" He spread out his hands in front of him.

"Don't call me that." She'd let him call her Livvy, thinking it was an endearment. But it was just like when the boys had teased her as a child. It was heartless. "Why?"

"You were so sick. I sat by your bedside every break I had, dripping water or broth into your mouth and begging God to spare your life. When you woke, you were not only weak, but you'd lost your memory. I wanted you to get stronger before you learned the news."

"So you lied to me?" Her voice cracked.

"I didn't lie. I never said they were alive." He shoved his hand through his hair.

Her heart thumped in her chest at the familiar gesture. "You did by omission. It's the same thing."

"She's got you there, ol' boy." Lloyd chuckled.

Drew ignored him. "Try to understand, Olivia. I wanted you to regain your memory. I thought it best if you didn't learn that information while you were so fragile."

"But I'm not weak anymore and you still didn't tell me." She dropped her head into her hands and rubbed her forehead. Her parents were gone.

Drew knelt in front of her. "I needed you to remember me, Li—Olivia. It's what has kept me going. The hope that your memories would return and we'd be back to how we were."

"The only thing she's going to remember is that we're overdue to get married. Don't play games with her. She's mine and always has been." Lloyd turned his attention from

Drew to Olivia. "Now will you go with me, Olivia?"

She lifted her head. "No. I'm not going anywhere with you."

♥♥♥

Relief rushed through Drew like cool water over a fresh burn. He'd been terrified she would leave with Lloyd. But she'd chosen to stay. It wasn't time to rejoice yet. There would be plenty of things she'd want to know and answers he'd have to give.

Lloyd glared down at her. "You're not going to stay here with him, knowing what you know? I'm not the one that lied to you. I warned you, Olivia. I told you he had developed some sick sort of infatuation."

Drew had had enough. He rose to his full six-foot-two stance, but held back his complete fury. "You heard the lady. She isn't going with you. But make no mistake, you are leaving."

Lloyd kept his eyes focused on Olivia. "You can't stay here with him. We're engaged. I courted you when no one else would. Staying here isn't only disloyal; how would I know of your virtue?"

Drew's legs shook with anger. No one could besmirch Olivia's name and get away with it. He couldn't think, and the only thing he saw was the pain that crossed Olivia's face. He tightened his hand into a fist and swung at Lloyd's jaw sending him backward and toppling over a chair.

Before Lloyd could rise, Drew lifted him to his feet and sent another blow to the man's chin. Lloyd staggered, catching his balance on the door frame. Drew would beat an apology and the truth out of him if need be. Blood dripped from the side of Lloyd's mouth and not an ounce of sympathy or remorse stirred Drew. He took a step toward Lloyd.

Olivia screamed. "Stop it. Both of you." Sobs rang out.

She pushed up from where she sat.

Drew reached out to help her. She jerked away and lost her footing, collapsing to the floor. His gut twisted. Dropping to the floor next to her curled up body, he stroked the hair from her face. "I'm sorry. I shouldn't have done that." Regret flooded him, but not for Lloyd's sake. It was Olivia's distress that caused his sorrow.

Another cry escaped. "Don't touch me." She whimpered. "Please, don't touch me."

Drew pulled back, a knife penetrating his heart. What had he done? She may never love him again. With her head cradled on her arm, protecting it from the wood floor, her body convulsed from sobs wracking her slight frame.

He longed to wipe her tears. "I'm sorry, I'm so sorry." He whispered the words, his heart begging for forgiveness and a second chance. "Please don't cry, Olivia."

He was an idiot. How could he do something so thoughtless when he knew how frail she was? He knew not only her body needed strength, but also her mind.

The squeak of the porch door opening and then a gasp brought Drew's head up. Mother rushed forward and fell to her knees. "Olivia, darling, what's wrong?"

His mother's eyes locked with his. He broke away, the pounding of footfalls on the wooden piazza steps garnering his attention. The snake had slunk away. If he cared for her at all, how could he leave her lying here distraught?

Drew had to make Olivia see the truth in the man. Lloyd Pratt had to be looking for something when he searched the remains of the Macqueen home. He just had to find out what it was that Pratt wanted. Was the man truly broke and he looked for cash? But then why go to someone you know and risk getting caught? Unless he'd heard of their deaths and wasn't worried about them showing up and catching him in the act of pilfering.

"Drew, help me get her into the house." Mother's voice broke through his thoughts.

Bracing himself against protests, Drew scooped Olivia's soft body into his arms. The warmth of her against him sent his temperature up ten degrees. He waited for her objection or the stiffening of her muscles but it never came. The sweet smell of roses sent his senses on overload and flooded him with memories of the past year. She must have come across her perfume decanter in one of the drawers and applied it.

The scent brought back recollections of her in his arms not so long ago when he held her for other reasons—reasons where tender, soft lips sought his as desperately as his did hers. He shook off the thought that made him want to kiss her until she remembered everything.

"Take her up to your sister's room, son." Mother held the door for him.

"Please, just take me to a chair. I'll be fine." She blinked away tears as her voice warbled.

Happy to turn the other direction from the bedroom, Drew headed for the parlor. The last place he wanted to take her was to his sister's room. With the way his luck had been running lately, she'd come home and tell Olivia what a scoundrel he was for defending Olivia's honor.

Keeping her head averted, Olivia didn't seem to be affected by the closeness of their bodies—the sweet temptation he might never lay claim to. He gingerly deposited her in the chair near where Mother stood.

He thought he might be sick. Had he destroyed any chance of winning her heart back? "I will say it again, Olivia, and I will say it every day for the rest of my life if it helps you forgive me. I'm sorry. I just couldn't let him talk to you that way."

She kept her beautiful blue-gray eyes turned away.

Drew straightened and spun on his heel. He had to get out, get away from her. She didn't want comfort from him, in fact, she wanted nothing he could give her. Mother would take good care of her, and he'd just have to find solace in that.

God where are you? You say all things work together for good for those who love You. The only person I see getting something good out of this is Lloyd. And he doesn't have anything to do with you.

He stepped out of the room and motioned for his mother to come.

"I've made a mess of things, Mother." He kept his voice low. "Olivia knows her parents have died. I never should have kept the truth from her."

"Wasn't that your father's decision that she needed time to heal?" Mother glanced over her shoulder toward where Olivia sat.

"Yes." Drew's insides heaved with the burden. "But that was when she first became conscious. I should have told her when she began asking questions. I was so worried that it would throw her into Lloyd's arms or cause her to never remember."

"It can be hard at times, but you must trust God. You shouldn't take things into your own hands. He always knows best." Understanding shown in Mother's eyes. "I'll go see what I can do. Try not to worry, dear."

Stomping out of the house, he made his way to the carriage. He'd take some time and go through the papers he'd brought back from Mr. Macqueen's desk. Maybe they would tell him something. Although, he doubted he would find anything, he had to try. He had to do something. He'd waited long enough for a miracle to come. It was time to take charge.

Reaching under the seat, he pulled out the drawers full

of desk papers, along with the poetry book he'd bought her for their first six months of courting. He'd found it in her drawer and should have left it there. Now he needed to do something with it.

Stacking the drawers, he carried them up to his room, avoiding the parlor. Stopping by his sister's room, he slipped the poetry book onto her small bookcase. Perhaps the day would come when he could give it to Olivia again.

The calm he sought didn't come from his room as he'd hoped. Dropping down into the chair by the window, he set the drawers between his feet and began what he hoped was a mind and heart numbing process. He needed something to help him keep his thoughts off Olivia and her reaction to his defending her honor.

Was it possible that even though she didn't remember her past, that something in her was frightened by violence? She may not remember the incident of Lloyd's abuse, but what if something deep inside of her still held that fear? What if now she was afraid of him instead of Lloyd? He prayed he didn't just drive her into the arms of her abuser. When he finished going through all the papers, he'd go back to her house and find anything of value and bring it to her. Somehow he had to show her that he cared.

Drew glanced across the room at the open wardrobe where he'd hung a picture of Olivia on the inside door. He'd had a photographer take her portrait one evening right before they entered the theater. She looked so lovely he couldn't resist the cajoling of the young man with his camera. And he was glad he hadn't, because at this moment that was all he had of her.

Reminiscing about Olivia wouldn't get his mind off her, it wouldn't get his task done either, nor would it help win her love and forgiveness. He pulled out the first piece of paper, a receipt for a hat. He set it aside and wouldn't allow himself to ponder if it was for one of Olivia's. Finishing the first drawer, he'd found many receipts, bills stamped paid, letters from clients, and solicitations for advertisements, but nothing that would tell him why Lloyd searched through Mr. Macqueen's belongings.

Drew leaned back and stretched his legs out to relieve the aching muscles in his back. This was a waste of time and he knew it. But he was sure Lloyd had a secret. Or was he just hoping Lloyd did so he would have a piece of ammunition to give to Olivia? Something—anything–that might persuade her that Lloyd wasn't the man she thought he was.

This was getting him nowhere. He tossed the empty drawer on his bed and began the tedious process of going through each paper, piece by piece. Pulling out the accounts book, he set it aside. Several letters later, he found one that revealed slight interest.

June 9th, 1885

Dear Mr. Macqueen,

I would implore you to check your accounts again. I came in to your office a month ago on my way home from work and paid Mr. Pratt. It was quite late and he offered to send me a copy of the policy rather than waiting for him to finish filling out the paperwork. However, I have yet to receive it. But rest assured I did pay for coverage with your company. I look forward to hearing from you and receiving confirmation of my policy.

Sincerely,
Timothy L.

Blane

He placed the missive in the growing pile of inconsequential papers. How easily he'd forgotten Lloyd had worked for Mr. Macqueen. Perhaps he should explore other reasons for Lloyd's appearance at the Macqueen's home after the earthquake. It was entirely possible that he wasn't there trying to steal something such as money or a deed. He could be trying to keep information from getting into the wrong hands.

Drew picked the letter back up and scanned it, taking in the date. Olivia's father would have addressed the issue with Lloyd had there been anything to the letter. He went to set the paper down and paused. But why keep it if it was of no importance? His gut told him that Mr. Macqueen kept the letter for a reason. It may have been something as simple as a reminder not to trust the man, but whatever it was, Drew intended on finding out. He finished looking through the rest of the papers, coming up empty-handed.

Carefully replacing the contents back in the drawer, he kept out the letter. Mr. Blane's concerns were intriguing, but certainly not forthcoming. After stopping by the bank to speak to Mr. Helms, a visit to the man might prove productive.

Chapter 12

Olivia folded the thin cotton blanket and stacked it on the pillow at the end of the cot before tugging off the sheet. It was time to leave. Her hands trembled at the thought of where she'd go and how safe it would be for her without her parents' protection. She needed to find Simon. But in a city disrupted by such a grave disaster, with homes like hers in ruins, and people living in the parks and squares in tents, how would she find him?

Her stomach swirled with queasiness. If Simon was alive and well, he'd have searched for her. He'd have knocked on every door in the city until he found where she stayed. Numbness swallowed her. God was her strength. He had to be, because she had none of her own. Yet, if He loved her, how could he leave her alone with no family? She should have died with them. They lived better lives than she had. Both Papa and Mama were generous with their time and their money. Mama could find a need that no other saw and would step in to fill it. Papa found work for anyone down on their luck who came by, whether it be at the agency or gardening around the house. He never turned anyone away.

And Simon…dear Simon. Olivia placed the neatly folded sheet on top of the others, leaving her cot barren. Simon always had a smile on his face and saw the best in everyone. He could bring cheer to a dreary day. But what did she have to offer? Nothing. So why did God spare her and not the rest of her family? Her life would be more of a punishment, knowing that she should have died in their place.

Drawing in a deep breath, she ran her hands over the

cotton sheet on the top of the pile. Where to go was the problem. She certainly couldn't stay at the Warwick's place. She was well enough to leave and all the patients who had been treated at the makeshift hospital had recuperated and gone their own ways, all but three people, her being one of them. The family had been kind enough to allow her to stay this long, and after what had happened between her and Drew she wasn't sure she could face him another day.

She folded her dresses and placed them on the cot before gathering all her underclothing and hair supplies and putting them in a gaily printed flour sack the cook had given her. The cheerful pattern stood in great contrast to the black dress she wore, as well as her mood. Her heart felt as if it were too heavy to carry in her chest. Giving up seemed the best way. But even that didn't seem to be an answer. Why couldn't Drew have just left her in the rubble of her home? Why did he have to come looking for her? If he'd have minded his own business, she'd be with her family right now instead of separated by a great chasm.

She shoved the last of her things into the sack with a little extra force then hit it again.

"Glad I'm not that sack."

Olivia let go of the bag and swung around at the sound of Drew's voice. A light thump sounded on the floor and she looked down to see half of her things spilt out on the wooden boards. She sighed and bent to retrieve them.

"I'll get them." He knelt down and picked up her brush and comb, placing them back in the bag. "I'm sorry about yesterday, Olivia. I shouldn't have hit Lloyd. Although he deserved it for what he said about you. Surely you remember that I'm not usually like that." He paused.

She didn't answer. She really didn't remember. But something inside her told her that what he said was true.

He stood and returned the bag full of her clothes onto the cot, resting his hands on the top. His brown eyes that had looked almost black yesterday when he was angry with Lloyd now had softened to a rich brown. He drew in a deep breath, and she sensed his next words would be hard for him.

"If I've ever regretted anything, it couldn't compare to the regrets I have today. I should have told you the truth as soon as I knew you would survive your injuries. My fear of losing you overruled my common sense. I should have known that keeping the truth from you would only hurt you and drive you away from me. I'm sorry. I know words are inadequate, but they're all I have."

He gently rested his hand on her shoulder, stroking her softly, speaking to her like they had a relationship. And something tugged at her to believe him. But what if Lloyd was right and Drew had concocted a relationship that never really happened? It was entirely possible that he had developed some sort of an attachment to her after caring for her. She *remembered* being engaged to Lloyd. She'd remember if they weren't engaged anymore. Something like that would be hard to forget. And if they had broken up, Lloyd certainly wouldn't be saying they were still an item.

"You're forgiven." Her words came out flatter than she'd meant.

"Am I really? Because you aren't very convincing." He seemed to seek out the answer in her face.

She shook her head. "I do forgive you. And I appreciate the fact you didn't try to justify your actions."

"It wouldn't have been a real apology then." He grinned, one side of his mouth creeping up higher than the other. "But I do think I had good reason."

His playful smirk flooded her with familiar feelings. Happiness. Contentment. Safety. And the urge to roll her eyes. Her heart slammed against her ribs. It was a frightening thing not to understand her emotions. "He was upset. He didn't mean those things."

"Mean them or not, he never should have said them. Especially when he *claims* to care for you."

"You mean love me? He loves me. We are engaged."

The muscle in Drew's jaw tightened. "That's what he *says*."

She lowered her brows. "That's also what I remember."

"But you've forgotten a year of your life. Don't you wonder what happened in that year?"

"You don't have to remind me what I've lost. That much I do remember. A year of my life gone. Just like that." She snapped her fingers. "But what I know is what I do remember—and that is I was and am engaged to Lloyd. He loves me and I love him."

Drew growled. "No! You say you want the truth from me and you get upset when I don't give it to you, yet when I try to tell you the truth you won't listen. You are an exasperating woman."

"You couldn't possibly understand how frustrating it is to walk around pretending life is the same when everything has changed—my family's gone along with my most recent memories of them. So call me what you'd like. I have to cling to that which I know."

His eyes clouded over and his broad shoulders dropped just enough for her to notice. "And I have to cling to that which I love."

Drew felt like a feather pillow that had gotten punched down to size. He stared down at her. With her shoulders thrown back, chin lifted, strands of sun bleached hair that had escaped her loose chignon, and her nose flaring in defiance, Olivia looked like a warrior queen ready for battle. That was one of the things he loved so dearly about her. But it wasn't nearly as charming when her bravado backed up her love for another man. He had to make her see the truth. "If you don't believe me, why haven't you asked my family?"

"They'll just tell me what you want them to."

"I hope you don't believe that. We all have more integrity than to do such a thing. They wouldn't lie for me."

She let out an unladylike snort. "Just like everyone told me the truth about my parents?"

Drew shuffled his feet. "That was different."

"Was it?"

It was different, but he wasn't going to be able to convince her of that right now. He'd really hoped that she'd grown to trust his family and would believe them. "That can't be the only reason you've never asked them."

Brushing the fallen strands away from her face, she looked defiantly at him. "Your parents have been far too gracious for me to insult them by suggesting their son lied to me. And isn't that what I'd be doing if I asked them if you told me the truth?"

"They would have understood."

"Maybe they would have, but I can see that it wouldn't have mattered. The Warwicks stick together."

Drew eyed the bag of personal items she still clung to and the truth dawned on him as he took in the bare cot and blankets and sheet folded in a pile. "What are you doing?"

She blew a puff of air up, dislodging a strand of hair from her lashes. "Talking to you. Isn't it obvious?"

"That isn't what I mean." He had a strong suspicion she knew exactly what he was asking. She fingered the bag and glanced away. Heat swept through his body. "Why are your things packed and your gowns folded?"

Her beautiful gray-blue eyes glimmered. She sucked in her bottom lip. A scoop of butter in a hot pan couldn't have melted any faster than his heart did. If only he could pull her to him and let her rest her head on his chest while she fought through the fog of confusion. If he could only convince her to trust him. How could he be so out of control of his own life? He typically made plans and proceeded forward until all was in order. But for the first time since he could remember, he wasn't in control of the situation and there was no way to make her come around to his way of thinking.

"I have to go, Drew. Your parents were kind enough to let me stay here well past being healthy enough to go out on my own. I won't impose on their hospitality any longer."

"Don't be ridiculous. You aren't imposing. You've been a great help to my mother."

"I'm not going to stand here arguing with you. I'm leaving before I overstay my welcome."

"Who's overstayed their welcome?"

Like diving in the cool Ashley River on a hot day, relief flowed over him at the sound of his mother's voice.

"Olivia is leaving. She thinks she's not welcome here anymore." Drew winked at his mother. She would be his saving grace. If anyone could convince this stubborn woman, it was his mother.

"That's not what I said." Olivia stomped her good foot.

"Honey, what's all this about?" Mother edged in beside her and wrapped her arm around Olivia's shoulder. Silver strands glistened in his mother's chestnut hair.

Olivia pursed her lips and scowled at Drew. Attempting innocence, Drew raised his hands, palms up. "What? I told her what you'd said to me."

"Ignore him, dear, and tell me what the trouble is." Mother gave him her warning glance that her family knew all too well.

Twisting the fabric of the bag in her slim fingers, Olivia's gaze never left her hands. "It's time I go. I appreciate all you and your husband have done for me." She looked up at Mother. "But I'm well now. I need to go home."

"This is your home, now. Yours is gone."

"You've already done far too much for me. I couldn't possibly continue to impose upon you." Small beads of sweat appeared above her upper lip and she stole a quick glance Drew's way.

He kept his mouth shut. Mother's earlier look brooked no argument. He would let her do the talking.

"My darling girl, you have never been an imposition, nor will you ever be. You're part of our family." Mother squeezed Olivia to her. "You have no home to return to right now, so please allow us to offer ours."

Not able to keep his tongue any longer, Drew spoke up. "She can stay in my room. I'll bunk with William or Christian."

Mother smiled, but he recognized the warning in her eyes. What was it about a mother? He was a grown man yet she could still keep him in his place.

One thing he knew for sure is that he would not give her the items he'd gathered from her parent's house. He'd spent the good part of the day there retrieving the salvageable items. But he'd not give them to her right now. If she sold the valuables he'd gathered, she'd use the money to leave. He'd return them someday. He smiled to himself, contemplating what a wonderful wedding surprise that would make.

The door banged and he glanced up to see Christian traipse through the hallway with two small puppies—one in each arm. The small brown-and-white creatures squirmed to get down, their fur and wrinkles bulging under his hold.

"Oh. How sweet." Olivia bustled over to Christian, smiling up at him. "Can I hold one?"

"Sure." Christian handed her one that had a white spot on its nose.

A twinge of jealousy knotted Drew's gut. Would she ever smile at him like that again? Would she ever let him tuck her in his arms like she snuggled the pup?

"She's so cute. What kind is she?"

Christian ruffled the dog's head. "Looks to have some spaniel."

Taking in the easy demeanor of his youngest brother, Drew noticed how at ease he seemed—something rare of late. Since the earthquake struck, both he and Christian hurt for the women they loved.

"What are you doing with those?" Curiosity got the best of him.

Christian shrugged. "I'm putting them out in the stables in one of the feed bins. The box ought to be large enough for a few weeks anyway."

Mother stepped over and stroked the one still in Christian's arms. "The question is why are you bringing them here?"

"Their mother died in the earthquake. Someone has to look after them or they'll die, too." Christian scratched under the pup's chin and the little guy closed his eyes in bliss.

Drew chuckled. "Are you going to change fields to veterinarian?"

"Doesn't sound like too bad of an idea. They don't argue with you and there isn't a dishonest bone in their body." Christian retrieved the puppy from Olivia. "I better get these critters settled in."

Mother swung around, her dress sending up a swishing

sound and the scent of gardenia perfume. "Well now, that settles it. Drew will give up his room and Christian will certainly need help with those babies. Drew, go empty your room and bring Olivia's bag up."

Drew could have skipped back to retrieve Olivia's belongings. Mother would win. He could hear it in her voice. Scooping the bag up, he grinned.

"But..." Olivia's voice trailed off.

"There will be no arguing. If we have room for two orphaned puppies we certainly have room for you. I'll not have anyone saying that the Warwicks opened their home to dogs, but cast out people in need."

"Oh, Mrs. Warwick, I never meant to imply that at all. No one would ever think such a thing of your family."

Drew climbed the stairs, a smile still on his lips. Things were looking up. Now if he could only keep Lloyd from coming by. The man was hiding something. He could feel it deep down in his bones. But what was he hiding?

Drew sat in the house glaring out at the piazza where Lloyd sat with Olivia, their voices and laughter floating in through the open door, tormenting him. He'd returned from the bank, learning that Mr. Helms had already started taking care of the Macqueen's Insurance Policies, happy to bring good news to Olivia. It was like a punch to the gut seeing Lloyd sitting with Olivia. The man hadn't shown up for two days, and Drew had hoped he'd fallen off the face of the earth. A spear of guilt stuck him at his ungodly thought. But Lloyd was nothing but a blackguard, so how could he possibly think good of him?

With his mood continuing to darken, Drew headed out of the room. Having to pass by the screened door to continue to the hallway, he could hear more of their words as he neared.

"You needn't worry, Lloyd. But it's very sweet of you to concern yourself about it." Olivia sounded relaxed which grated on Drew.

"I concern myself with everything that affects you." Lloyd's voice was as smooth as snakeskin.

"And that means so much to me." Her voice softened. "But what I mean is that Drew has already taken care of that."

Drew stopped. What were they talking about, and what had he taken care of?

"Really? And why would he do that?" An edge laced Lloyd's words.

"Now don't you start." She sounded like a schoolmarm. "Drew was concerned about important papers and personal information in Papa's desk being ruined by weather or falling into the wrong hands."

"I see. So he took it upon himself to do the job? How interesting. Did he find your father's account book?" A chair creaked and Drew imagined Lloyd leaning forward waiting for Olivia's answer.

"I don't really know what all was in Papa's desk. But if it was in there, I feel sure Drew would have taken it. I could ask him for you if you'd like."

"No. That's not necessary." The chair creaked again— probably Lloyd leaning back and digesting the information.

A ray of sunshine split through Drew's gloom sending his lips into a grin. So, Lloyd was interested in the account book. He must have a good reason, to be sure. Ready to dash up the stairs and see what he could discover, Drew reined in his urge in hopes to learn more from the conversation.

"Where did Drew put your father's things? Surely he gave them to you." Lloyd's tone insinuated that Drew was up to no good.

A pause stretched between them and Drew wanted to peek out and see what was holding up Olivia's answer.

"I don't know where they are. But I'm sure they're in safe keeping. It's not as if this family is in need of money if you're suggesting he'd try to steal something from my father."

She defended him. His heart beat to a happy tune.

"You never know a man's motives, Olivia."

Drew almost choked at Lloyd's last statement. He had to be talking about himself. Catching sight of Christian approaching him, he put his finger to his lips and slinked away from the continuing conversation and toward his brother.

Once far enough away, Christian spoke. "What was that all about?"

"Just doing a little eavesdropping." Drew couldn't keep the grin off his face. She defended him.

"So who were you listening to? As if I need to ask. And why the smirk?"

"Just that Lloyd is giving away his secrets. Whatever he is hiding is in the account book. And to think, I discarded that to the side, thinking that couldn't be what he was looking for."

Christian let out a low whistle. "Embezzlement?"

Drew cocked his head and raised a brow. "That's what I'm thinking."

Chapter 13

Lloyd kept the smile on his face, glad Olivia couldn't see the turmoil within him. Negotiating the account book and any other incriminating evidence out of Drew's hands and into his own had to be a top priority. He was too close to being free from worry to have Warwick spoil things. He needed the man out of the way.

He smiled remembering his conversation with Middleton, the man who had gotten him into this mess. *Maybe it is time to bring in my sister.* His smile faded. That hadn't been exactly how the conversation had gone. More like, *if you can't get this done yourself then maybe it's time to call in my sister.* Why did he ever let himself get involved with a bunch of gypsies? He should have just taken the beating right then and there. Maybe if he had come in bloodied and begged long enough instead of storming off he could have convinced Mr. Macqueen to let him borrow the money. Surely the man would have had some sympathy for him then instead of trying to break off his engagement to his daughter. What was done was done. He was in up to his neck now and if he didn't do something quick he was going to drown. Maybe literally, with a millstone tied to his ankle somewhere in the cold, deep harbor.

Would it help to bring in Constance Middleton? Her brother sure thought her capable. And Drew once fancied her. Who knows, she actually might want to get back her old beau. He didn't know what plot they were devising.

If he hadn't gotten so far in debt from gambling, none of this would have happened—he wouldn't be worrying over how he was going to get his hands on an account book and he never would have lost Olivia in the first place. When he'd taken the money from Macqueen's Insurance business it was just to keep from getting his head bashed in. He planned to return it as soon as he hit a winning streak.

A winning streak that never happened. Things just got worse when he told those gypsies how he intended to pay them back. Lloyd shook his head. He knew Constance in the most intimate of ways. How was he supposed to know her brother was some sort of a criminal and would entangle him into this embezzlement scheme? And now he was in deep. One thing he knew for sure was that he didn't want to go to prison. Regardless of the fact that they pressured him to take the money from the Macqueen's insurance firm, there was no evidence to prove that it was *their* idea and not his. It'd be his words against theirs. And if he ever fingered them, he knew he'd wind up in an alley—dead. That was a guarantee.

Getting a book didn't seem like it would be too hard for hardened criminals, and if Drew got hurt or worse…well, all the better for him and Olivia.

♥♥♥

Olivia strolled along the Battery, her arm looped in Lloyd's. Hardly a limp was visible. And unless she stepped on a large stone or uneven ground, her pain was minimal. Memories of days gone by when they took this same walk filled her thoughts. She should be thankful she still had Lloyd. Her heart hiccupped and she pushed the thought away. If God was punishing her, He very well could take Lloyd from her, too.

Trying to get her mind off God's anger, she took in the tents pitched around the area. The salty air filled her lungs and the occasional pigeon cooed for something to eat. A dozen or so of the canvas dwellings had been set up in no particular arrangement. The mostly white tents were spread out through the city of Charleston, giving shelter to those who'd lost their homes. She shuddered. She could have easily been sleeping in one of those. Maybe God had shown her some mercy after all.

"Do you think Charleston will ever be the same?" She glanced over at Lloyd. His light gray trousers fit loosely on him. He'd unfastened the top button of his crisp white shirt. The vest he wore peeked out of his dark gray coat. He'd grown a short beard and she decided she liked it. It seemed to mask the pointed chin of his oval face.

He shrugged. "I don't really know. But quite frankly, I don't much care. As soon as we get married I thought we'd move far away from here."

She gasped. "Move? You never asked me about that."

He looked down at her, sending an air of arrogance her way. A sliver of fear shot through her.

"Why would I? The decision is mine. You'll come with me."

She swallowed. "But what if I don't want to move?"

"Why would you want to stay? You have no family or home here." He looked more shocked than annoyed.

Anger smoldered inside her at his callousness. "Because this is home. All my memories of Mother, Father, and Simon are here. If I leave…it's like I'm leaving them. And I don't know where Simon is. He could come back. "

"They're gone. They left you, not the other way around. You don't have to feel guilty about that. I sure wouldn't."

"But I love Charleston." She stalled and swept the bay with a gesture of her hand.

"What makes this city so special? We'll move to an even grander metropolis." He tugged her forward.

"I love everything about this wonderful city. I love the Ashley and the Cooper Rivers. Fort Sumter out there that looks over the city. I love this Battery that we promenade on. The people here are some of the friendliest people I've ever known."

He snorted. "They're the only people you've ever known. People are people. It doesn't matter where you live."

"Then why leave?" She fired back.

"Look at this mess. I can't for the life of me think of one good reason to stay." He stopped and swung her around, clamping his hands tightly on her shoulders, his rough thumbs exploring the bare skin at the base of her neck. Lidded eyes swept from her head to her toes and back up. He seemed to consume her, and she squirmed inside, feeling as if she'd just been violated. "Let's leave today. We'll go somewhere and get married. It'll be an adventure."

"But I don't want an adventure. This earthquake has been enough of one. Besides, I'm in mourning. Can't you tell?" She glanced down at the black dress she donned—thankful she'd saved it along with a nicer gown after mourning her grandmother.

"That's the beauty of this, sweetheart. No one will know your parents and brother died. We can go on as if they hadn't. And just for you, when they get this whole city cleaned up, we'll return, and if you want to move back to Charleston we will."

She jerked out of his embrace. "I-*I'd* know. And there is always the possibility that Simon is alive and can't get to me."

Lloyd pushed his shoulders back. "I didn't want to add to your pain because I thought you'd accepted his death. Simon is dead. I have it on good authority. He was found down in front of your father's insurance business."

Her insides quivered. "How did he die?"

"The building crumbled above him and the stone fell—"

She pushed her hands to her ears. "I don't want to hear any more."

He waited for her to lower her arms. "You see, there is no one keeping you here. You can come with me."

"I couldn't—wouldn't want to pretend my parents were alive so I could go on with all the fun things of life. It's not right—I love my parents and brother too much."

He reached out and gently clasped her lower arm. "So, what if you continue wearing your black? We could marry. People would understand. After all you have no family, no home, no place to go."

She shook her head and attempted to pull away, but his hand tightened on her arm. "You're hurting me." She blinked. A memory. A fist swinging. Fear shot ice through her veins. What was it? She fought to get it back, to not let it slip into the recesses of her mind. Her hands began to tremble as an ominous sensation filled her. "I want to go home."

He loosened his hold on her arm without letting go. "You don't have a home. That's what I've been telling you. That's why you need to marry me."

She tugged free. "Then take me back to Dr. and Mrs. Warwick's."

"Excuse us."

Olivia spun around to see two dragoons looking intently and holding their horses' reins.

"Can I help you?" Lloyd moved to stand beside Olivia.

"Are you Lloyd Pratt?" One of the dragoons asked.

Lloyd lifted his head and narrowed his eyes. "Who wants to know?"

The two dragoons looked at each other and then the same one spoke. "We were riding through the streets keeping an eye on things and saw a bunch of kids running from your house. Thought you might want to know."

"What. Someone robbed me?" Lloyd started to walk away, heading in the direction of his house, but stopped and glanced from the dragoons to Olivia.

"Go ahead. I'll see the little lady home." The talkative dragoon winked at her.

Lloyd looked to her, uncertainty furrowing his brows.

"I'll be fine, Lloyd. Take care of what you need to." Olivia forced a smile. "Just be careful."

"I will."

"Want some assistance?" The second dragoon spoke for the first time.

"That might not be a bad idea." Lloyd turned to go and the officer followed beside him.

The middle-aged dragoon staring down at her offered his arm. "Gideon Sharpe, miss. You can call me Gideon. May I have the honor of escorting you home?"

Olivia took his arm and cocked her head to look up at him. "Do I know you?"

"We've met before. But you probably don't remember an old coot like me." He chuckled.

She was sorry to say she didn't remember him. It very well could have been that they'd met the past year and that was why she didn't remember, but she'd never tell him that. For some reason her memory loss embarrassed her. It felt like she wasn't whole. And truly, she wasn't. But it seemed so personal. Too personal to share with someone she wasn't close to.

People would look at her differently if they knew. Some might even shun her, want nothing to do with her because she was different. She watched the ground in front of her as she walked to keep from twisting her ankle.

"You okay, miss?" Concern filled his voice.

His words woke her from her reverie. "Oh, yes. Do you think Lloyd and your friend are in any danger?"

He chuckled a deep rumbling in his chest. "No, I suspect they'll be just fine."

"You and your friend are very kind to help us out like this. Poor Lloyd didn't know what to do. I could see it in his face."

Gideon grunted. "He looked very sure of himself moments earlier when he was hurting you."

Olivia took her attention off the ground to meet his gaze. "You were watching?"

"I saw enough to know he needed to go his separate way."

Olivia widened her eyes. "Are you saying that no one broke into his house? You-you lied?" Her legs began to wobble and she willed strength back into them. This man was an officer of the law–he wouldn't harm her even if he had lied to them.

He shook his head with exaggeration. "Nope. Never lied to him. I said we were riding through the streets keeping an eye on things and saw a bunch of kids running from his house. Now, he may have interpreted that as they were running from inside his house, but I never said that. I just said they were running *from* his house, as in *away* from his house." A mischievous grin split his lips.

Olivia couldn't contain her giggle and it spilt forth. He was a knight rescuing a damsel in distress. She noticed a slight limp as he escorted her along the way. It seemed perfect that any knight wearing his full armor would walk stiff or almost as if he had a limp. Her heart warmed. "Are you married, Gideon?"

He broke into a full smile. "To the prettiest girl this side of the Mississippi."

Olivia sighed. "She's a lucky lady."

"She sure is." He gave her a wink.

He saw her all the way to the front door where Drew was exiting. He raised his brows in question then stuck out his hand to her companion.

"Captain Sharpe. We meet again." He shook his hand. "So you're escorting beautiful young ladies home now, huh? What's Ellen going to say?"

Gideon chuckled. "She'll never know unless you tell her."

Drew held the door open for her. Turning to face her knight, she smiled. "Thank you for seeing me here safely."

He gave her a slight bow, then Drew swung his arm around Gideon's shoulder and they descended the steps and walked away from the house, all the while speaking in hushed voices. It wasn't necessary. She knew very well what they discussed. A glance back her way as she closed the door told her that Drew was none too happy.

♥♥♥

It was her first Sunday back to church since the earthquake. Missing pieces of plaster left dark mosaic designs on the walls and ceilings. Large decorative wood beams were absent from the sanctuary ceiling and two of the pews below had been removed from their places and pushed against the side wall. Light filtering through the open windows glistened on the recently polished pine seats. Olivia swept the room with a careful eye, looking for other signs of damage. Small cracks traced around the walls, much like at the Warwick's place, marring the painted surface.

Sprinkled throughout the sanctuary were mourners in their black attire, a grim reminder to all of the devastation outside. Like her, they were probably attending service for the first time without their loved ones.

She glanced next to her where Drew sat, his attention

not wavering from the preacher at the front. Shifting in her seat, which suddenly seemed uncomfortable, Olivia couldn't remember ever wishing church would get over. But something had changed. How could she sit in God's house acting like she had every right to be here when she truly had none. She should have died in place of her parents. They were the good Christians, not her. They were always the ones who turned the other cheek, went the extra mile for their neighbor, and gave the coats off their backs, not her. What had she ever done for anyone? She'd always wanted to be like her parents, but sitting here in God's house, she realized she never tried to be like them. She always felt she belonged in church because her parents were so good. But now...

Now, sitting in church made her feel like she was dirty. God didn't want her here. This place was for people He loved. She glanced over at a woman dressed in black with two small children, wondering if she felt the same way. Probably not. God hadn't taken everything away from her. The woman had her children and—as young as she was— maybe her parents, too.

She had no one. No family to love her. No one to take care of or to care for her. She was alone. Because God didn't love her. She squirmed as the feeling of a thousand ants marched up and down her body. If only she could run out of the building away from God's condemning eye.

Drew reached over and covered her gloved hand with his and squeezed. Heat shot through her, warming her face. She glanced around—concerned someone might see the intimate gesture.

Understanding filled his kind smile, and he withdrew his hand. The loss of his warmth left her longing for the comfort he'd just given her.

♥♥♥

Drew leaned back in the landau, eyeing Olivia. What had made her so jittery in church? His lovely Olivia used to drink in every word the preacher spoke while jotting notes in her Bible. And on the ride home, she'd want to discuss, expound, question, and sometimes debate every aspect of what she'd just heard. Never one to take every word the preacher spoke as gospel, Olivia would dig into the scriptures referencing every passage with another to back it up.

Something had changed. He prayed her amnesia didn't affect her belief in God. Surely, not…her relationship with the Lord started long before her forgotten year. He raised his brows, piercing her with his stare. "What had you so antsy?"

Her long lashes flickered and brushed her cheeks. "Me?"

He glanced around the empty seats as if searching for another of his family members who'd yet to climb in the vehicle due to fellowshipping.

She rolled her eyes. "Very funny."

"What was going on in that head of yours? You usually are like a horse with blinders on the way you stay focused on the preacher as he gives the message." He hoped it was just a distraction of some sort. The last thing he wanted her to say was that her heart had changed toward the Lord. Giving himself a mental shake, he thrust the thought away and waited for her reply.

"How would you know my tendency in church? I've never been here with you before. As a matter of fact, today is the first time I've ever visited this church."

Drew's heart lodged in his throat and he struggled for words. Of course, she wouldn't remember the church because it was a part of his life and during the time period she had no recollection of. How long could he go on playing this part…this lie? His hand went to his shirt pocket that held her ring—his hope, his dreams.

Her memory wasn't returning, and Lloyd continued to take advantage of the situation. Regardless of how the blackguard treated her, she continued to insist they loved each other. All the while, Drew tried to be patient and allow time to bring his life with Olivia back to normal.

He jumped down out of the landau, eyes holding her to her seat. "If you truly believe that, Olivia, then come with me. I can prove you've been here—with me. There are dozens of people who will vouch for my words and they aren't family, since you believe my family would lie to you."

"Why? Did you ask one of your friends to lie for you?" She snapped the words out like a twisted wet towel cracking the air.

He reached in and snatched her hand. "Come on. You can ask anyone you see. Anyone. Just try me, Olivia. You won't give me the time of day to prove what I tell you is true, yet you'll take a man who abuses you at his word."

Instead of coming forward, she scurried back against the far side of the vehicle, attempting to tug her hand away. Her face drained of color. She reminded him of a cornered mouse that knew there was no escape.

"Leave me alone." Her words cut him deeper than a sharp knife.

He released her hand, wishing he could hit something. He'd welcome the pain it would bring to his hand because maybe, just maybe it would help him forget the piercing ache in his heart.

Swinging around, he marched toward the road.

"Drew. Where are you going?" JoAnna's high voice penetrated the early afternoon air.

"You're walking home?" She hurried up to him.

"What gave it away?"

"Well, aren't we in a dour mood? I guess you weren't listening to the sermon. Sounds like maybe you need to sit through a week of Sundays."

He stopped and thrust his fists on his sides. "What do you want, Jo?"

She shrugged. "I just wondered why you were leaving alone, that's all."

"Because I need the fresh air *and to be alone*."

"Is it Olivia?"

He snorted. "I had my whole life planned out. I'd graduate, get my medical license, work beside Father, marry, and have children. Then in the blink of an eye, all of that is lost and I have no control over it."

JoAnna's eyes softened and she gently touched his sleeve. "I'm sorry, Drew. I really am. Do you want me to talk to her?"

He wanted to tell her she'd done enough, but she was being too thoughtful to take out his frustrations on her. "No, there's nothing you can do. She thinks you and everyone else in our household will lie to her and tell her what I want you to say. It'd be best if you didn't say anything to her when it comes to me. The less said the better."

"You're not giving up are you?"

"Oh, I wouldn't call it giving up. Just giving in. I can't force her to love me again. She can see no wrong in Lloyd no matter what he does to her. I kept one thing from her, trying to protect her, and she doesn't trust me. It doesn't make any sense." He started to turn.

She stopped him by tightening her hand on his arm. "Want some company?"

He gave her a sad smile. "Not today, sis. I need time to think."

"You're not going to let Mr. Pratt have her are you? I

know what she's doing is hurting you, but I love Olivia. I don't want her to fall prey to that… that rake."

He removed her hand from his arm and squeezed it. "Watch your mouth. Mother hears you say something like that, and you won't see the light of day for that same week of Sundays. And to answer your question, no, I'm not going to leave her to the machinations of Pratt. I may not ever gain Olivia's love again, but I promise you, Lloyd Pratt won't have her either. I won't see the woman I love mistreated."

"Are you sure I can't say anything to help? I feel sure she'd believe me." Pleading filled her words.

He let go of her hand. "I'm sure. It's best this way. Don't tell her anything. That way she can't accuse me of trying to get you to lie for me."

Drew walked away, feeling his sister's gaze on his back. He swallowed the lump in his throat, reminding himself men didn't cry. Pushing his shoulders back, he started the trek home, knowing he had to move on with his life. He couldn't make her love him and he certainly wouldn't marry her if she didn't.

Chapter 14

Olivia huddled in the corner of the landau, jumping when JoAnna showed up at the door where Drew had left. He'd looked so angry with her that it was a good thing she hadn't been standing because she was certain she'd have collapsed from wobbly legs.

Climbing in the carriage, JoAnna chose the seat across from her and smiled before looking away. Olivia returned her smile. "Where's your brother?" She croaked out the words.

"He said he needed some fresh air and would walk home." JoAnna stared out the window.

"Oh." Olivia ran her gloved finger along the edge of the cushion. If he was so frightening to her why did she feel disappointed that he wouldn't be riding with them? Olivia glanced out the window closest to her to see if any of the other Warwicks were near. They weren't. "Can I ask you a question?"

JoAnna eyed her cautiously with green eyes. "What would you like to know?"

"Drew keeps telling me that we were engaged when the earthquake hit and that Lloyd and I had broken off our engagement a year prior. Is that true?"

Drew's youngest sister wouldn't look her in the eye. She brushed at some wrinkles in her skirt then plucked off her gloves, one finger at a time and laid them in her lap before looking back out the window. "I'm really not free to talk about that." She gave her a timid smile. "You must know how much I love you and wish I could."

Olivia observed the beautiful red-headed Warwick, noticing for the first time the difference in her coloring and the young woman's brothers. Taking after her mother's beauty, JoAnna was not only lovely, but seemed the most forthright. Another trait Olivia had noticed of Mrs. Warwick. If any of the family would impart the truth to her it would be JoAnna. So why did she feel she couldn't share? Was it because she'd have to lie or betray her brother? "I understand." But she didn't. Not really.

It left her to draw only one conclusion. A conclusion that at the moment she didn't like too well. She wished her insides didn't get so fluttery when she was around Drew. Then perhaps what she was ascertaining wouldn't trouble her quite as much. And the draw she felt to Drew left her feeling unfaithful to Lloyd.

What she didn't understand was why neither man could appreciate the fact that she was confused and struggling to understand her emotions and her lack of memories.

"My brother's a good man." Loyalty burned behind JoAnna's eyes.

"Indeed. Then why won't you share with me what you know?"

She hesitated and Olivia could see the battle that waged within the youngest Warwick. Guilt filled her at making her choose between family allegiance and her, but she wouldn't release her from the question. Too much was at stake.

JoAnna bit her bottom lip. "Drew asked me not to." She rasped.

Olivia furrowed her brows. Those words were all she needed to hear. They sealed Drew's fate as sure as the words "Drew lied." The poor thing tried to protect her brother while not telling an untruth. Nothing like her brother who didn't seem troubled to lie to get what he wanted.

Well, he may want her, but he'd never have her. She should have trusted her memories and Lloyd, then she'd never have let feelings toward Drew grow. "I'm sure he did." Anger singed each word.

"No, it's not like that."

Olivia reached forward and patted JoAnna's white knuckled hand clenching the seat edge. "I didn't mean to take it out on you. Let's change the subject to something more pleasant." She smiled.

"Although I'm not free to talk about my brother, you must know he is a wonderful man and cares for you deeply."

"I'm sure as a brother he is." Wonderful in JoAnna's eyes. But care for her? Maybe in the strange attached way that Lloyd had described. But she really wanted to ease the young woman's concerns. JoAnna seemed almost distraught by the whole conversation. Olivia wished she'd not brought up the matter, but then she'd not have discovered the truth.

"He would be wonderful to you, too." She sighed. "I think you're trying too hard to remember. Sometimes trying too hard with things only makes it worse. I don't know what you're going through because I've never lost my memory and I've never had two men in love with me, but I think if it were me, I'd let them prove their love to me. What does the past matter? It's the future that's before you. The past is the past and can't be changed, but the future, well, it holds all your hopes and dreams."

♥♥♥

Olivia fluffed her pillow and laid back down. Her mind wouldn't stop sorting through her circumstances. How could she possibly stay here at the Warwick's home if she believed that Drew lied to her? She tossed the thin blanket off and rolled to her side on the large poster bed. She'd opened the upper piazza door, allowing the light of the moon to leave shadows dancing on the wall. She breathed in the sweet aroma of the fall gardenias as it rolled in on the night breeze. But even that couldn't mask the scent of Drew that permeated the room. Everywhere she looked she saw reminders of him. It irritated her that she would even notice his things or the scent of woodland spice. Despite the verity that she'd washed the sheets and hung them on the line to dry, allowing the sun and fall air to freshen them, the scent of Drew still seemed to rise from the mattress. There was something oh so familiar about it, but like all her other memories, she couldn't put a finger on it. It was most likely a popular cologne for men, that was all. But still her stomach swirled with each inhale. No wonder she had trouble sleeping.

She drummed her fingers on the sheet. Drew's jacket, not yet needed in the early fall weather, hung on a hook. A beautiful mahogany wardrobe consumed a goodly portion of the opposite wall. Two doors the length of the cabinet were separated by drawers. She'd forbidden herself from peeking in and seeing what all Drew kept in it. That was none of her business and she reminded herself that he was generous enough to give up his room and one door of the wardrobe for her—the least she could do was respect his privacy. She looked away to avoid temptation.

Her gaze landed on the painting of a woman welcoming home her hero. The intricately carved gold frame seemed appropriate to hold the picture of the happy couple. Mosquito netting and darkness kept her from enjoying the picture as she did in the daylight hours. Did Drew choose the picture? Did it stir longing in him like it did her?

It didn't matter. She was engaged to Lloyd. She closed her eyes and tried to bring Lloyd into her mind's eye, but try as she might, his short, black hair melded into brown, wavy locks that smelled of woodland spice, and she was once again staring into the all-consuming eyes of Drew Warwick.

Flopping once again to her back, she attempted to think about the puppies Christian had brought home in hopes of getting her mind and senses off the traitorous road they were on. Lord have mercy on her. Why did this man haunt her thoughts day and night? She wasn't loyal to Lloyd. She didn't deserve him with the way her mind wandered to improper places. She was an engaged woman, not free to admire a handsome man and then ruminate on him as if he were hers.

Giving up on sleep, she swung her feet to the floor. The ankle improved daily and she rolled it as she sat on the edge of the bed before standing. Not even a twinge of pain. Treading across the room, she stood in the doorway that led outside to the upper piazza. She made out the tree line and houses across the way. A whippoorwill sang his cheerful song above the chirp of the crickets and cicadas. If only sleep would overtake her. She took a deep breath, filling her lungs with the strong scent of gardenias.

A flash of memory like lightening burned across her mind. She was sitting on the grass, with Drew lounging beside her, when something had suddenly crawled up her leg. She had screamed and bolted to her feet. Swishing the skirt of her dress back and forth as she jumped up and down, she had begged for his help to get it off. Drew rolled to his back laughing as the grasshopper fell from the inside layer of fabric.

Olivia grasped hold of the door frame to keep herself upright. It couldn't be. She saw Drew because she was surrounded by his things, his scent, his family—no other reason. It was Lloyd on the grass with her, surely, not Drew. She swayed as she closed her eyes trying to put Lloyd next to her, but every time she tried, it was Drew.

Drew closed the door as his last patients left. He waved to the couple and climbed in his own vehicle. He'd not planned on seeing patients today, but had stopped by the office to pick up his favorite pen so he'd have it for church on Sunday. He was in town to collect the cases he'd ordered for the ancestral wedding book and knife. To his disappointment, the larger of the two cases hadn't been ready for pickup. He drew in a breath of refreshing air to ease his frustration.

Early fall had arrived and the air cooled to a comfortable degree somewhere in the seventies he'd guess. With the amount of people still sleeping in the tents around town, Charleston people could be thankful that the quake hadn't struck in the dead of winter when the temperatures often ran in the low forties at night. A thin blanket would keep people warm for now. He could only hope that people would be in their homes before the weather changed or they'd be inundated with sick patients.

The warm sun's rays shown down from a robin's egg blue sky. Hammers echoed throughout the city demanding people not slumber late this Saturday morning. He snapped the reins, sending the horse lurching forward as he listened to the now-familiar sounds of a town rebuilding itself. The streets were once again clear of brick, stone, and debris, allowing horses and vehicles to maneuver through the city without detours or risk of peril coming to them should they brave the shorter route.

It would take a lot of hard work to bring Charleston back to her former glory, but it would be done. One thing was for sure, there was no shortage of work anymore— shortage of housing, but not of employment.

Even as he approached his family home, the street was alive with barking dogs and activity. It seemed even the animals rejoiced that things were progressing toward normal and the old routine.

Drew maneuvered the vehicle to the side of the house. Barks, meows, and what sounded like a lamb came from the back yard. The stable area—to be specific. Drew shook his head at Christian's new championing efforts. They looked more like a veterinary office than the home of doctors.

He trudged into the house, case in hand, where the last cot had already been moved out of the living area and Father stood on a ladder examining a crack in one of the walls.

"So, what is your assessment? Surgery or just some stitching up?" Drew leaned his shoulder against the wall.

"From what I can tell, it looks like some plaster and paint should fix it up fine." His father climbed up another rung and proceeded in his examination.

"I see. You do realize we won't be able to find anyone knowledgeable and free to come right away. I don't think there's a mason or carpenter within a fifty miles radius of Charleston that hasn't been put to work."

"You're right. Ebenezer and I are going to do it after he gets his house rebuilt." Father climbed down the ladder before scrubbing his hands together in an attempt to brush off the powder.

"He was able to get his hands on some supplies then?" Ebenezer was not only their driver, but also their handyman. Drew hadn't realized how much they relied on the man. Ebenezer had been a slave in his younger years just like Mrs. Benninger. He was a hard worker and a loyal employee.

"He has. And he needs to get back to work to earn money for his family. Hard to say how long it could take him to get a roof over his family's heads. That's why I decided we are going to have a house raising."

"You're going to help?" Drew asked with skepticism in his voice.

"Don't sound so doubtful. I'll have you know I have many hidden talents."

Drew chuckled and turned to leave. "Let me know when we start."

"Before you go, I'd like to talk to you." Father stepped forward and clasped Drew's shoulder.

"Nothing serious I hope." He frowned at his father's tone.

"That would depend on what you call serious. Why don't we go into the study and talk?"

Drew followed his father into the only room in the house that looked like his father. Ancient medical tools hung in frames on the wall or adorned his father's desk top. Bone drills, hooks, bone forceps, and even uvula-crushing forceps were amongst the equipment Drew had once found fascinating as a child. Now he found them appalling.

Father said he kept them to remind himself how far they'd come in medicine. He'd also said being a doctor back in ancient times wasn't for the fainthearted. Drew thought about the pain the patients had suffered—all in the name of being healed—and shuddered.

His father took a seat and waited as Drew situated himself across from his father. Father leaned back in his chair. "I see you got the case for Brithwin's knife."

"Yes, but I'm sure that isn't what you asked me in here for."

"No. No it isn't. What are your plans as far as Olivia?"

Drew startled. Father didn't usually question their personal affairs. "Did Mother put you up to that question?"

"No." He leaned in, placing his elbows on his desk. "I'm asking because *I* want to know."

"I see." Drew set the wood-and-glass case on the desk

and crossed his arms in front of his chest. "I don't have any actual plans in regard to her."

"Are you going to continue to pursue her?"

He flung his hands up. "You have got to be kidding me, Father. Would you have pursued Mother had this been her?"

His father raised his brow.

Drew pushed up from the chair and began pacing the floor. "I have done everything I can to get her to believe me, but because of my lack of good judgment with the news of her parents, she refuses to listen to anything I say."

"I initially told you not to tell her. You can't blame yourself for that."

"But I chose to keep it from her when I knew she needed to know because it was easier than seeing her in pain over the loss of her parents."

"Still no news on Simon?" Two worry lines formed between his father's eyes.

"No, nothing yet. But as strange as this is going to sound, I believe Simon will show up. I can't tell you why, but deep down I think he's alive. I've been to every morgue, talked to everyone I could think of who might know something, and Simon has never shown up."

"For Olivia's sake, I hope you're right."

"Me too, Father. I just hope and pray she will remember and that she can forgive me." He pulled back the silky sheer curtain and peered out the window.

"Drew, you have always had a need to be in control of a situation regardless of what it is. When you were younger, I brushed it off as being the oldest of three boys. As you grew into a young man, I continued to make excuses for you. You are a hard worker and determined to conquer everything you do. But Olivia is not a mission or an undertaking. She is a woman with feelings."

Drew scowled. "You don't think I know that? I love her. I want her to be my wife. Believe me, she is much more than either of those things."

Father tented his hands, gazing over them. "I'm just trying to give you some fatherly advice here, son. I know you love her. But it's almost like she is a mission of yours."

"What am I supposed to do? Just sit back and hope it all works out? I don't want to lose her to Lloyd, or anyone else."

"You can push too hard and push her right out of your life."

"Oh, so I'm just supposed to stand by and watch her walk away from my life?" Drew blew out a gush of air and sat back down.

"Olivia has not been herself this past week, and when I asked your sister if she knew anything, she shared with me what happened last week at church. Do you think by dragging her into a church where she doesn't remember a soul and forcing her to listen to people tell her that you two were a couple is going to win her heart? If you think that son, you are sorely mistaken." Father's voice was compassionate. Shame filled Drew at his behavior. It was desperation that led him to that. Why couldn't his father see how maddening the situation was?

"I admit I shouldn't have done that. But I'm done. I give up. You're right—I can't force her to love me again."

Tenderness filled his father's eyes. "I didn't say to give up. You need to turn this burden over to the Lord. This one is too big for you, and it's time you learned that you can't solve everything in your own power. Most of your life you've been fortunate enough that through hard work and determination you conquered your mountains. I have let it go and let you do your own thing, but it is time for you to realize God's will in your life is most important. You may be able to make things happen like you want. But it doesn't mean that is what's best for you."

"So you're saying I should walk away and if she remembers great, but if not, move on? Could you have done that with Mother?"

"I'm saying lay this at our Lord's feet. Pray and give the burden to him. I know you love Olivia. But maybe God is using this tragedy to show you she isn't the one He has chosen for you."

Drew's scowl deepened. "If she's not the one, then I don't want to get married. She's the only one I want." Frustration which had grown steady within him each day since he lost Olivia expanded to the bursting point.

"No. If God has someone else for you, she'll make you happier and give you more fulfillment than Olivia. I can promise you that." His father's tender gaze went to a picture of Mother hanging above the fireplace. "Yes, I can promise you that."

Drew dropped his head in his hands. "I feel so lost…so empty without her."

"And that is a normal feeling. But you can't let her come before our Lord. And I'm afraid that is what I'm seeing happen here. Your desire for her is consuming you."

"I can't just let Lloyd have her. He doesn't love her. He's using her. Did I tell you I think he's guilty of embezzlement with her father's company?"

Father pushed back in the chair and rubbed his chin. "I think Lloyd does care for her. But I hadn't heard about the embezzlement. Do you have proof? Absolutely, protect her. She has no one else looking after her now. But do it as a friend. She needs friends right now. They are easier to trust. They give and don't expect anything back."

"I thought to expose Pratt for the scoundrel he is. Then maybe she'd forget about him." Drew rubbed his temples with his index fingers in an attempt to massage away the oncoming headache.

"Just be careful how you go about it. If you do it the wrong way, you'll just push Olivia away. Use wisdom, son."

"It's not that easy proving something like this. Especially in the chaos our city is in. I've been to the bank, but they won't talk to me because I'm not Mr. Macqueen. And I can't tell Olivia what I'm trying to do. So that door has been closed. I have to try and contact some of the people who have filed and received money for claims and see if the people even exist."

"You're not a detective. Maybe you should give this over to the police." Father gave him a concerned look. "If he's caught up with criminals they could be dangerous."

Drew let out a mock laugh. "And what am I supposed to say? I think Lloyd Pratt is an embezzler because he was seen digging through the belongings of his once-fiancée's home and ran? I don't think that will motivate them to work on the case."

"I see what you mean." His father frowned. "Take caution, Drew. You never know what people will do when they feel threatened that their freedom may be taken away. I don't want to find you injured or dead somewhere."

That wasn't his desire either. Drew headed to the drawing room, glad to get the conversation with his father behind him. Once there, he retrieved the precious knife, the emerald eyes of the hawk staring up at him. Hadn't Brithwin, the owner of the knife, and Royce, her husband, faced overwhelming odds? From the stories told to him, it was hard to believe the couple ended up with such a deep love. He could only hope that he held some of the same good fortune that they did. Father had always told him that his tenacity was much like his grandfather's, who was like *his* grandfather. Perhaps it skipped a generation all the way back to Royce.

He fastened the beautiful, detailed knife into the case and hung it back on the wall. The wedding book on the table below beckoned to him. He fingered the cover before gingerly flipping it open. His eyes scanned the marriages and dates. He could only hope that one day Olivia's and his wedding would be entered.

Chapter 15

Maybe JoAnna was right. She should just move forward—, erase the slate, so to speak. Olivia tucked a loose strand of hair behind her ear as she squatted down to sit on a low wooden stool in the stable. She cuddled the puppy with the white spot on his nose. She held him against her chest, cooing. The little guy licked her chin, puppy breath filling her nostrils.

Eight feet away, Christian bent over a colt, securing a splint on its leg while his weight was suspended from a rafter with a rope and a sort of sling wrapped under his belly. Olivia tilted her head to watch. "Where did you get him?"

Christian lifted his head, while still bent over at the waist. "A friend told me they were going to have to... put the colt out of its misery. I couldn't let that happen."

"Will he get well?" She wished she hadn't asked because she didn't want to know the answer unless it was yes.

"His leg will heal. Not sure how much work he'll ever be able to do." He ran his hand down the colt's back. "He's a beaut though. A pure Egyptian Arabian. I couldn't let him die."

"You should have been a veterinarian." She looked around the room where the feed and tack was kept. Menageries of animals were in makeshift pens, both injured and healthy. "What made you become a doctor?"

Christian chuckled. "If you haven't noticed that seems to run in the family."

"Is that why you went to medical school? Because your father and brothers did?"

He shrugged. "I guess I always knew I would. I really don't remember making a choice."

Running her hand down the pup's silky hair, she stilled the squirming bundle. "Do you regret the course you took? I mean if you don't remember choosing, do you ever wonder why you chose it?"

He regarded her for a moment. "Are we talking about me?"

Heat filled her face. Since Drew had stomped off after church over a week ago, she'd hardly glimpsed him. She'd hear him come in late at night, and before she got down to breakfast he'd already left. There hadn't been a chance to talk to him about her memory of him…of them. But then she had a hard time trusting her random memories that seem to flash before her eyes at any given time. So often she couldn't even make sense of the vision she'd seen. "Of-of course we are."

He nodded and turned his attention back to the colt. "I guess because it felt right. You could say I had peace."

"But you love animals. I don't see your father or brothers out here in their spare time tending to these furry critters."

"I do have a soft spot for God's creatures. But right now it keeps me busy and my mind off things I don't want to think about."

She wished she could do the same. Throw herself into something to keep her from thinking about her life. She certainly didn't have any peace in her life right now. She rolled the pup onto his back and rubbed his tummy. "What did you name the puppies?"

"He's Spot." He gestured with his head toward the other pup cuddled up next to a saddle. "He's Spotless."

She huffed. "Those are terrible names." She put the little guy next to his brother. And tried to brush out a large soiled spot where the pup had laid on her black skirt, leaving it brown.

Christian grinned. "Still think it's a poor name?"

Olivia giggled. Even Christian's problems didn't keep him down. She'd do well to remember that.

She stepped out of the stable and into the late September sun. The rays beat down on her unprotected head and face. She paused and soaked in its warmth, not caring about the ill effects it would have on her ivory skin. Peace. When was the last time she'd felt that? God's peace seemed almost like something foreign to her. It was as if her memory loss had stolen that too.

She sobered and trudged up the stairs crossing over the piazza. She needed something to fill her time and help keep her mind off Drew and Lloyd.

Guilt twisted her insides that she hadn't spoken with Drew about her memory of them. It had taken everything in her not to talk to JoAnna or Mrs. Warwick about her flash of recollection. She wanted to ask them to fill in the voids, but her conscience wouldn't let her. She'd tried to reason with herself that Drew had scarcely been around, but she knew she could have stayed up or even left a note and he'd have made himself available.

Why was she afraid to speak to him? She should be happy that he was telling the truth. But that would mean that Lloyd lied. It was the most frustrating thing she could ever remember.

The smell of baked apples and cinnamon met her as she opened the door of the house. Olivia followed the aroma to the kitchen where Mrs. Benninger had just pulled out an apple cobbler. She peeked in the doorway as the cook looked up from her masterpiece.

"Smells delicious. Do you need any help?"

A grin split the old woman's face. "Do ya mean eating

or cooking?"

The gentle teasing lightened Olivia's spirit. "A little of both."

"You can have some cobbler after dinner, but JoAnna is looking for you so I don't think you'll have time to do any work."

"Do you know where she went?"

"Nope. Stuck her head in here just like you did and then she disappeared."

Olivia swung around and nearly collided with Drew's chest. Strong hands clasped her arms and steadied her. Their gazes met and his soft chocolate eyes seemed to be trying to read her thoughts. She sucked in a stabilizing breath.

Tearing her eyes away, Olivia stole a glimpse over her shoulder all the while feeling the warmth of Drew's hands seep through her cotton blouse.

Mrs. Benninger watched with brows raised and hands on hips. "What is it about my apple cobbler that brings everyone out from their hiding places to come by and check on how I's doing? I think I'll just stop making it so's ya'll will stop pestering me and slowing me down in my work."

Drew released her arms and threw his hands up, snapping his attention to the cook. "I was just coming to find Olivia." He smiled. "And I have, so I won't disturb you any further."

"See that you don't." Mrs. Benninger said with a twinkle in her eyes.

Olivia stepped out of the doorway and off to the side to put some distance between her and Drew. "What did you need me for?"

He put his finger to his lips and guided her away from the kitchen with his hand on the small of her back. When they reached the hallway he stopped.

"I wasn't really looking for you. Just trying to keep the cook happy." He winked.

Olivia gasped and threw her hand to her chest in faux surprise. "Why Drew, I can't believe—"

"What can't you believe?" JoAnna came around the corner. If she hadn't known better, Olivia would have sworn Drew growled.

She flashed him a smile. "I'd like to talk to you, later." She lowered her voice. "Alone."

His eyes turned smoky and immobilized her. Pushing her hand against her stomach, she tried to swallow, but her throat had gone dry.

"Are you going to tell me?" JoAnna reached where they stood.

Drew sighed. "She was just saying she can't believe what terrible timing you have, JoAnna."

"That's *not* what Olivia was talking about." She gave her brother a swift swat before turning to Olivia. "Come on, sis, we have a party to get ready for."

Sis? Olivia's heart warmed at the thought of having a sister. She looked back at Drew. That would mean he'd be her…husband. She shook herself mentally. "Party? I wasn't invited to a party."

"Sure you were. I just forgot to mention it. And dear brother Drew is going to be our escort. Won't that be fun?"

"No one asked me about this." His brows rose so high that wrinkles formed on his forehead.

"Will you, dear brother? I felt sure you would want to keep an eye on Olivia and your baby sister. You never know what kind of nefarious men might show up at a party and try to take advantage of two beautiful young ladies."

"You know how much I enjoy those kinds of things, JoAnna." He heaved a sigh.

"But you wouldn't trust Olivia's or my safety to

anyone else would you?" JoAnna challenged.

His eyes locked on Olivia. "No." He let out a sigh. "I suppose I can endure it to keep an eye on you...two." Olivia squirmed under Drew's perusal. "What time do I need to be ready?"

"Seven o'clock." JoAnna grasped Olivia's hand and pulled her toward the stairs. "Come on. Let's go get ready."

Olivia let JoAnna pull her while sneaking a glimpse at Drew still standing at the end of the hall.

"You didn't say where the party is." Drew raised his voice as they reached the banister.

"At Pastor Meynardie's residence." JoAnna giggled and sped up the stairs dragging Olivia along.

When they reached the second floor, Olivia stopped. "That wasn't nice to make Drew come, JoAnna. He obviously doesn't care for social activities."

JoAnna pursed her lips together, but Olivia could still see a glimpse of a mischievous grin. "He'll enjoy it with you there." JoAnna let the full smile emerge. "Besides he can be such a prude. Don't you remember how..." She shook her head. "Trust me. Plans like this have been long in the making. He'll be a better husband, I mean man for it."

Olivia' face flamed. For heaven's sake why did that embarrass her? "But if he doesn't want to go and it's just to a church get-together, I'm sure we don't need a chaperone."

JoAnna flounced toward her bedroom several doors down from where Olivia stayed in Drew's room, and called over her shoulder. "Don't worry, he'll get either Christian or William to go with him." She stopped at her door. "Probably Christian since he doesn't meet a stranger. But that man seems to be in a mood of his own lately."

When she'd disappeared into her room, Olivia went to the banister and leaned over it. "Drew?"

Footfalls sounded on the oak flooring below then

softened as they fell on the hall rug. Drew tipped his head up and soft brown curls fell back away from his face. "Yes?"

"You really don't have to come if you don't want. I'm sure we'll be safe from nefarious men." She giggled.

Grinning, Drew cocked his head. "Well, I don't want to be called a prude so I'll go."

Olivia gasped. "I didn't say that. That was your sister."

"Hmmm, I didn't hear you argue with her. But if you don't want me there—"

Olivia stomped her foot. "Oh! You're impossible."

He winked up at her. "I do try."

She rolled her eyes. "Would you like to get your things from your room before I go in so that you can get ready?"

He started up the stairs. "That's a good idea." He reached the top and stopped in front of her. "I really don't mind going."

He was close enough that if she leaned forward she could rest her head on his chest. She blinked, feeling awkward, and nodded. After disappearing into his room he reemerged with clothes draped over his arm. "Thank you."

Once he was out of sight, she hustled into the room. Opening the wardrobe door where her clothes hung, she ran her hand over several dresses. Pausing at the burgundy gown made of silk and nun's veiling, she pulled it from the cabinet. She ran her fingers over the fine Egyptian lace. It was the last gown she and Mama had picked out together. She drew it to her, kicking out her leg to admire the row of knife pleats around the bottom. The gown sported a fine bustle in the back and princess drapery in the front.

Before she could return it to the wardrobe there was a knock at her door.

"Are you presentable?" JoAnna opened the door a crack and peeked in.

"You may enter. I was just about to find you to see if you needed help with your dress and have you help me with my buttons."

JoAnna pushed into the room, letting out a squeal and she rushed over to her as she still held the dress against her.

She reached out and touched the silk fabric. "It's beautiful. Drew isn't going to be able to take his eyes off you all night."

Olivia forced a smile. "This isn't the gown I'll be wearing." She hung it back in the wardrobe and pulled out a black gown. "I'll be wearing this."

♥♥♥

Drew stood in a small circle of friends, but his eyes continued to be drawn to the loveliest woman in the room. Olivia, even in her black silk crepe gown, looked like God's perfection of women, she exuded such beauty. Their eyes locked and her cheeks flushed. She'd just caught him watching her.

She lowered her head, lashes fluttering against her cheeks, a timid smile on her lips. Hands on each side of her gown, she swished it back and forth in an adorable nervous fashion. Forcing his attention back to the conversation at hand, Drew lifted a glass of punch off a servant's tray.

Tom Bruely, a longtime friend of Drew's, pushed up a pair of round wire-rim glasses that had slipped down his thin nose. "I must say, I'm thankful for Captain Brown's generosity. I not only have a bed, but meals too."

"Captain Brown?" Drew swirled the punch in his glass, trying to stay focused on what Tom was saying rather than hoping someone would join Olivia, JoAnna, and the pastor's wife across the room.

"Yes, he's the master of the U.S.S. Wisaria. It's a 167-foot lighthouse tender vessel, complete with side paddle wheels and steam powered."

Drew chuckled. "Sounds like you've had a few tours of the ship."

"To be sure. But it beats staying in the Northeastern Railroad passenger cars. I understand the mosquitoes are terrible there. At least the breeze off the water keeps those pesky things away. Where are you two staying?" He glanced between Jonathon Riley and Drew.

Jonathon, a cocky new resident of two years to Charleston, took a sip of his punch. "I'd be stayin' at Robert Graham's."

"I heard that he's housing almost one-hundred-fifty people in his stable, many with mattresses." Tom replied.

"It's true. Right generous man, Graham is. Although I forwent a mattress so Susan Mathers could have one. And she was extremely appreciative." Jonathon gave a wink and turned to Drew. "Where are you staying?"

"I'm fortunate in that I only spent a few nights in the open air before returning to my own room. Our home had been set up as a makeshift hospital until a week ago." *He wasn't actually in his room,* but he wasn't going to start explaining all that.

"I wonder why the good Lord showed you so much favor. Last I heard 40,000 of our 60,000 Charleston residents were sleeping in their yards, streets, or the city squares."

Drew stole a glance at Olivia, wondering what she wanted to discuss with him and praying it was something he'd want to hear. "I've had more than a roof over my head stolen from me. I'd trade losses with either of you."

"I'm sorry, Drew. I forgot about Olivia. Such a shame." Tom shook his head.

"Guess I missed this. Olivia finally see you for the scoundrel you are? Maybe I should give her a go. She might like a change." Jonathan smirked.

Drew felt the full blow of Jonathan's verbal punch.

Tom winced. "Give Drew some consideration. How would you feel if your girl couldn't remember you?"

Now it was Drew's turn to wince. He wished he never brought it up.

Jonathan let out a guffaw. "No girl I've ever courted forgot me."

"I'd be willing to wager on that." Tom shot back with a chuckle.

"Olivia will remember. It could happen at any time. All her lost memories could come rushing back at once. The brain is a complicated thing to understand." Drew wished he could believe his own words.

Glaring at Tom, Jonathan seemed to ignore Drew's comment. "The women like me. Why, I bet if I went over there and asked your sister or Olivia to the theater they'd say yes."

Drew ground his back teeth. "Don't bother because I'm telling you right now the answer is no."

Jonathan raised his brows. "You afraid I might be able to win your belle?"

Drew opened his mouth to speak, but Tom jumped in. "Just ignore him, Drew. Jonathan probably believes Wiggin's claim that he predicted this earthquake *and* his prediction that tomorrow Charleston along with Atlanta, New Orleans, and Mobile will be destroyed by a massive earthquake far greater than the one we had."

"He did predict this one." Jonathan argued.

"No, he claims to, but has yet to give any proof of it. Anybody can lay claim. He needs proof. He's a crank, a lunatic, and he's frightening gullible people needlessly." Tom growled.

Drew was glad to see that Tom had steered Jonathan off the subject of Olivia. He owed the man a favor. Seeking out Olivia, he scanned the room to find that she and his sister had moved nearer to the refreshment table. Mrs. Meynardie had moved away and spoke with another group of ladies closer to her age.

The women in the church seemed to be avoiding Olivia like she had some contagious disease rather than amnesia. His hope that someone would chat with her and mention his name in connection with hers faded—unless the pastor's wife said something, which he highly doubted.

Returning his attention to the continuing disagreement about Wiggin's reliability, Drew caught a glimpse from the corner of his eye of someone approaching Olivia. His body went rigid.

What was Lloyd doing here?

Chapter 16

Olivia flinched as Lloyd strolled up and took her arm, guiding her away from JoAnna. She thought that JoAnna was going to object, but the challenging look Lloyd blasted her way silenced any argument.

To her knowledge, Lloyd had never attended Bethel Church. And for that matter, she couldn't remember Lloyd attending church at all unless she begged him to. He always had an excuse as to why he couldn't. Her brow furrowed at the memory. So what was he doing here at a church function?

"Let's go outside and talk." Lloyd turned her toward the door.

She skidded to a stop. "I'd prefer to remain indoors."

He scowled at her. "I'd like to talk to you in private."

A chill swept up her spine and she glanced around the room. Drew's eyes smoldered as he moved his gaze from Lloyd to her. She swallowed and looked back at Lloyd wishing that Drew would come rescue her. She still hadn't had a chance to speak with him. Christian and Drew had accompanied JoAnna and her in the carriage, leaving no time for a private conversation.

She'd told him she wished to speak to him, so it would be his responsibility to make it happen. She was home all day long, every day. It shouldn't be too difficult for him to find her.

"There's no one around. What do you wish to speak to me about?" She kept her voice steady.

"I want you to move out of the Warwick's home. We're engaged. How do you suppose that looks? Not to mention I don't trust Drew." Lloyd glanced in Drew's direction.

Olivia was tempted to peek and see if Drew was still glaring their way. Remembering that she had wished to speak to Lloyd, too, she pushed her shoulders back. Knowing Drew stood across the room gave her the confidence she needed to spit the words out. "I am glad you brought up our engagement. You see I had a flash of recollection this past week."

Lloyd looked as if she'd slapped him. "So your memories have returned?"

"Not all. But I'm certain more will return soon. It's given me hope."

He eyed her carefully. "So what exactly did you remember?"

"I remembered a time when Drew and I were sitting in the grass together."

"That means nothing."

She lifted her chin. "We were alone."

He shrugged.

"You said Drew had developed this fascination with me *after* the earthquake. Yet, apparently I was seeing him before."

"I said that to protect you."

She unlooped her arm from his and turned to face him. "From what? What could you possibly have been protecting me from?"

His gaze shifted over her shoulder to what she hoped was Drew. "What he had done to you." He returned his gaze to her. "I admit I wasn't completely honest with you. You and Drew did see each other for a period." He scratched behind his ear. "But he was unfaithful to you and you broke it off. It hurt you badly and I wanted to spare you from that pain."

"I-I don't believe you." She glanced over her shoulder

to see Drew still brooding. Her stomach warmed, locking eyes with the man she had decided she'd enjoy getting to know better. He always made her feel safe. He sent her stomach into a flurry when she saw him, and she could never keep her mind off him. She'd just determined he had told her the truth and she wasn't ready to let him slip out of her good graces. She wanted to believe Drew. "You're lying."

He paled. "How could you say that to me when I'm the one who told you the truth about your parents? Drew was the one who lied to you."

"He was protecting me."

"He was protecting himself."

She gave an unladylike snort. "Drew gained nothing by keeping that from me."

"You never know what secrets Drew keeps." He snarled.

"Excuse me." The reverend stepped up to them and stuck out his hand. "I'm Reverend Meynardie. And you are?"

Lloyd glanced down at the reverend's hand as if he had leprosy before finally acknowledging him and shaking his hand. "Lloyd Pratt."

"Well, I'm glad you came by today. I don't believe I've seen you in our services before."

"I only stopped in to speak to Miss Macqueen, I'll be on my way." Lloyd's tone was clipped.

"Don't let me run you off. I'm as pleased as punch that you came by. We'd be honored to have you come to our Sunday service this week. I'll be preaching on Judas Iscariot. That always bodes for a good sermon and sometimes a sound convicting if I don't say so myself." A smile spread over Reverend Meynardie's face.

"I must go." He turned to Olivia and grasped her hand

bringing it up to place a kiss on the back of her glove. "Think about what I said."

♥♥♥

Olivia sat next to JoAnna and across from Drew on the ride home. Drew leaned forward. "Did you enjoy yourselves?"

"Oh, yes. We had a lovely time. Wouldn't you say, Olivia?" JoAnna's voice held a smile.

"No nefarious characters to deal with I hope?" Drew teased.

Olivia giggled.

"Are you talking about Lloyd?" Christian asked.

JoAnna kicked Christian and he let out a yelp before rubbing his shin. "What'd I say?"

"Nothing." Drew answered. "Our little sister just needs a bit of restraint. I think she's been spoiled by the whole lot of us."

JoAnna held her own, bantering with her two brothers during the ride home while Olivia's stomach churned from the time Drew stepped into the carriage. She had to try to speak to him when they reached the Warwick's place. Just thinking about asking for time alone with him in front of Christian and JoAnna caused half of her anxiety. Perhaps he would remember she'd requested to speak privately with him and he'd seek her out.

Christian pulled back the short curtain covering the carriage window. "I'm going to ride around back and see how my patients are doing."

"I want to see them." JoAnna wiggled in her seat. "Do come too, Olivia. I know the one puppy has stolen your heart."

And he had after holding him in her lap the last time. Out of the corner of her eye she glimpsed Drew watching. Was he waiting to see what she'd do?

"Please. You know you want to." JoAnna begged.

Christian winked at her. "Yes, please come Olivia. I've had about all I can deal with of JoAnna tonight, and if you don't come to keep her company she's going to be asking me a hundred questions about the care of these animals."

JoAnna went to kick him again, but he seemed to be expecting it and moved quickly, causing JoAnna's foot to thud as it connected under the seat. She let out a gasp then grasped Olivia's arm. "She's coming."

Olivia didn't have time to argue. Christian rapped on the parquet ceiling then opened the door, telling the driver they would be getting off at the carriage house. He closed the door and turned to Drew. "You might as well come too."

Drew got out first and helped his sister and Olivia alight from the carriage. Christian entered the room he'd set up for the stray and injured animals, and by the time they got in, he was checking on a three-legged cat. Olivia went directly to Spot. What a name for an adorable little puppy. She'd have to think of something different to call the little guy. Sitting down on the crate next to where the puppy slept, she scooped him up into her lap.

The pup let out a yelp. Olivia cooed. "What's wrong little guy?" She stroked his back. On her second swipe, she ran her hand down the puppy's head and he whimpered again.

Olivia looked up to see if anyone else had noticed, but Drew had joined Christian as he examined the cat with the amputated leg. JoAnna had plopped on the straw-strewn ground in her beautiful gown. Olivia nearly gasped. Should she remind her that a young lady shouldn't risk ruining her dress by sitting on the ground? Seventeen was old enough to know what was proper. She finally decided against saying anything. JoAnna cuddled what looked to be a perfectly healthy cat on her lap.

Returning her attention to Spot, she searched in the area her hand had been when he cried out. The side of his neck seemed swollen. She leaned in to get a better view and accidently pressed on the area. He squirmed and let out a pitiful cry that ended up in a howl. That drew everyone's attention.

"What pray tell was that about?" Drew's attention was on the puppy.

"I'm not really sure. He seems to be sore in either his neck or his front shoulder. I just touched him and he cried." She longed to stroke his fur so as to comfort the little guy, but feared hurting him again.

Drew knelt down next to her and began gently feeling around the area where Olivia had mentioned. The pup whimpered. Drew's brows lowered and his forehead furrowed. He moved on his knees to the front of Olivia and tilted his head, getting a better look. "Let me take a peek at you."

His tender tone sent Olivia's belly into a swirl. How could she have ever doubted his kindness? Gingerly slipping his hand under Spot, Drew kneaded the area. The little guy let out more cries of distress. He parted the pup's hair and let out a low whistle.

"What is it?" Olivia leaned forward and bumped heads with Drew. "I'm sorry."

"He's been bitten by a snake."

"A snake!" Olivia and JoAnna shrieked.

Christian turned around. "Fang marks?"

"One set is all I see." Drew spread the fur in other areas searching for more bites.

"I wonder what species of snake." Christian turned back to bandaging the three-legged cat's stump.

"Wish we could tell, but there is no way to know."

Olivia looked up into eyes like warm melted chocolate. "Do you think he'll die?"

"Unless we know what snake bit him, we can't know for sure. Some are more lethal than others." Drew patted the pup's head.

"Do you think it could have bit any of the other animals?" JoAnna asked.

Drew turned. "JoAnna, get off the ground. Do you realize that snake could still be in this room? You could be sitting on it."

JoAnna let out a scream that surely could be heard all the way down Meeting Street. With a jump that was anything but ladylike, JoAnna bounded to her feet, sending petticoats and her silk peach gown flying up to her knees. "Is it there? Was I sitting on it?"

Drew let out a chuckle and Christian joined in. Olivia glanced over to the place her friend had vacated. "I don't see anything, Jo."

JoAnna stood by the door staring at her. "You called me Jo."

Olivia blinked. "I did, didn't I? I hope you don't mind." The room had grown strangely quiet. Her gaze traveled from JoAnna to Christian who was now eyeing her, to the man in front of her who no longer gave his attention to the puppy. "What?"

"You used to call me Jo, but you haven't called me that since the earthquake." JoAnna's voice came out hushed.

"What made you use her pet name?" The intensity in Drew's eyes nearly sent her into a swoon.

She couldn't pull her eyes away. It was as if he'd mesmerized her. "I-I don't know. It just came out."

She wanted to tell him right that instant about her memory of the two of them. If she just blurted it out and didn't think about whom else was in the room with eyes locked on her maybe she could do it. She swallowed, trying to find her voice, but her throat stuck together and no words would form on her tongue. Drew would be happy for her…for them. JoAnna and Christian wouldn't judge her for her doubts. She should tell them now. She drew in a fortifying breath.

"Don't be disappointed, Livvy." His voice was so tender it stole her heart. "Just that you are remembering to use pet names is a good sign. You don't have to remember using them. Your mind is healing. It all points to healing. Keep your faith. God will see you through it."

JoAnna let out another scream. Only this time it was blood curdling.

Christian jumped a foot then glared at his sister. "For pities sake, JoAnna, what is your problem this time?"

"S-s-snake." She pointed near where Drew knelt on the floor.

Olivia froze. The snake slithered through the yellow straw, it's copper and yellowish colors an efficient disguise. Drew's hand slid from Spot to Olivia's hand. He squeezed. "Just sit still. It just wants to get away from us." Olivia nodded. All other thoughts flew from her mind except that the slithery creature would pass within inches of Drew's leg bent on the ground.

JoAnna continued her screeching while leaping up on a barrel. Christian went to her and put his hand over her mouth. "Please, I can't take anymore."

Drew grinned. "She's so dramatic. At least we know who the culprit is that bit this little guy." He patted Spot's head again. "And it's good news. Copperhead bites are rarely fatal. He'll be sick for a few days, but he should recover."

Olivia glanced over at the snake as it exited the door of the storage room. "But he's so big. How can you be sure?"

"A full grown copperhead is actually better than a baby. The adults know how to control their venom and don't put more in than necessary." Drew stood up.

A masculine scream came from out in the stable area. Christian and Drew burst into laughter.

"Lord save me!" Ebenezer's cry reached into the animal's sick room.

Drew stepped out the door. "What you doing on that crate, Ebenezer?"

Christian, having already removed his hand from his sister's mouth, grinned. "Between you and Ebenezer, that poor snake was probably scared to death."

"Snakes can't hear." JoAnna attempted to brush dust and straw from her soiled gown.

"How do you know that?"

"They don't have ears do they?" JoAnna frowned.

"Hmm. I don't know. Want me to go get the snake so we can see?" Christian took a step in the direction of the door.

"No." JoAnna's voice went up in a fervor pitch.

Drew came back in, a grin on his face and his eyes twinkling.

Olivia wished she could remember everything. If only she could make the memories come back. Not just one, but all of them. When Drew was near her, she felt so safe. She didn't want to leave his side. If she could only get a chance to talk to him alone. Maybe she should just ask him.

"What are you going to do with Spot?" JoAnna asked.

"He'll sleep in here where he always does." Christian picked up Spotless and put him in a small cage and closed the door.

"Oh, but he's sick. Can he sleep with me?" Olivia gave her sweetest smile.

Drew cocked one brow and watched his brother.

Christian shook his head. "Women."

"Is that a yes?" Olivia waited intently.

"I guess it can't hurt. But if he has any accidents, you have to clean them up." He came over and looked at the wound. "Just try not to bump him in that area. It'll be sore and probably swell a little more."

The elder Dr. Warwick stepped into the room. "Was that you I heard screaming like a banshee?" He looked over at his daughter.

A deep red blush filled her cheeks. "There was a snake, Papa."

"And every neighbor within a quarter mile knows it. Why don't you head on into the house and ready for bed. I'll keep an eye out so no snakes will attack you."

JoAnna slid off the barrel and glanced over to Olivia. She could see the question in JoAnna's eyes, asking if she'd go with her. But Olivia wanted to talk to Drew. Dr. Warwick cleared his throat.

"Yes, sir." JoAnna kept her eyes locked on Olivia.

Guilt and new friendship won over Olivia's desire. "I'll join you."

A smile spread across JoAnna's face. She turned to the others. "Goodnight."

Olivia hugged the puppy gingerly to her and followed JoAnna into the house and up to the landing at the top of the stairs before going their separate ways to their rooms.

The blanket on the bed all bunched up made a fine spot to put the little fella down while she readied for bed. Once she'd washed her face and got into her night rail, Olivia snuggled down in her bed with Spot curled up, sandwiched between the bend of her arm and her side. Poor little guy. He was too sweet to have to go through such a terrible thing. He was probably curious about what was slithering across his floor and went to investigate when he got bit. She ran her hand down his silky puppy fur. Spot seemed like such a terrible name for him. She'd have to come up with a new name before he started responding to it.

Closing her eyes, she sighed. She'd waited too long to tell Drew that she was remembering feelings and even had a memory or two. Once she shared that news with him, she felt certain he'd want to spend more time with her. The heat in his eyes left little to the imagination of his feelings for her. Gentlemanly respect for her was the only reason he didn't force his attentions on her. He was an honorable man, she could see that now. And she believed it, regardless of what Lloyd told her.

Lloyd was another problem she'd have to deal with. She couldn't spend more time with Drew while Lloyd believed them engaged. It wouldn't be right. And she wasn't so sure she believed Lloyd about the postponement of their engagement. Both men couldn't be telling the truth and Drew seemed the more honorable of the two. Yes, tomorrow she needed to set things straight with both men. She needed to move forward with her life.

She whispered a prayer, not sure if God cared enough to listen. *Lord, if you still love me will you make a way for me to speak with Drew and Lloyd tomorrow? Show me which man you have chosen for me and let me feel peace within your answer.* Spot nuzzled his head under her arm. *And please help this little guy get well.*

If only she knew if God had heard her prayer. She settled her mind allowing sleep to creep in. Tomorrow would tell.

♥♥♥

Drew wasn't in one of his best moods, never getting to speak with Olivia the previous night. He came around the corner of the study as someone rapped on the front door. He glanced around, but either no one was downstairs or they didn't hear the weak knocking. Irritation slashed through him. Catching Olivia alone was a challenge. Jo seemed to have attached herself to Olivia like a bloodsucker, and right this minute he knew Jo was upstairs and Olivia was out checking on Fang as she'd renamed the sick puppy, claiming he deserved a much fiercer name since he'd faced down a copperhead snake and won.

Drew let out a growl and stomped to the door. Why was a simple thing like finding time alone with Olivia so hard? Her wanting to speak to him privately had his hopes up that maybe her heart was changing toward him. It just seemed that one thing after another kept them apart or in someone else's company.

With a quick jerk he pulled the door open. He blinked at the image in front of him. Over a year had passed since he'd laid eyes on her. And ten more could go by before he cared to again.

"Hello, Andrew." Her voice was sickeningly sweet. "Aren't you going to invite me in?" She glanced past him.

Drew heard a noise behind him, but refused to take his eyes off the woman in front of him. "I don't think that's necessary, Miss Middleton."

"Oh, come now, darling, we're way beyond that. You can still call me Constance."

Drew stiffened. "I think not."

Her lip jutted out. "I will only take a moment of your time."

"We have nothing to talk about." Drew was ready to close the door on her. She was one of the last people he wanted to see.

She gave him a sly smile. "Don't you want to meet your son?"

Chapter 17

Olivia swallowed the gasp that nearly escaped her lips. Son? Drew had a son? She withdrew behind the cover of the door, knowing she should leave and not eavesdrop. The woman he called Miss Middleton had seen her, she was certain. Her heart pounded so rapidly in her chest she could hear it in her ears. She'd only been moments away from telling Drew she wanted to get to know him better. But a child— a child changed everything. He needed to marry that woman. It was only right.

"Please allow me to come in, Andrew. We need to talk." Miss Middleton's tone was pleading. Olivia didn't have to see her face to know the woman felt desperate.

"We have nothing to discuss. That's not my child." The irritation in Drew's voice sent a wave of pity through Olivia for the little boy. How could he be so cruel to an innocent child?

Constance sniffed. "How can you say that? Look at him. He has your hair color and brown eyes. You can't deny him."

Olivia had heard all she cared to. Her stomach revolted and she feared she'd lose her breakfast, as meager as it was of toast. She'd given her bacon and eggs to Fang. Dashing up the stairs, she headed for her room. Drew's room. Inside, she leaned against the door. What was she to do now? She couldn't entertain the idea that she and Drew could ever be together. These feelings she was remembering would have to stop—somehow.

Pushing off the door, she sauntered toward the bed, wanting to fall on it and cry into the pillow. Why should she feel so distraught over this? A few weeks ago she didn't believe Drew, thought that she was engaged to Lloyd. Now here she was, heartsick to find out Drew was a father. She collapsed onto the bed, not bothering to pull back the hand-stitched quilt. She buried her head into the pillow and let out a sob.

But this must be God's answer to her prayer. Maybe that was the whole reason why she'd lost her memory because she was supposed to be with Lloyd, not Drew. The thought didn't comfort her. Just when she let her feelings go to explore the possibility of loving Drew, God snatched it all away. She wasn't sure she wanted Lloyd, even if God did take Drew from her. As nice as he tried to be to her, he could never compare with Drew. And the feelings he stirred within her were nothing like the fire that burned through her veins when Drew spoke to her or touched her.

She rolled to her side and wiped the tears with the back of her lace-trimmed sleeve. Tears continued and blurred her vision. The open door of Drew's wardrobe caught her attention. She blinked away the tears, trying to see what was attached to the inside of his door. She dabbed at her eyes again, attempting to focus. It was a picture.

A quick glance at the bedroom door told her it was still shut and she was alone. She pushed up to a sitting position and reminded herself that a promise to herself was still a promise. She'd vowed she wouldn't go through any of Drew's things when he'd been generous enough to let her use his room.

While she was outside with the puppy, Drew must have come in and left the wardrobe door open. If only she could see from where she was whether the photograph was of Constance or perhaps Drew's little boy. She bit her bottom lip. Full of indecision, Olivia slid off the bed and took one step, then another, toward the open door. It needed to be closed. Why, she couldn't just leave the wardrobe standing open. Drew would want her to close it to keep the dust off his clothes.

With one hand on the intricately carved mahogany door, Olivia raised her head to peer at the photograph. Her fingers tightened on the wood to steady herself. Still, her legs wobbled beneath her. Shaky hands pulled the picture from where the edge was wedged between two pieces of overlapping wood. "Oh, Drew." The tears returned, blurring the photograph of her. "You do love me."

Sinking to the floor, she buried her face in her hands, letting the photograph fall from her grasp. The memory surfaced like a missing puzzle piece lost amongst the floorboards. A piece for her to place in the picture of her life—her missing year. But now it mattered not. It couldn't. Drew had a responsibility to the child…to the mother of his child. She had to forget these feelings he stirred within her.

If she was to believe her memories and what he had told her—that they had courted the past year—he'd been a father even then. Did she know? Surely not. God forbid that she could be such a horrible person that she would come between a woman, a son, and father. But the woman—Constance—she was certain she'd looked beyond Drew and had seen Olivia approach and hesitate in the hall. And yet the woman spoke of the child being Drew's as if it were common knowledge.

She had to have known before her memory loss. What had made her such a self-serving person? She prayed no more memories would surface. As much as she had wanted her past returned to her before, it would only mean sorrow now. She didn't want to know what a terrible person she was, she didn't want these feelings for Drew. Remembering would be much more painful than not knowing.

She opened her eyes and the picture stared up at her from her lap. Remembering the moment, the laughter, the cajoling young man who'd talked Drew into having her picture taken in front of the theater and Drew's response played out in her mind's eye as if she sat in the theater watching. Another piece of her heart broke. She could add it to the pieces she'd lost when her parents and brother died.

Why did God allow her to live after taking her family? Their life meant something. She wished she'd have died in their place. This had to be all God's punishment. A clamp tightened on her lungs and the air sucked from them. She would become a better person. She'd gain God's love back.

Pushing herself off the floor, she gathered the picture and slid it back between the wood. She went to the wash stand and splashed water on her face and then wiped the dampness away. She needed to talk to Lloyd.

♥♥♥

Horror filled Drew as he stared down at Constance and the young boy in her arms who couldn't have been much more than six months old. What game did this woman play now? He certainly didn't want to invite her into his home, not with Olivia here. He'd have a hard time explaining things to her. Olivia already didn't trust him. And he felt he was finally making some headway on that.

"Why don't we sit out here on the piazza?" Drew extended his arm out toward the bench. He'd really like to tell her they had nothing to discuss, but if Constance was going around telling people he was the father of her child, they needed to talk.

Constance sat down and awkwardly put the baby in her lap. She looked down, straightening the white lace trimmed collar around the child's neck. Lifting her head just slightly, she peered under arched brows. "I've missed you, Andrew."

Drew grunted. He hadn't missed her. He hadn't thought about her in a very long time. Not since she'd tried desperately to seduce him. He shuddered at the memory and how close he'd come to giving into his carnal lust. She'd been persuasive. He'd even say relentless in her attempt to persuade him to be with her intimately. After he discovered she'd been unfaithful to him and was pregnant with another man's child, he saw through her machinations. She'd wanted to claim the child was his. Another instance where being in control had served him well.

He'd broken it off with her the day he'd learned the news. Though his heart was sick, he couldn't abide her unfaithfulness. He assumed she took his advice and went away to have the child where no one would know her or the circumstances. So why would she come back with the child… and to him? People could put two and two together. Her disappearing and returning with a child. It wasn't hard to surmise. So what was her game?

He eyed her and couldn't help but to compare her to Olivia. Constance was attractive with her oval face and sandy blonde hair and light blue eyes. But even in her fetching pink silk gown, she couldn't compare to Olivia's beauty in her black mourning clothes. And were he to compare the integrity and character of the two women, there was no question who would come out on top.

"What's this nonsense that the child is mine?" Drew cut right to the point.

She batted her eyes and glanced toward the shut door. "You could be his papa."

"You and I both know that isn't possible."

"He needs a father, Andrew." She patted the baby's head, reminding Drew of the way a person would pat a dog.

"He has a father. Why aren't you having this conversation with him?" He couldn't believe the nerve of her. After what she'd done to him. Betrayed him with another man. How could she ask *him* to step into that man's shoes?

She had the decency to look down. "He took off. I never should have—you were the best thing that ever happened to me. I made a mistake, Andrew. I was lonely. You were working all those hours. What was I supposed to do?"

"Remain faithful. I hadn't been out of medical school a year. I had to prove myself more than most, because of who my father was. I didn't like being gone and apart any more than you did." But he counted it a blessing that he found out her character—or lack of it—before he'd gotten too serious. He shuddered to think if he had married her.

She pursed her lips in a pout. "I said I was sorry. Can't we let bygones be bygones?"

Drew wanted to argue that she hadn't apologized, but he wouldn't get in a boxing match with her exchanging verbal blows. He owed her nothing. "We can," he replied.

She smiled, her brows rising.

"But things will never be as they were. I'll not bring up your…indiscretion, but I'll not entertain any delusions of romance with you, either. I've moved on and I won't have you complicating my life."

Her smile turned to a scowl. "Why? Is there someone else in your life?"

"That, madam, is none of your business." He was becoming annoyed with her. And the last thing he wanted was for Olivia to see her sitting here. What he really wanted to do was find Olivia and see what she had wanted to talk to him about. He wasn't sure what had changed in Olivia, but whatever it was, he was glad for it.

"You see, Andrew, that's where you're wrong. I have a great investment in you. Or I plan to anyway." She gave him a cunning smile.

"You're dreaming dreams that are never going to

happen, sweetheart." It was time for her to go. Did she really think he'd take her back after all she'd done? He stood. "I don't think we have anything else to discuss."

A triumphant gleam filled her eyes. "Oh, my Andrew. You're wrong again. Two times in one day. You must be slipping."

He narrowed his eyes. "What's that supposed to mean?"

"You didn't ask me what our son's name is."

"He's not *our* son."

"Guess anyway. What do you think I named him?" She bounced him on her knee even though the child had not made a sound.

The boy stared back at Drew through brown eyes. He had a round face with an extra layer of fat giving him the look of two chins. The boy was cute. "I really have no idea."

"Just guess." She bounced in her chair, jarring the boy.

Drew blew out a puff of air. "Lloyd." He wasn't sure why he said it. Maybe because right at this moment he was angry with both Constance and Lloyd.

Constance blinked and stared at him. "Now why would you say that?"

"Forget I said it. I tire of your game, Constance. What is it you want?" He looked down on her from where he stood.

"I want you."

Her declaration nearly took his breath away. "It's too late for that. You should have thought about that before you—" He wanted to put this whole unpleasant encounter behind him.

She lifted her chin. "His name is Andrew."

Drew's gut churned. "Why would you name him after me?"

"I still love you. I've always loved you."

He snorted, the bile rising in his throat. "You had a strange way of showing it."

"And imagine me coming back to town after being gone since you broke our engagement and having a child with me." She paused and looked at him as if waiting for him to understand something. "I named *our child* Andrew."

Drew's eyes widened. Surely she wasn't trying to blackmail him. He clenched his back teeth. "We weren't engaged. And stop calling the child ours."

She tittered. "Oh, but it's been such a long time. People forget and it's amazing how suggestions can make them remember something wrong. Especially if it means juicy gossip. And the gossipmongers do thrive on it. Why, I'd venture to say they could have the news around town in no time. The disaster may even help my cause. Nothing like a good scandal to get one's mind off things."

Chapter 18

The sound of pounding hammers echoed on the afternoon air. So many unfamiliar sounds caused by the reconstruction of Charleston had Olivia's nerves on edge. She glanced off to her right as crews of men worked to replace the whole front side of a house. Rooms had been left exposed to sun, rain, and dirt, along with anything else, for the past month. She hurried by, but the men paid her no attention.

She'd not been out walking since the earthquake. Every time she'd gone anywhere, it had been in a carriage with one of the Warwick family members. She'd snuck out today to be alone. She needed time to think and knew they wouldn't approve of her going out by herself. What could she tell them? That she had overheard Drew speaking with the mother of his child earlier in the day and needed time to get her thoughts together and her emotions under control?

It was better they not know she left. No one would miss her if she returned before supper. Besides, she worried they would see the shame inside her. It appeared God had turned his head away. He'd ignored her prayer and left her to fumble around and try to figure things out on her own. And she would. God hadn't heard her last prayer. She'd repented and begged for His guidance. She'd sworn to live a better life, but still He turned His head the other way. She'd lost everything just like Job. But she didn't have the faith to believe God still cared.

She couldn't stay at Warwick's forever. It was time she took responsibility and started thinking of what she would do. Her father's parents lived in California. She could go there, but she'd never met them before. She bit her lip.

Would they even want her? She was a grown woman and they'd have to be in their sixties. She might be a financial burden they couldn't afford. And then there was always the problem of how to travel so far alone, as well as where she'd get the money for the trip.

Sighing, she stepped around a fissure in the sidewalk caused by the quake. A carriage pulled up alongside her and stopped. The door flung open and Lloyd jumped out.

"Just the woman I was coming to see. How are you, my dear? I've missed you."

She'd wanted to talk to him, too. But that was when she'd remembered spending time with Drew—when she believed Drew told her the truth—when she thought that maybe she and Drew would have a chance of a life together. Memories of her prayer ran through her mind. *Show me which man you have chosen for me and let me feel peace within your answer.* What if God hadn't ignored her? What if this was her answer? Could God have allowed her to hear Drew's conversation with the woman so she would know which man was right for her? She took a long blink and drew in fresh air. Confusion enveloped her. Why couldn't things be clearer? She just wanted a simple answer. God seemed so far away that she couldn't tell if He listened or if everything she'd said fell on deaf ears.

She turned to face him. "Hello, Lloyd. It's good to see you."

He flipped down the step. "Come take a ride with me."

"I'd rather walk. You are welcome to join me though." Riding in a closed carriage wasn't proper. Did he really think she would? Or was that something she'd been doing the past year of her life? She hoped she'd never brought shame to her mama and papa.

A spark of annoyance flickered in his eyes and disappeared. "I'd love to, my dear."

"You were coming to see me?"

"Of course. Who else would I come to visit? Certainly not Drew."

She hoped he hadn't come to try to talk her into moving away again. That last conversation hadn't gone well. "Speaking of Drew, I'd like to ask you some questions."

He slid his arm around her waist and she flinched. Skittering away she took hold of his arm. Again a flicker of irritation or perhaps anger emerged in his eyes and was gone as quickly as it came. "What would you like to know?"

"The truth." She swallowed and concentrated on steadying her voice. "I want to know the truth about us." She looked ahead but could feel his eyes on her.

"All right. What do you want to know about us?"

"Why did our engagement *really* get postponed or was it truly broken?"

He walked along, looking ahead with her hand still on his arm. She'd begun to think he wasn't going to answer her. They passed a warehouse where men still worked. One whole section had fallen out. It looked as if someone had cut out a fifteen foot square of bricks and deposited them on the ground.

"It was Drew. That's why I despise the man. He relentlessly pursued you, flirted with you, and wooed you with his family wealth until he wore you down." He laid his hand over hers on his arm. "Understand though, sweetheart, I don't blame you at all. It wasn't your fault. It was his. He knew you were engaged to me."

The words that fell from his mouth had conviction. She cocked her head and looked at him. He sounded truthful. "So I broke off our engagement?"

He swallowed and she could almost imagine he had

tears in his eyes. "Yes. But it wasn't your fault."

It most certainly was. If she broke off the betrothal, it was her choice. "But I get the feeling you don't work for my father anymore...or you didn't before he died. Was it because of me?"

"It was too painful, seeing people I cared for every day. Men that I thought one day would be my father and my brother. I just couldn't. I had to quit and move on. You were lost to me."

They turned the corner to avoid lumber that had been tossed into a pile. Dust floated in the air and attached to the black fabric of her skirt and she sighed, knowing her choices of black garments were limited. Her insides twisted. He sounded as if he were telling the truth. Part of her wanted it to be a lie. Her heart wanted Drew to be the wonderful man she'd thought he was. But he was out of reach for her. Lloyd wasn't.

"I saw a picture at the Warwick's. Drew had requested it taken of me at the theater." She wasn't really sure why she said it.

"Do you remember?" He cocked his head, his eyes locked onto her.

"Some." Tears stung the back of her eyes. She swallowed. She couldn't let them fall.

"Are your memories coming back faster?"

"I've only had a few. Mostly I get feelings like I should know something or someone. Drew says I'll remember."

"I'm sure you will, sweetheart. I'm sure you will." He ran his thumb over her gloved hand. But his caress didn't send pleasant shivers down her spine.

"Were Drew and I courting when the earthquake struck?"

Silence reigned again. They turned onto Church Street, and Saint Philip's Church with all its glory stood before them. A large portion of its belfry tower had fallen to the ground like a broken crown. Tired of the destruction everywhere, Olivia looked away. The beauty of Charleston had crumbled around her just like the beauty of her life.

"No."

Just no? Not an explanation or anything? "Why?"

He stole a glance her way, but never met her eyes. "You found out he'd been unfaithful."

Could it have been the woman at the door today? "What is her name? The woman that…"

"It doesn't matter. It will change nothing. The only thing you need to know is that Drew Warwick is a man who cares for no one else but himself, and he'll walk on whoever he has to in order to get what he wants."

She would find out later if these two women were one and the same. She had a sick feeling they were. "So I ended it?" Still none of what he said brought back memories, glimpses of the past, or even feelings of something she should remember.

"He didn't like it, though. He wouldn't give up on you. I worried for your safety. Since the day you came back to me, he has hated me. That's why I want you out of that house. Away from the Warwicks."

"I don't believe he hates you." But he certainly disliked Lloyd.

"I worry for you. Where do you sleep?"

Her heart banged in her chest. "In Drew's room."

"What?"

"It isn't like it sounds. Drew has moved down the hall and shares a room with his brother."

Lloyd gave her a calculating look. "And where is the room you sleep in and where is the room that Drew sleeps in?"

"They are both upstairs. I am in the room all the way to

the right and Drew is at the opposite end of the hallway, the last room. JoAnna and Mr. and Mrs. Warwick have rooms between us. So you see, there is nothing to concern yourself with."

He frowned but looked pleased with himself. "Do you think that would make me agree with this arrangement? Not when you, my dear, are anywhere near Drew Warwick at night."

"Then I'm to understand that you and I were courting again when I lost my memory?"

"We were. And we were looking forward to setting a new date for our wedding." Lloyd swung around in front of her, stopping her in her path, and dropped to his knee.

Olivia glanced around. Men were working on both sides of the street. Several carriages pulled by horses could be seen rolling down the street toward them. What was Lloyd thinking? Words lodged in her throat, but nothing came out.

"Marry me, sweetheart. I want to take you away from all this. You remember our love for each other. We are a good match, you and I. Things will be just as they were."

"I-I don't know. I need time to think." Think about why those memories weren't stirring the love she thought she once had for him, why her heart only leapt for Drew and why when she closed her eyes she saw Drew, not Lloyd.

"What's there to think about? You love me, don't you?" He pushed to his feet and grasped both her hands in his.

"I don't know what I feel anymore. I'm so confused."

His hands tightened on hers, sending spears of pain through her fingers. Depravity filled his face. "It's Drew, isn't it?"

Beneath his grasp, fright seized her body. Unable to

control the trembling, she tried to pull away. Glancing up, she knew he felt her fear, for evil delight slithered into his eyes.

"No." Her heart raced in her chest. "I'm confused. I can't remember my past. I've lost my parents. I-I need time."

His grasp loosened. "I tire of waiting, Olivia. And I don't approve of you staying there."

She pulled her hands free. "I understand."

He smiled, but she knew it was to cover his irritation. "What? That I tire of waiting or that I don't approve?"

"Both."

He batted at the dirt on the knee of his trousers. "What are you going to do about it?" It sounded as if it were a challenge.

"There's not much I can do about where I live, unless I wish to move into a tent." She raised her chin, refusing to show any more trepidation.

"You can marry me and you'll have a home."

He wasn't listening to her. "I can't make a decision to marry when I am struggling with my life." She swallowed, knowing what she was about to say would most likely make him angry. "If you must have a decision now, then it will have to be 'no'."

A vein pulsed in his forehead. "I can wait. Just don't make it too long."

♥♥♥

Drew gathered some of the supplies that were going to be needed over at Ebenezer's on the morrow. He gave up looking for a missing hammer and turned to William. "Do you know where the other hammer is?" As usual his mind wasn't on the job at hand, but on the woman who owned his heart. Unconsciously, he reached up and touched his hand to his shirt pocket, feeling the engagement ring he still longed to put on Olivia's finger.

William hefted a bucket of nails from the floor of the carriage house and made his way to the wagon. "Father was out front of the house on a ladder. He might have had it with him."

Drew turned to go. He'd not made it to the back of the house when William called out to him. "Better grab the ladder too."

Making his way around the far side of the house, Drew heard voices. One in particular stopped him in his tracks. Olivia. They'd all been concerned when she didn't show up for supper. But he'd been even more worried when they discovered she was nowhere on the grounds. He'd hoped that with her recent softening to him that she wouldn't see Lloyd anymore. Apparently, that wasn't the case. If only he could make out what they were saying, but he was too far away and around the corner which didn't play in his favor. He stuffed down the desire to rush around and rescue her from the creep and instead he waited until he didn't hear voices anymore.

Drew stepped around to the front of the house, fully expecting to see Olivia gone and Lloyd strolling down the sidewalk, but what he saw was enough to send his blood into a fever. Lloyd towered over Olivia and as quick as a bird snatching an insect in flight, Lloyd had swooped down and stole what belonged to Drew.

The blood pounded in Drew's ears. He clenched his back teeth and curled his fingers into fists. Olivia ducked her head and disappeared through the front door. Smirking, Lloyd spun on his heel and headed toward the road. It was just as well because Drew was beginning to think he might truly hurt the man.

Finding his father gone and the hammer in the grass, he snatched it from its resting place before hauling up the ladder to his shoulder and stomping back to the wagon. Unsavory thoughts of Lloyd ran through Drew's mind. Anger mingled with guilt churned in his gut. He was a doctor, a healer, how could he have so much anger toward another individual? He'd sworn to only do good and never do harm, but he seriously would not be grieved to see Lloyd dead. And what scared Drew the most was he almost wished it on the man.

His father's words came back to him. *You need to turn this burden over to the Lord. This one is too big for you, and it's time you learned that you can't solve everything in your own power... it is time for you to realize God's will in your life is what is important...I know you love Olivia. But maybe God is using this tragedy to show you she isn't the one He has chosen for you.*

Drew nearly sank to his knees. Thankful he'd not made it back to the stable and carriage house yet, he set the ladder down and leaned it against a tree. He had lost control, and it was tearing him apart. His father was right, he did need to give this over to the Lord before he did something he would forever regret.

Lord, this is more than I can manage. I will do my best to leave Olivia in your hands and trust you with her and with my heart.

Feeling no better, nor sensing any relief, Drew pushed off the tree and carried the ladder and hammer to the wagon. He may not feel any respite, but he'd do his best to leave this right where he put it—in the Lord's hands.

Drew could have woken the crowing roosters, he'd gotten up so early. With the wagon having already been loaded the night before, Drew, William, and Christian arrived at Ebenezer's place to smell the aroma of bacon wafting from open fires at the nearby square filled with tent refugees.

Ebenezer's chimney had fallen from its foundation, landing on the house and bringing down a goodly portion of the roof by the looks of things. But it was the front wall of the house that looked like someone had taken the wood and played a game of jack-straws with it. Sheets had been hung across the unwanted opening, keeping out some dust and giving a sense of privacy. Drew stared at it in disbelief. Oh, he'd seen many houses and businesses that looked much the same. This house had actually fared better than many, including Olivia's. What had him in awe was the understanding that he and his brothers were going to help rebuild it.

William, Christian, and Drew stood where they had jumped down from the wagon, all of them with arms crossed, as they assessed the damage. Father had made them learn basic repairing around their home growing up. One of them was always sent to help Ebenezer with a job. But this—Drew rubbed his hand over his chin—this would be like *building* a house, not making repairs.

Christian chuckled and William scowled at him. "What do you find so humorous?"

"Just wondering what this is going to look like when we get done. We're supposed to put people back together, not houses."

"Wasn't it Father that volunteered us?" William tipped his head and looked down the row at his two brothers. "And what was it he said that kept him from coming this unusually hot October Friday morning?"

"Whatever it was, I don't believe him." Christian's eyes twinkled with laughter.

"At least the bricks have all been moved and stacked into neat piles." Drew's back ached just thinking about the task.

Ebenezer came from the back yard carrying two

buckets of water, sweat already beading on his charcoal forehead in the humid morning air. "What you boys standin' there for? Don't you see there's work to be done?"

William groaned. "He's going to be a tough taskmaster."

Drew couldn't agree more. Ebenezer was one of the hardest working men he'd ever known. When he'd helped him as a boy, Drew would fall into bed at night feeling muscles he never knew he had. And he had an inkling that he was about to experience that part of his childhood all over.

Jumping in to help Ebenezer, Drew and his brothers went to work. They spent the better part of the day trying to salvage the good pieces of wood to reframe the front wall. By noon, he looked like he'd been in a fist fight, his hands were so bloodied up from the work. It had been worth every scrape and cut, though, when lunch was delivered by Olivia and Mother. Olivia had fussed over his hands, insisting on cleaning them up. Unfortunately, she seemed as worried about his brothers' conditions as she had his.

Father arrived before they'd left and spent the rest of the day helping. When they finished for the day, all the good wood had been sorted and set aside waiting for tomorrow when they would start framing up the front wall.

Drew lay next to his father in the back of the wagon as Christian steered toward home with William on the seat beside him. Drew stared up at the cloudless blue sky losing its light. "Times like this I can appreciate being the oldest."

His father chuckled, hands clasped behind his neck. "Definitely has its advantages."

Reaching the stables, Drew hopped down and hurried up to the room he shared with his brother so he could clean up for supper. After changing his clothes he made his way down, hoping to find a few minutes alone with Olivia, but she wasn't there. He sent a prayer that she'd be the first one down and he'd get his time with her privately.

He sat in the study with the door open, knowing she'd have to pass by to get to the dining room. But luck wasn't with him. When the light patter of feet sounded on the stairs it was accompanied by the chatter of Olivia and Jo, soon followed by his brothers. With a sigh, he pushed up from the chair he rested in and found his place at the dining table.

Once the women had taken their seats, the men followed suit. Christian asked the blessing and the food was passed.

Mother scooped a spoon of mashed potatoes onto her plate. "Did you get much done today?"

The question seemed to be up for grabs. Drew took the bowl from his mother and answered. "We got the area cleaned up and things ready to go. I think tomorrow we will see some real progress."

"I know Ebenezer appreciates all your hard work." Mother smiled, pride filling her eyes.

"I hope he feels that way when we get finished." Christian grinned.

"You boys will do a fine job. I have no doubt." She shifted her gaze to her husband. "With your father working alongside of you, it won't be anything but perfect."

Father reached over, placing his hand over hers and squeezed. "It's all good experience. One never knows when they might need to know these skills."

"That's right, dear. Why, you built our first home with your own hands."

Father let go of Mother's hand and picked up his fork. "And I wouldn't change those meager beginnings for anything. They were hard times, but I'm thankful for every one of them. They made me appreciate what we have now."

Mother turned to Drew. "I almost forgot. You received

a letter from that investigator. It's on the hall table." Her eyes darted to Olivia.

Olivia had just taken a sip of her water and didn't seem too concerned about the missive.

Silverware clanked around the table and forks scraped against china plates as everyone seemed to want to suddenly eat rather than talk.

Olivia set her glass down. Her eyes pierced Drew. "You had a visitor today."

Mother shifted in her chair. The apology he saw in her eyes left him uneasy. He smiled, not feeling the emotion. "And who would that be?"

"She said her name was Miss Middleton." Olivia didn't release him from her penetrating glare.

The clanking of silverware quit and Drew swept the table with his gaze, noticing everyone had stopped eating, all focused on him. He cleared his throat. The food he'd just swallowed soured in his stomach. "I see, and did she say what she wanted?" He knew what she was up to. He just hoped she hadn't been brazen enough to say something incriminating to Olivia.

Chapter 19

Drew lounged in a chair in the study after dinner, flipping the letter over in his hands as he thanked the Lord that Constance hadn't said anything to Olivia other than request she let him know that she'd stopped by. He didn't know why she didn't, but he was mighty relieved that she hadn't spouted the same lie to Olivia that she had to him. Olivia would have no way of knowing that it was a falsehood. He didn't need anything else to explain.

"Are you going to open it?" Christian stared at him from across the room.

Drew tore the letter open and scanned over the short note.

"Well?" William asked.

"Looks like he hasn't been able to find the people he's looking for. Not too surprising with so many people displaced from their homes. But he said that he does have a witness that claims there was never any damage to his neighbor's house." Drew lowered the letter to his lap and looked up.

Christian let out a low whistle. "Well, if that doesn't sound like embezzlement, than I don't know what does."

Olivia splashed water on her face from the wash basin and stared into the mirror. How well could she trust these memories that were returning? Now that she didn't want to remember anything, it seemed like she was getting more and more little glimpses into her past.

She refused to let any feelings grow for Drew. He may not have lied about everything, but one thing she did know—he kept the truth from her, and that was as good as a lie. She could never marry a man she couldn't trust. She blotted her face with the towel. He belonged with the Middleton woman, anyway. He had a duty to her and their child.

She tossed the cloth over the bar to allow it to dry. Drew was lost to her forever. She had to accept that in not only her mind but also her heart. The only way she knew to do that was to concentrate on Lloyd. A sense of desperation and frustration started to grow within her. How could she turn to Lloyd when her heart didn't stir like it did for Drew?

Drew, Drew, Drew. Everything came back to Drew. She pushed the thought of him away, focusing on her new memory. When she had passed the study last night on her way to sit out in the evening air and think, she'd heard Christian say something about embezzlement. The word triggered a memory and nearly took her breath away.

Papa, Simon, Mama, and she were at home and Simon had said that someone had embezzled money from Papa's insurance company. The details were lost in a fog and as late as she had laid in bed last night and tried to clear her mind so she could recall the particulars that Papa and Simon had discussed, it was all for naught. But this morning she had a thought. She wouldn't call it a memory because it was more like an intuition or a suspicion that Lloyd was involved.

Guilt seized her for jumping to such a conclusion. How could she be so unfair? Lloyd was the only person she had left in her life. The Warwicks had been wonderful to her, but she couldn't stay here forever. And there was no other man besides Drew interested in her. With Papa and Simon both gone, she had to make a good match or who knows what might happen to her. Her family's house was destroyed, the building her father rented for his insurance business was severely damaged, and she had no home and no way to support herself. She had to marry.

All of her life she thought to marry for love just like her parents, but that option was quickly fading. She'd loved Lloyd once. Surely she could love him again. But before that possibility, she had to find out whether Lloyd's involvement in embezzlement was more a memory than intuition or a figment of her imagination.

It was well after eight in the morning when Olivia neared Lloyd's house. Lloyd always went down to one of the local cafés to eat breakfast. She hoped some were open and that hadn't changed. The hammers and men's voices echoed over the empty street. It was sad that no children played in the yards or ran up and down the cobbled avenues. But she supposed that was best today. She glanced around and trusted that the workers would be too busy to notice her. Knocking on the front door, she waited, tilting her head to hear any sounds from inside.

No one came to the door as she had suspected. That was why she chose this time of day. Lloyd would be out. With her insides quivering she turned the knob on the door and peeked in.

"Hello. Are you home, Lloyd?"

She waited. No answer came. Throwing one last glance over her shoulder, she slipped through the opening on wobbly legs. "Lloyd?"

The ticking of a clock was her only answer. The last thing she wanted to do was spend much time there. She passed the dining room. It looked as if it was never used—dust gathered on the table. She stuck her head in the kitchen as she held her breath. It was empty. She really didn't even know what she looked for, but if Lloyd had embezzled, she supposed any information she wanted would be in his room or in his office if he had one.

She'd never been in his house when they were

engaged, it just wasn't proper, but at the moment she'd wished she'd had the opportunity to have gone through the house at least one time. Then maybe, just maybe she could pull from those memories. That is, if they had come back to her.

Backtracking and exiting out the other side of the dining room she took a short hall. On the left, stairs led to the upper floor and on the right an archway opened into the great room. Indecision gave her pause. She glanced at the stairs. Feeling fairly certain that Lloyd's room would be up on the second floor, she hiked up her gown so as not to step on it and went up.

Four doors adorned the hallway walls and all were open. Gliding toward the first room, her feet tapped lightly on the wooden floor. A slightly musty smell met her as she neared the first rooms. The room on the right looked to be an extra bedroom. She glanced through the doorway across the hall. It looked to be a place of storage as odd pieces of furniture sat haphazardly in the middle of the floor. She moved on, forcing one foot in front of the other.

Her heart thudded in her chest as she approached the next rooms. The one on the right appeared to be where Lloyd slept. She ignored the one across and tiptoed in, even though she knew no one was at home. His bed sat between two windows on the far side of the room. A small table with a lamp had been placed next to it at the head of the bed on the left side and next to that another door. A wardrobe stood sentinel across from the bed. Beneath one of the windows stood a small square table with some papers and a billfold on top, and next to that a chair.

Hurrying over, she flipped through the papers, but they were only receipts. She opened the billfold to find money tucked in the pocket. She set it down and turned, hands still on the table. Where else to look? Perhaps one of the drawers of the wardrobe. She crossed the room and tugged on the first drawer. It slid open with a loud squeal of wood on wood. She peeked in. Men's unmentionables filled it. Her face heated.

A door slammed downstairs. Olivia froze. Her heart raced, sending blood pounding in her ears. She pushed the drawer and stopped as the wooden side rubbed against wood threatening to give her away. Her throat went dry. Leaving the drawer open was her only option. She'd pray that if it was Lloyd, he wouldn't notice.

Footfalls sounded on the steps and panic rose within her. Her gaze darted around the room for a place to escape. It had to be Lloyd. What would he do when he found her in his house snooping around his belongings? And if he found her in his bedroom…she gulped…would he think she suggested something? Her legs nearly gave out beneath her as footsteps neared. She ran to the door beside the table and opened it so she could slip through, not knowing where it would take her.

It was an empty room with no escape and no place to hide. At one time the room had probably been used for a nursery with its single window. Pushing the door almost shut, but not enough to latch and take a chance of Lloyd hearing the click, she pressed herself against the wall opposite the hinge side of the door and waited. She sent up a silent prayer he'd not notice the open wardrobe drawer or that the door was not shut all the way.

If she hadn't been leaning against the wall, her legs would have given out. They weren't much stronger than a newborn babe at the moment. She ground her back teeth to keep them from chattering. Every movement of her body, both internal and external, echoed in her ears as if announcing her presence.

The wardrobe drawer squeaked shut. He was in his

room. She listened for movement, but none came. He must have been taking in the room. This was it. Would he come to where she hid? She took a deep breath and closed her eyes. When she opened them she stared at herself in a mirror.

Lord have mercy on her. If he opened the door he would see her in the mirror. There was no other place to go. The sound of footfalls drew closer. He approached the room. She slid down the wall to a squatted position and pulled the fabric of her black skirt as close to her body as possible.

The handle rattled and she imagined his hand on it. She pinched her eyes together. If he saw her she didn't want to know. She almost snorted at her foolishness, but caught herself before the sound escaped.

The hinges creaked as the door slowly opened. Her eyes shot wide. Had the door made that sound when she'd slipped into the room? Had he heard her? Did he know she was there and played some game of cat and mouse with her? Her body trembled until she didn't think she could remain in the same squatted position.

Olivia held her breath for fear her breathing would give her away. Could one's heart pound so loud that another could hear it? She prayed not.

The door started to close and then paused in its position before opening back up. He took a step, half of his black shoe stopping on the threshold of the door. Another pause ensued. She couldn't stop her body from trembling. She prayed he didn't lean in the room for if he did she'd be found out. He grunted, his shoe disappeared, and the door slammed shut.

With her lungs begging for air, Olivia fought the desire to gasp. Instead she slowly drew oxygen into her lungs. Afraid to move, she remained squatted on the floor. Lloyd's footfalls left the room and she strained to hear if they went down the hall and onto the steps, but the closed door kept her from knowing his whereabouts.

Olivia remained huddled in the same position. She didn't know how much time had passed. Fifteen minutes, an hour. Waiting always skewed time. She thought she heard the front door shut. What if it was a trick to get her to come from hiding? She pushed herself to an upright position, her knees and ankles aching from crouching so long.

Once the blood had returned to her limbs, she hurried over to the window to see if she could see him on the street.

The placement of the bedroom window didn't allow her that advantage. She'd have to wait. Returning back to her position against the wall, Olivia began counting to keep track of the time. When what she calculated to be ten minutes had passed, she slowly opened the door and peeked out.

Lloyd was nowhere in the room. The billfold was gone and the wardrobe drawer closed. There were five others she hadn't looked in, but she didn't have the courage to go through them. The only thing she wanted to do was to escape.

She peeked down the hall and all looked clear. Before tiptoeing past each room she looked in while trying to conceal her body around the corner. A sense of relief swept through her as she passed the last rooms and reached the steps.

Just down the stairs through the hall and dining room and a little farther to the door and she'd be free. She carefully made her way through the downstairs and to the door. Her hand clasped over the handle. What if he waited outside for her? Her mind raced. She was allowing her imagination to run away from her—probably from guilt.

Drawing in a deep breath to sustain her courage she pushed the door open just enough to slide through the opening and closed it behind her. She rushed down the porch steps and out to the sidewalk, her heart still thudding in her ears.

Once past the next house she let out a sigh. She'd made it. She slowed her pace. After all she went through, she knew nothing more than she did this morning. Olivia suddenly became aware of heavy footfalls moving quickly toward her. In her relief for being out of Lloyd's house she hadn't noticed. She picked up her pace, but before she made it more than a few steps large hands seized her from behind.

♥♥♥

Drew reached out and closed his hands on the black sleeves of Olivia's upper arms. Now he would find out what brought her here—and more than that he wanted to know what she wanted to talk to him about several days ago.

When he'd glimpsed Olivia sneaking out of the back door and not saying a word to anyone, he had to follow her. He gave his father and brothers a vague excuse about needing to do something and he'd be to Ebenezer's straight away as soon as he took care of it. It was all true, though he knew it had looked like he tried to avoid work at Ebenezer's.

Not only had curiosity gotten the best of him as to what Olivia was up to, but it had been impossible to find time alone to talk with her. Her leaving had seemed the chance he'd been waiting for and he'd decided right then not to let it slip through his fingers. He'd do extra time this evening at Ebenezer's to make up for it if need be.

Olivia had seemed as skittish as a child coming to the doctor's office with the way she had kept looking over her shoulder, which made following her all the more challenging. Staying back and out of sight had caused him to lose track of her twice. But when she turned on to Lloyd's street he knew her intended destination. He had almost turned around and walked away.

But now that he had caught up to her and could feel the warmth of her body seep into his hands, he was glad he hadn't given up the pursuit. He wanted to pull her to him. He wanted to kiss her like he used to.

The trembling of her body beneath his touch brought his senses back to the moment at hand. She'd frozen in front of him. No sound left her lips and she'd not even turned around to see who held her.

"Olivia?"

She swung around, and fear melted from her features. "Drew." The words came out in a whisper. "What are you doing here?"

He frowned. "I was wondering the same thing about you."

"I-I took a walk."

"Alone? And so early? Don't you think you should have had someone come with you? I would have escorted you." But he knew she didn't want company. He'd saw her knock on the door and then slip in Lloyd's house. And he'd also saw Lloyd enter just minutes later. Had they set up some sort of rendezvous? But Lloyd had gone in and come out in a couple minutes and Olivia seemed nervous as she exited the house several minutes later. And even now she seemed jumpy.

She glanced over his shoulder in the direction of Lloyd's house. "I needed to be alone so I could think. I can't think around you. I mean I can think, I just think of the wrong things. No, no, no. Not wrong things as in *wrong*. Just things I shouldn't be thinking of—"

Drew grinned. Even as upset as he was with her for

going in Lloyd's home, he couldn't help but smile. This was his old Olivia. The one who always wanted to explain everything so nothing could be misconstrued, all the while digging herself into a deeper hole.

Olivia's blue-gray eyes grew stormier than the Atlantic during a hurricane. She stomped her foot. "Drew Warwick, you stop that this instant."

Drew let go of her arms and lifted his palms up in question. "I didn't do anything. I was just listening to you."

She glared at him. "You know that smirk of yours makes me ramble."

"You…" His heart beat in staccato causing his voice to falter. She remembered. He loved to tease her and get her so flustered she babbled aimlessly.

The frown lines on her forehead softened. "Is something wrong?" She placed her hand on his arm.

The familiar touch sent a thrill through his veins. He blinked, looking for some sort of recognition. Something that told him she remembered him…before. "You remembered."

She cocked her head and the lines furrowed her beautiful ivory skin again. "Remember what?"

"You said my smirk makes you ramble. You remembered." He could see her sorting through his words.

"I know that." She stared off blankly. "But I don't know how I know it."

His heart sunk. But maybe it was the beginning of her recovery. "But it means you knew me before."

"Yes, it does."

"So now you know I didn't lie to you."

She bit her bottom lip. "I know *some* of what you've told me was the truth."

Drew took her arm. "Let's walk."

She nodded.

"But now that you know we weren't strangers, why would you doubt anything I've said?"

"Everything I've been told conflicts. I have to work through this…on my own."

"Is that why you went in there?" He jerked his head back toward Lloyd's home.

The blood seemed to drain from her face. "I don't want to talk about it. And please, would you keep this between us?"

He tamped down the urge to batter her with questions. He didn't want to upset her. The best way to handle this was to keep a closer eye on her comings and goings. And hopefully that way he would learn what she was up to. If she didn't want to talk about this, then now was a good time to discuss what she wanted to talk to him about. "All right, I'll do that for you. But tell me, what did you wish to speak with me about?"

She scrunched her face in question, but then dawning lit her features. "It isn't important now."

"It is to me."

"Things have changed and it is no longer relevant."

Drew's hair bristled on his neck. "Does it have to do with Lloyd?"

Her lips pressed together in a thin line.

Drew groaned. "I know. You don't wish to talk about it."

He should have made a way to speak with her sooner. Now he had lost that chance to find out what had seemed so important at the time.

Their conversation the rest of the way home was minimal, about the weather or some such nonsense. The most interesting thing they discussed was the damage they saw from the earthquake. How could this be happening? He had made a way to speak to Olivia and now there seemed to be no words to say.

His prayer came back to him. *I will do my best to leave Olivia in your hands and trust you with her and with my heart.* Was it so wrong to want to be in charge of his life, making his own decisions? He wanted to be the one in charge of his destiny rather than leave it to God. Trust left him feeling too vulnerable.

Drew opened the door of his family's home and waited for Olivia to go in. He needed to get to Ebenezer's place. He'd already wasted enough time. Wasted in some ways, but not in others. He enjoyed his time spent with Olivia, but it hadn't turned out fruitful. Following her had been productive. It just left him wondering what exactly Olivia was up to.

Drew could hear Olivia's gown swishing behind him as he strode toward the back door of the house where he could be on his way. He passed by the parlor.

"Drew." Mother's strangled voice stopped him where he walked.

He backed up and bumped into Olivia. His mother's pale face made him forget to apologize to Olivia. His heart skipped a beat. "Is everything all right, Mother?"

The color in her already fair skin had drained as she sat motionless on the settee by the large picture window. He stepped in the room with Olivia on his heels.

An unwanted female voice greeted him. "Hello, Andrew. I've been waiting for you."

Chapter 20

Olivia sat in the small room off from the carriage house and stable where Christian kept his menagerie of animals, wondering if she should attempt going to Lloyd's again. He'd come by and seen her once since she almost got caught snooping around his house. He hadn't seemed the least bit suspicious, but he was highly agitated when she wouldn't agree to marry him or leave the Warwick's.

The truth was she should leave. She knew that, but deep down she had to admit to herself that she didn't want to. She kept making the excuse that she had nowhere to go, but she hadn't once looked into any possibilities either. Mrs. Warwick was like a mother to her. She was the closest thing to one now that Mama was gone. And Dr. Warwick, though quiet, seemed always concerned for her. JoAnna had become the sister that she'd always wanted. Christian and William treated her like a little sister. She smiled. Well, maybe a little nicer than a little sister.

And then there was Drew. He was the reason she should leave. She couldn't look at him without her heart getting involved. Every moment she spent with him she put to memory. As much as she tried to be angry with him and not care for him as more than an acquaintance, her emotions wouldn't obey. She had no right to care so deeply for a man that was a father to someone else's child. The child needed him. And she begrudgingly admitted to herself so did the boy's mother.

Sitting down, she scooped up Fang and put him in her lap. He licked her chin and then nuzzled down into her gown. The bite area was still swollen, but he didn't seem much bothered by it anymore. Spotless came over and laid his head on her leg, looking up at her with black little eyes. She stroked his silky fur, allowing her hand to glide over him and cool her palm. The smell of fresh straw filled the room and she allowed herself to relax.

"Hello again." Miss Middleton stepped into the small room and curled up her nose.

"Good day. Can I help you find someone?" Olivia smiled though she didn't feel it inside. When Drew and she had come back from their walk and found Miss Middleton in the parlor with Mrs. Warwick, Miss Middleton had barely been civil to Olivia. Drew didn't stay around, claiming he needed to get over to Ebenezer's place and help out. Once Miss Middleton realized Drew wasn't staying, she excused herself and left. Olivia was relieved to see her go. She didn't want to get to know the woman any better.

"I was looking for you, Miss Macqueen."

"You've found me." Olivia ran Fang's downy soft ear through her fingers.

"I thought it would be nice if we became friends. We seem to be about the same age."

Miss Middleton looked and sounded more businesslike than someone seeking out a friendship. Olivia certainly wanted nothing to do with the woman who had a child fathered by Drew. There were far more things that set them miles apart than they had in common. "Where's your little boy?" Olivia knew her words sounded waspish, but still they slipped out.

Challenge shone in the woman's eyes. "Andrew is with my sister. I named him after his father."

Olivia cringed. Andrew? She named the boy after his father? A smirk played on Miss Middleton's lips. She knew she had the upper hand with Drew. What man wouldn't choose the mother of his son over a woman who couldn't even remember him? Olivia shook herself mentally. What was she thinking? This was no competition to see who could win Drew. As much it tore at her heart to admit it, Miss Middleton had every right to expect Drew to marry her. "I'm sorry. I don't believe I'd make a very good friend right now."

Miss Middleton glided over to her and patted her shoulder as she pulled out a handkerchief edged in lace and placed it on the stool and sat. "I know it has been a hard month for you with losing your parents. And that's why I think you do need a friend. It seems this good family has taken you in like one of their own, and when Drew and I marry we will almost be like sisters."

Olivia stiffened. She and Drew marry? Her heart wrenched within its cage. Wasn't this what she was just thinking? So why did it cause despair within her? Olivia scooted Spotless's head off her lap and gently placed Fang beside his brother before she stood and brushed off the hair and straw from her gown. Tears stung the back of her eyes and a large lump formed in her throat. She swallowed. "Thank you for your kind offer, Miss Middleton. I'm overwhelmed by your kindness. If you'll excuse me, I just remembered something I need to do."

Olivia sashayed out the door and toward the house, knowing she had just been the epitome of rude. One was supposed to turn the other cheek, but in this case, Olivia had taken to the road of the old scripture of an eye for an eye. The woman had been unkind to her when she'd met her in the parlor talking with Mrs. Warwick a few days ago. She was only returning the favor. She couldn't be this woman's friend. Not when she would become Mrs. Drew Warwick, and in Olivia's heart of hearts that was who she wanted to be.

Just another sign that God no longer cared about her. He slowly seemed to be stripping from her life anyone who meant something to her. She picked up her pace, desperate to get to her room before the dam waters broke.

Drew strode down the sidewalk still fuming over Constance showing up when he wasn't home two days ago. The nerve of the woman coming by and speaking with Mother, implying that the child she had was his. He certainly had not suspected that from her. He was glad he hadn't softened and taken her back the day she had come crying to him, begging his forgiveness.

When he'd found out she'd been unfaithful to him, it killed any deep feelings he'd ever had for her. Perhaps because it wasn't truly love. As angry as he had been with her for betraying him, he'd prayed about it and was reminded how Jesus had forgiven the adulterous woman and how Joseph decided to put Mary away silently. So he told Constance to go away and start a new life with her baby. He'd even given her money and promised to keep her secret. He'd not even told his parents why he'd broken off their engagement.

So when Mother had stared at him, face drained of all color, he knew keeping the truth from them had been a mistake. After assuring her a half dozen times that there was no way the boy was his, she finally seemed at ease. It pained him to think that his mother would ever doubt him.

But for Constance to return a second time while he wasn't home…and he was confident that she knew he wasn't, and to seek out Olivia while she was in with Christian's animals, bringing her to near tears according to JoAnna, was almost more than he could abide. The woman needed a set down and if she continued, he would be more than happy to give it to her.

Drew shook off the unpleasant memories and turned into the private investigator's office. A pretty young brunette with spectacles looked up from behind a desk. "Can I help you, sir?"

"Drew Warwick," Drew snatched the bowler off his head. "Could I speak with Mr. Fraser?"

"He hasn't come in, yet." Her brows furrowed. "I'm a little concerned. He usually lets me know if he is going to be late."

Drew pulled out his card from his inside pocket and handed it to her. "Would you have him contact me when he comes in?"

She took the card and gave a wavering smile. "I will…" she glanced down at the card, "Doctor Warwick. Have a good day."

Drew picked up his pace on his way back to the office. It seemed that patient flow ran in spurts of busy. He understood the sickness. Certain times of the year there seemed to be an influx of colds, influenza, and stomach ailments. That was to be expected. But with the amount of collapsed and partially-collapsed buildings, combined with the work being done on them, they had been extra busy these last few months with injured workers.

Walking in the waiting room, Drew was met by five patients waiting to be seen. He smiled, said good morning, and hurried back to the examination room, making sure all was ready. Shedding his coat and hanging it on the hook beside the door, he returned to the hall, noticing that both his father's door and William's were closed.

Within the few short minutes he'd walked back to his sick room, making sure all was set up before returning to get a patient—another injured man had joined the ranks. Drew let his gaze stop on Mr. Maloney, sitting in the waiting area. He held a bloody cloth to his hand as more blood dripped on the floor. "Mr. Maloney? What'd you do?"

"Cut my finger." He moved his hand and winced.

"Why don't you follow me back and I'll take a look at it."

Mr. Maloney took a seat in the chair and Drew carefully unwrapped the cloth from the appendage. Not expecting what he saw, Drew flinched. "What were you doing?" He examined the tip dangling from the finger.

"I was tearing down a wall and a slate from the roof gave way and sliced my finger."

Drew gritted his teeth as he looked closer.

"You've sliced through the bone and—"

"Yes, yes, I know. What can you do for me Doc?" The color drained from Mr. Maloney's face.

"It only hangs on by the skin. I'm afraid all I can do is stitch it up. You've lost your finger." Drew got up and retrieved the things he'd need to clean and stitch up the man's hand.

"At least it weren't one I use all the time." The man turned his head away as Drew went to work on him.

"It is only the tip. You'll still have some use of the appendage." The man was fortunate it was only his small finger and not a thumb.

The rest of the day continued in a busy blur. After seeing several people with bad coughs and one with pneumonia, all complaining how quickly it progressed, he finished up with another man who'd injured himself while working on home repairs.

All his patients having been seen, Drew was ready to get home. Father still with his last patient, said he needed to stop at a man's house to check on him. William was out the door before Drew could ask him any questions. His brother had been spending more time away than at home lately.

Weary from the long day, Drew decided to walk home rather than accompany Father to the patient's home. Olivia was on his mind, and he looked forward to talking to her. He'd left early this morning and hadn't had a chance to see her before he'd rushed out the door to the investigator's office.

He kept a brisk pace up all the way home. Inside, Drew drifted through the hall, glancing in the rooms that he passed in search of Olivia. Finding the rooms empty, he headed toward the kitchen where he could hear Mrs. Benninger banging pots and pans and humming.

He stopped just inside the kitchen taking in the lone woman. She turned, locking eyes with him and letting her song fade on her lips. "Dinner ain't gonna be ready for over an hour, so don't you start telling me how hungry you are."

Drew grinned. For some reason Mrs. Benninger still thought he was a growing boy, always hungry. "It sure does smell good in here. If I stick around in here too long I will be starving."

"Well, then git out of my kitchen and let me do my work. Go on." She shooed him away with her hands.

"I'll go as soon as you tell me if you've seen Olivia."

"Olivia, your momma, and JoAnna baked cookies and took them down to one of the tent parks for them poor folks without a home."

Disappointed, Drew removed himself from the kitchen and headed back through the house. He'd hurried home for nothing. He made it halfway up the stairs to change his clothes when a crash came from down the hall. Taking the remainder of the steps two at a time, he couldn't imagine what had fallen, unless he or William had left the window open and a breeze had knocked something off a table. He strode down the hall, hoping it wasn't his cologne.

He frowned as he reached William's and his room. He never closed the door and it didn't seem that windy out. Turning the knob, he pushed it open. A man whose shoulders looked to be twice as broad as Drew's swung around. A plum colored jagged scar ran from the corner of his eye across his cheek, stopping near the corner of his mouth.

"What are you doing in here?"

The man growled and charged toward him. Drew planted his feet firmly on the floor, determined not to let the man past him. The man didn't look like he was going to stop of his own accord, so Drew prepared. Just as he reached Drew, Drew swung his fist into the man's gut.

Pain shot through his hand and up his arm. He wondered if he'd hit the wall or a human. The blow didn't seem to faze the man a bit. One glimpse of the mongrel's fist and the bicep behind it and he knew how it was going to end. Throwing his arm up to block the man's punch, pain spiraled down Drew's forearm.

The front door slammed. The intruder gave a quick hard shove, knocking Drew off his feet as he bolted past him. Drew scrambled up and gave chase. JoAnna screamed and plastered herself against the wall on the stairs. Drew flew past her in pursuit. Down the narrow hall, Mother stood with her hand on her chest. Attempting to pass her in hopes of catching up with his thief, Drew didn't stop.

He made it to the door when his mother's words reached him.

"Drew, let him go."

Drew peered down the road at the swiftly retreating man before glancing over his shoulder at his mother moving toward him. He pushed the screen. "He's getting away." He couldn't let the man go. If nothing else, he wanted to know what he was looking for. He was on the sidewalk when his mother called out again.

"Andrew Joshua Warwick, you stop this instant."

Drew's feet turned to lead. He was twenty-three and

his mother could still make him obey her. Infuriated that he didn't follow through, still he couldn't bring himself to disobey his mother. He pivoted around. "The man was up in William's room going through our things."

She stood on the piazza by the steps with hands on her hips, reminding him of many a day when he was but a boy and about to get a very stern scolding. "I don't care. If you chase him down he might hurt you. Someone who comes into a home when not invited looking for money or valuables is not someone with whom you should trifle."

JoAnna joined Mother and stood beside her.

"My intent was to bring him to justice. Now he's gotten away."

"I'd rather that than something terrible happen to you. People like him would not think twice about hurting you."

"Mother, don't worry. I'm a grown man, and I did give him something to think about." He wanted to shake the numbness out of this hand, but his pride restrained him. He hoped he could uncurl his fingers come morning.

She patted his arm. "It didn't look like he found anything to his liking. He left empty-handed."

Drew placed his hand over his mother's, hiding a wince at the effort. "You might want to keep the house locked if none of the men are home." JoAnna's face had drained of all color. He'd never seen her at a loss for words either. "You all right, sis?"

She nodded. "Do you think he'll come back?"

Drew gave her a side hug. "Now that he's tangled with me I don't think we have to worry about that."

He winked at her and bent over giving her a kiss on her cheek. "I think I'll go make sure he didn't pocket anything."

Inside the bedroom, Drew looked around, but nothing seemed terribly disturbed except for William's golf clubs, which had been knocked over. That was most likely the noise that had drawn his attention originally. There were plenty of valuable things lying around that a common thief would have taken. The man had to have been looking for something specific. Drew headed down the hallway, sticking his head in his parent's room and then JoAnna's, making sure nothing had been disturbed before going on to his room which Olivia now used.

Pushing open the door, he nearly gasped. The drawers had been pulled from the wardrobe and emptied on the floor. His and Olivia's clothes mingled together. The bed had been stripped of its blankets. The nightstand drawer had been yanked out and tossed haphazardly on the floor. Furniture had been moved.

Drew picked up the wardrobe drawers and slid them into their holes. Quickly, trying not to think about what he was doing, he placed all of Olivia's clothes and personal items back in the wardrobe, hoping he'd put them away how they were supposed to be. He doubted he had succeeded. He could see Olivia's blush creeping up her face when she discovered he had picked up all her unmentionables.

Drew retrieved the last item that had been tossed to the floor, a book, and slid it in beside the other three on a shelf. That was when he knew why he'd had an unwanted visitor. With haste, he returned to William's room and went straight to the bed. He knew it was going to be gone before he'd even looked. He'd hidden Mr. Macqueen's account book because he wasn't ready to tell Olivia why he had it. Telling her that he believed Lloyd embezzled from her father wouldn't be easy, and she—in all probability—wouldn't believe him. He needed proof. He'd been looking through it trying to find what he needed. And since Olivia hadn't asked for anything from her father's desk, he'd kept it in the room he slept in.

Drew lifted the mattress and slid his hand beneath it, feeling the wire springs that supported the mattress. Even though he knew, his heart lurched when all he felt was the cold metal. Tilting his head, he peered beneath the cushion and scanned the space for the evidence that would finally indict Lloyd for the scoundrel he was.

Chapter 21

Mrs. Benninger's words filtered through Drew's frustration as he dropped to his knees to get a better look. *"Olivia, your momma, and JoAnna baked cookies and took them down to one of the tent parks for them poor folks without a home."* Drew had to remind himself he needed to breathe. How could he forget about Olivia? He'd seen both JoAnna and Mother, but Olivia hadn't come home with them. Bounding to his feet, he dropped the mattress, the urgency of indicting Lloyd not so important anymore.

Why hadn't Olivia come in with his mother and sister? "Jo." Drew took the steps down two at a time, keeping his balance with the hand rail.

His feet hit the landing as JoAnna came around the corner. "What?"

"Where is Olivia?"

"Is that all you want? You frightened me. I thought we might have another intruder in the house." She folded her arms in front of her.

"Where is she? Mrs. Benninger said she was with you and Mother." He wished he'd not given in to Mother's pleading to let the man go.

"Really, Drew. You are overreacting. She did go with us, but when we walked past her old home she asked if we would mind if she stayed there a little while. I offered to stay with her, but she wanted time alone."

Drew grabbed his bowler off the hall table and thrust it on his head as he headed out the door. "Lock the house."

JoAnna laughed. "I don't believe my eyes. You Drew, my pragmatic brother, are being melodramatic."

"Just do as I say, JoAnna." He pulled the door shut.

The door squeaked back open and JoAnna's head popped out. "It was probably someone down on their luck because he lost everything during the earthquake. You surely scared him so bad that he's on his way out of Charleston as we speak."

Drew glared at his sister. Why couldn't the chit ever just do as he said? She had to question every single thing he told her.

The smile fell from her face. "Oh, all right. I'm locking it now." Her red curls were the last thing he saw before hearing the click of the lock.

He spun on his heels and dashed to the back where his horse was stabled. Barking met him at the entrance. He passed by the small room where Christian kept his animals. With little effort he tossed the saddle on his Morgan horse, Stitches, threw himself into the saddle, and headed toward Olivia's family home.

Drew dug his heels into Stitches' sides, weaving around carriages and slower horses. A few yells to slow down flew his way, but getting to Olivia was all he could think about. He had to believe that Lloyd wouldn't hurt her or allow any of his thugs to, assuming the man who broke into his room was hired by Lloyd. But what if Lloyd wasn't the mastermind behind it all? What if he was a pawn in a much larger game? Egad! If that were the case, her life could be in serious danger.

Leaning forward, he urged his mount on with coaxing words. The few minutes it took to get to Church Street seemed like an hour in the dentist chair. The crumpled remains of the stately manor finally came into sight. He'd never get used to seeing the destruction of Olivia's home, and he could only imagine how hard it was for her. His Livvy was a pillar of courage. She'd lost everything, her family, her home, her memory, and still she pushed on helping his family. Her character and attitude encouraged everyone around her.

Encouraging. A word that would not describe him. Father was right. He spent too much time trying to control every situation to be of any encouragement. What did he think? That he was God? That he, Drew Warwick, should ordain everyone's steps or do it himself? Drew berated himself. Hadn't he said he'd leave Olivia in the Lord's hands? And here he sought her out.

But it had nothing to do with winning her over, he argued with himself. The only reason he came to find her was to make sure of her safety. Even Father had said to look after her because she had no one else who would. A small figure materialized amongst the rubble—her black dress disguising her amongst the debris.

Drew leaped from Stitches and dropped the reins, ground-tying him. Agonizing sobs rent the air. As he neared, the shaking of her shoulders and her head buried in her folded arms resting on her bent knees became visible. His chest cinched. If only he could take her pain away.

♥♥♥

Having given in to the weakness overtaking her knees as memories flooded back, Olivia had crumpled to the ground weeping over the life that had been. When she accompanied JoAnna and her mother to the square to give away cookies to the less fortunate in tents, she'd asked to return by Church Street so she could once again see what was left of her home. But when she went to pass by, her heart begged her to stay. The ladies were agreeable for her to have some time alone. They seemed to understand her need.

But as she had walked around the house and then the back yard, little things began to elicit memories. The white iron bench under the Live Oak Tree was where Drew had asked to court her. He'd plucked a rose from her mother's rose bush, pricking his thumb on the thorn. Then cutting all the thorns off, he handed it to her. He said he never wanted to do anything that could hurt her. She remembered the cracked wooden picket that Simon had tripped and fallen into when he chased her with a cicada bug. She remembered the first kiss Drew gave her on the piazza steps.

The tears came along with weakness that filled her body. She'd been so terrible to Drew, insisting she and Lloyd remained engaged. Her stomach twisted until it gave way to nausea. How could she have forgotten Drew, yet remembered such a scoundrel as Lloyd? Drew had been so kind and patient with her—his gentle nudges trying to get her to remember all they had shared. And she'd scoffed at them. Thrown them back in his face. Even lashed back in anger over his insistence. He didn't deserve the trouble she'd given him.

Instead, she praised Lloyd, defended him, sworn of their love. A man who had been unfaithful to her. She swallowed a sob, trying to get a hold of herself. A man who had stolen from her family. A man who had abused her.

"Olivia?" Drew's baritone voice found its way through the fog in her mind.

She lifted her head and brushed away the tears with her black glove. "Drew." His name came out as a whisper.

He knelt beside her, hesitating. Doubt filled his eyes and he seemed to be battling a response. But then his arms surrounded her and he gently pushed her head to his shoulder. "Shhh, love. It will all be all right. Time will heal your pain."

He thought she cried for the loss of her family. And perhaps some of the tears shed were for them. But she'd had time to grieve their loss, and although the sorrow remained in knowing she'd never see them again on this earth, there was peace in knowing they were together with the Lord. The agony that tore her heart apart wasn't death. It was the knowledge that she must live every day of her life without the man she loved—without anyone to love her—Drew, her family, and even God.

He pulled her hat from her head and pressed his lips to her hair. "I'm sorry I can't take away your pain. If I could shoulder it all, I would. I'd give my life to make you happy."

Another cry ripped from her throat. She couldn't bear it if he was gone. But he had a child who deserved to have a daddy. She couldn't take that from Drew or from Andrew.

"I didn't mean for you to see me like this." She sniffed, trying to get a hold of her emotions.

His hands ran over her hair and she reveled in his closeness. They slid down to encompass her cheeks and he tenderly pulled her head away from his shoulder and looked deep into her eyes. It was as if he could see the memories brimming to the surface and she wanted to look away to conceal them, but the love in his eyes kept her tied to him.

"Don't ever feel that way. You can share anything with me. I'll always be here for you, Olivia. Always."

His gaze lowered to her mouth. Her body trembled. She ran her tongue over her lips, tasting her salty tears. Before she could tell him no, his lips were on hers, consuming her and demanding more. Her arms wrapped around his neck of their own free will and she moaned. How could she have forgotten this? Forgotten him?

A small child yelled in the distance bringing her back to her right mind. She pulled away, missing the contact even as their lips parted. "I—I—" she stuttered as his finger came up and silenced her words.

"Don't say it. I know I shouldn't have, but I'm not

sorry and I don't want you to be either."

"We can't," she looked down at her hands. "It's wrong." But if felt so right.

"It's not. We are adults. I love you, and I think you are discovering that you care for me."

She shook her head and pushed away, stumbling to her feet. "No, it's Lloyd I love. We are to be married." How easily the words slipped out even now that she knew they weren't true.

Pain filled his eyes at her words. She wanted to take them back, but couldn't. He had an obligation, and she wouldn't stand in his way. Nothing good could come of their love. Not now. Not ever.

"Forgive me, Olivia. I overstepped myself." He stood, pulling back his shoulders.

She had hurt him. But it had to be this way. Now that she knew the truth, remembered their love, it was too easy to give in to the feelings raging through her. If she had any doubt about telling him the truth, it had vanished. For if he knew she'd regained that part of her memory, she couldn't be sure that she would remain strong enough to walk away. And she had to. Not only for Drew and Andrew, but for herself.

If there were any chance that God cared even a little bit about her, how could she take a chance and throw it to the wind? She'd not give God any more reason to turn His back on her, and letting Drew know that she loved him would do just that. She had to prove to God that she would not put her own desires above what she knew was right. Maybe then He could forgive her. Maybe then she'd get to see her family again someday.

"I should get back. Your mother is probably worried about me." She tugged her hat back on her head and straightened the plain black gloves on her hands.

Drew stiffened, and she wondered about his abrupt change to such a simple comment. His hand slid to the small of her back and he urged her forward. "Yes, we should be getting home."

He retrieved his horse, and then offered her his arm as they started back toward his house, the horse following obediently behind them. An awkward silence continued as they made their way back to the Warwick's home. How would she face each member of the family now that she remembered them? She could only hope that they would not see through the charade that she was about to play.

It was urgent that she get away from them before she made a mistake and they found out her secret. But before she could leave, she had one thing that must be done and that was to prove Lloyd's guilt. The return of some of her memories would have to be kept from him, too. At least until she had the proof she needed to put him away. Now that her father and brother were gone, it was up to her to see justice done.

The account book was all she needed in order to move forward. But how to ask Drew about it without drawing suspicion on her? "Did you ever return to my family home and see if anything of value survived? I'm sure Mother's jewelry would have survived. I can't believe I didn't think about this before. I know you gathered my father's things from his desk."

The look in his eye made her think he struggled to answer her question. Had he forgotten he told her he'd return to her home and rescue anything worthy? She should have reminded him. With well over a month gone by, if there was anything left worth salvaging, it would be ruined from the weather.

"I hadn't decided if I would tell you this, but since you have brought it up I feel I must."

Cocking her head, she glanced up at him as they walked. "Yes?"

He caught her gaze with his and drew in a deep breath. "You mentioned the things I pulled from your father's desk." He shoved his hand through his hair. "That is what really brought me here."

"I don't understand." He appeared so serious it sent an ominous shiver down her spine.

"Along with all the papers in your father's desk, I found his account book."

This had turned out easier than she'd imagined. She'd not even had to ask him about the item in question. Now she was very thankful she hadn't asked right away. "I see. I was wondering about that book just today."

His brows rose. "You were?"

She nodded and broke off their eye contact. The man was mesmerizing. It was time to leave the Warwick's home. There was no other answer. "I thought I'd like to look through it. It would have been some of the last things Papa wrote in."

"Your father's account book is gone."

"How can that be? I thought you brought it home with you."

"I did. I came home today and found someone going through William's room. He ran off when I saw him. But not before stealing the accounts book." He paused, rubbed his hand. "I tried to stop him with my fist in his belly, but nearly broke my hand instead. I wondered how anyone could have such an iron gut. Now I know he stuck the account book there. I suppose in case he ran into anyone, he hoped they wouldn't discover until later that he'd taken it."

Olivia's hand went to her chest. "You weren't hurt were you?"

He gave her a half grin. "Only my pride."

"I'm glad that's all." She took in his enticing smile before allowing her eyes to wander. A crisp white shirt lay beneath his dark brown tweed jacket that pulled across his shoulders. Lighter brown than his jacket, his trousers were tucked into high polished riding boots. He cut a fine figure. A lightning bolt of desire sizzled through her veins, warming her tummy. How could she go on pretending she didn't love him?

"Do you know why he might have wanted it enough to come steal it in full daylight?"

She couldn't look him in the eye as she avoided giving him the answer he sought. "I suppose it had something to do with Papa's business. Why else would someone steal it?"

"Indeed." His voice came out hushed, tempting her to look his way.

"But you said that's what prompted you to find me. Why would the stolen book make you look for me?"

"Because Mother and JoAnna had just returned when the intruder dashed out. When I realized you hadn't returned with them, I feared you and he may have crossed paths as he fled. One doesn't know what thoughts run through a criminal's mind. He could have harmed you or taken you with him." The words quivered on his tongue, whether from anger or concern she couldn't tell.

"As you can see, I am fine." She tried to make light of the situation.

"And I am immeasurably grateful. But I have good news amongst the bad. I had hoped to surprise you when your memories returned, however, I feel I should tell you now that you've mentioned your family heirlooms."

"And what is that?"

"I did return to your family home and spent a full day searching through the rubble. Amongst the silver and other things that I could salvage, I believe I found your mother's jewelry."

Olivia's heart went to her throat. She would be able to wear a necklace that hung around her mother's neck and a pin that clasped over her mother's heart. It was more than she had dreamed. "Thank you for looking after me, Drew. It's comforting to know I'm not alone…not that I'm alone. I have Lloyd, but he is not always around." Her blood pounded in her temples. Already she'd almost had a slip of tongue. She must remember that she and Lloyd was still an item for pretense's sake.

♥♥♥

Lloyd eyed Constance as she paced across the parlor in his home, her deep blue gown swishing as she spun around to face him, reclining in the chair. "I'm telling you, Lloyd, she loves him. I can see it in her eyes, hear it in her voice." She brushed her bangs from her eyes. "A woman can see these things in another."

Lloyd tightened his fists. No reason to take his anger out on Constance, she was just the bearer of the unwelcome news. Besides, he'd have her brother to account to, and that wouldn't end well for him. If he didn't want to know what she thought, he shouldn't have asked her. "What of me? Has she said anything?"

Constance plucked a glove from her hand, one finger at a time. "Not even your name, I'm afraid. She's too much in love with Drew."

"What did she say?"

"Very little. The mention of Drew and me sent her scurrying away faster than a mouse from a snapped trap." She laughed. "Little does she realize the one we are setting for her."

"*I* am not a trap. I just want what is rightfully mine, and that is Olivia." And, of course, to be free of this whole ugly embezzlement issue.

"Oh, calm down, Lloyd. I wasn't implying anything more than she is naïve."

"What about the child? No one has questioned you on him?" He forced himself to relax and stretched his legs out in front of him.

"Of course not. I told you no one here knew my child died at birth. I couldn't bear to come back. Too many bad memories." She worked on taking off her other glove.

"How does your sister-in-law feel about you borrowing her child?"

Constance rolled her eyes. "I'm not borrowing my nephew. I'm simply spending time with him, giving my sister-in-law a much-needed break. And Nathan runs the house with an iron fist. She really has no say. I'm just doing what dear brother has asked. Besides, how else could I bond with the child?"

Lloyd let out a deep laugh. "You are clever, my dear. I'll give you that."

"Yes, well, I have done my part. What are *you* going to do?"

"Drew needs to be out of the picture to get Olivia's mind off him. I can see that now."

"He isn't responding as I had thought. Reputation of his family and their business used to be one of his top concerns. But even my threats of a scandal don't seem to affect him." She thrust her hands on her hips, the white gloves dangling from one hand.

"I'd hoped you could win him over." Fire flared up in him at the thought of Drew.

"You've done no better with Olivia."

"True, you seem to have the same problem with Drew as I have with Olivia. But if he isn't going to respond to your advances, I've thought of other ways I can take care of the problem."

She narrowed her eyes. "What's that supposed to mean?"

"This is all a means to an end—Olivia marrying me. I need Drew out of the way. If you can't do that, I will."

"No. That wasn't the agreement. I *want* Drew and you want Olivia. You can't just do away with him. I won't let you."

Lloyd laughed. "Do you really think you can stop me? Even if you could, you couldn't stop your brother."

Chapter 22

Olivia couldn't keep putting off moving somewhere else. She was beginning to sound like the little boy who cried wolf. But she had nowhere to go and no money to use. The only option would be to head to California to Papa's parents. She'd never met them, but surely they'd take her in if she could find a way there—assuming they still lived. Papa had never said he'd heard otherwise. But with the house destroyed, she may not be able to find their address.

If she wanted to leave, she needed to wrap up the business of Lloyd's embezzlement and then start searching out her grandparents. Leaving before seeing justice served would haunt her the rest of her days. She pushed off the bed. The only place to find evidence of Lloyd's wrongdoing would be at his house. She didn't want to tell Drew, but if the account book had been stolen, then it was Lloyd who'd it taken. She had no doubt of that.

Lloyd should be off doing whatever it was he did with his day. Now would be the perfect time to make a visit to his home and see if she could find the book. Olivia crossed the room, passing by the window overlooking the gardenia-laden backyard; she halted before easing her way closer to the window. Drew's back was to her and Constance faced him. Arms folded in front of him and feet planted apart, he looked angry. Constance glanced toward the house. Olivia slid to the side of the window out of sight and waited a minute before peering around.

Constance's hands were to her face as if crying. Drew's arms fell to his sides. It didn't look as if they were arguing now. As the thought flashed through Olivia's mind, Constance flew against Drew's chest nearly knocking him off balance. His arms wrapped around her.

It was more than she could watch. Olivia spun around and fled through her bedroom door passing JoAnna as she left the room.

"Olivia, are you feeling unwell? You look pale."

She started at seeing JoAnna. "I just need some fresh air." Olivia dashed toward the staircase. She was out of the house as quickly as her feet would take her, determined to get proof against Lloyd so she could put this part of her life behind her permanently.

Maybe she could get the money owed to them from Lloyd and then take a train to California. Where did Papa say they lived? Sacramento? No that wasn't it. It was San something. She looked up at the cloudless blue sky in an attempt to distract herself.

San Jose. That was it. She exhaled in relief. She'd see if Mr. or Mrs. Warwick could tell her anything about the city.

Picking up her pace, she arrived in front of Lloyd's home while she still pondered the problem of getting to California. She'd been so lost in her thoughts, she'd not seen the man walking toward her until it was too late.

"Olivia. Just the woman I wanted to see." Lloyd's long strides ate up the sidewalk between them.

She blinked, not believing her eyes. "L-Lloyd, what a surprise."

He laughed. "A surprise? You are standing in front of my house."

She glanced toward the two-story gray wooden structure. "So I am."

Wrapping his arms around her, he gave her a tight hug. Nothing like the caring hug Drew had given to Constance. "You *did* come to see me, didn't you?"

What other reason could she give for strolling alone

past his home? "I hadn't seen you in a few days."

"I've been busy." He released her as abruptly as he'd embraced her. "Your timing is perfect. Come in and we can visit."

"It-it wouldn't be proper."

He snorted and grasped her hand, pulling her along. "You didn't come all the way here to stand outside."

She tried to tug her hand free, but he only tightened his grip, sending pain up her arm. "I thought we could sit on the bench out here."

He glanced around carelessly. "What bench?"

To her horror, there was no furniture outdoors. "Then I must go." She dug in her heels, but his strength was no match.

"Go? But you just got here. And now that you see I have no bench, you will need to come in to sit down." He'd made it to the front door dragging her along.

"Lloyd, please. It isn't proper. What will people think? It could ruin my reputation." Recollection flashed through her mind's eye. The rage she'd seen in his face the day he'd taken his full anger out on her had been singed into her memory. She should have known it would happen eventually. He'd given hints all along, but he'd made her feel like she deserved what he gave her. But the day that he took out his frustrations on her, she knew that all her father had told her was true.

"You are going to marry me anyway. What does it matter what people gossip about?" He pulled her through the door.

She gasped, her legs being as wobbly as the first time she'd crossed the threshold when she worried about being caught searching his home. "Drew—I mean Lloyd—"

He swung around, his face contorted in anger. "Did you call me Drew?"

More memories flooded her mind. She winced at the image of him taking his fury out on her, all the while knowing he could do it again. Easing his anger and reasoning with him would be impossible at this point.

Olivia managed to pull from Lloyd's grasp when he turned. She made it to the front door before he grabbed her by her hair. But panic drove her. Pain seared through her scalp as she yanked the door open and burst out onto the porch. In an attempt to run, she stumbled on her dress. Hiking it up, she ran.

Fear kept her running, even though she never heard his footfalls behind her. She was sure he ended up with her hat and a handful of hair, but she didn't care. She'd gotten away. Her hair fell down her back and she must look a fright, but she was safe. People were returning home from work, and that was the only reason she could imagine that Lloyd didn't chase her down the street.

She ran until she reached the Warwick's home. Trying to catch her breath, she paused before opening the door. If she could just make it to her room without being seen, she could fix her hair and no one would know. Entering the house, she hoped the parlor remained empty as she dashed up the stairs and into her room.

Behind the closed door, she collapsed onto a chair and sobbed.

Drew strode home, his thoughts busy with all the reading on head injuries he'd done since Olivia's accident. Some people were never the same after coming out of a coma brought on by severe head trauma. It was almost too much to bear thinking that she would never again be his Olivia.

His hopes had risen when JoAnna came to him long after Constance had left. Joanna had seen Olivia at the window in her room. Oliva had rushed out distraught. He dared to hope that she was troubled by what she had seen between Constance and him. He'd embraced Constance merely to console her when she had told him her little boy had fallen terribly sick. He'd comforted her the only way he knew to when she'd burst into tears and fallen on his chest.

He felt sure that the embrace wasn't the cause for Olivia's abrupt departure. Something else had sent her fleeing to the streets and away from the Warwick place. If he wanted to be truthful with himself, he'd admit that it was more than likely thoughts of Lloyd that drove her to go see him. Thankfully, JoAnna had followed her until she was certain Olivia was headed to Lloyd's.

Drew's mood soured. How could Olivia choose that scoundrel over him? He needed to get in contact with the investigator and show Olivia what kind of man she gave company to. The week had been too busy and he'd not had time to get back down and talk to the man. But in the morning he'd go—before heading out to Ebenezer's place.

Inside, Drew dropped down on the blue-and-gold brocade armchair by the front window and let his head fall back. He reminded himself he'd given Olivia to the Lord. That brought reality crashing down, sending his father's words back to haunt him. *...it is time for you to realize God's will in your life is what is important. You may be able to make things happen like you want. But it doesn't mean that is what's best for you...lay this at our Lord's feet. Pray and give the burden to him. I know you love Olivia. But maybe God is using this tragedy to show you she isn't the one He has chosen for you.*

As much as he didn't like to think about it, there was always the possibility that Father was right and Olivia wasn't the woman for him. He'd never truly given Father's words much weight until tonight when Olivia had chosen

Lloyd over him. Well, he'd walked away this time. It was in God's hands.

He jumped up from his chair, feeling as if he'd go crazy if he sat a moment longer. He'd go to Evan Frasier's home and see what information the investigator had uncovered. Trying to convince himself that he only did this to protect Olivia, he went to find the *Sholes' Directory of the City of Charleston.* He strode to the bookshelf he and his father had built years ago and plucked the book from its resting place.

Father had charged him with protecting Olivia, and seeing Lloyd put away for embezzling from her father could be considered safeguarding any money that may come her way. He did what any honorable man would do for a woman who had no one to look out for her. Finding the address, he headed back outside into the cooling air. Maybe it would cool the anger inside him.

Why did he even care about a woman who would choose another man over him? Pride alone should make him turn away. It wasn't as if he didn't have a woman waiting with open arms. Not that he wanted a woman who'd been unfaithful, but at least *she* wanted him. And as she sobbed on his chest over her son, hadn't she told him how sorry she was for her unfaithfulness? And didn't she say that now she realized that he was the best thing that had ever happened to her? What a wonderful man he was?

He needed to love someone who appreciated him. Olivia could see the man he was even if she didn't remember him as hers. Nothing about him had changed since they fell in love. She'd lived with his family for well over a month, surely enough time to stir old feelings. The same thing that drew her to him before should draw her again. But whatever the reason, it hadn't. So he had to believe something had changed.

Maybe when he kissed her it didn't stir anything in her and maybe Lloyd's kiss did. He ground his teeth. Could he really have imagined the passion he felt from her with that last kiss? His gut knotted. Everything he thought he knew must have been a lie. He had to get the woman out of his mind.

Drew rounded the corner heading toward home and nearly ran into Constance. "Constance, what are you doing out alone? It'll be getting dark soon."

She sniffed and dabbed a handkerchief under her puffy eyes. "I needed to clear my head."

Drew frowned. Just like him needing the fresh air. Something they had in common. "Did you stop at my house?"

She tipped her head up and tears glistened on her lashes. "No."

"Has Andrew's illness become worse?"

"No. I'm not sure what is wrong with me."

Drew took her elbow. "Let me walk you home and we can talk on the way. Maybe that will help."

"Oh Andrew, this is why I feel so guilty. No matter what I have done in my past or to you, you have always forgiven me. I need to—"

"You've already apologized. I don't want to hear another word." He stopped and turned her toward him and chipped her gently under the chin. "You hear me?"

"But—"

"No buts. All is forgiven. From this day forward you are accountable, but the past is the past and I don't want to hear another word."

Constance ran her tongue over her lip. "If you say so—"

A warning screamed inside of him to look away, to not let her get to him. And then her gaze fell to his lips. He wanted to numb the pain, to forget the woman he really loved. But not like this. She leaned in, never taking her eyes from his lips. He knew she meant to kiss him.

Pulling back, he skimmed his hands up to her shoulders. "Let's get you home." He'd not let her use her skills of seduction on him.

The sun had set by the time they reached Constance brother's home, where she was staying. Constance glanced over her shoulder toward the picture window at the front of the house, drawing Drew's attention. The lights were on and he imagined they were beginning to get concerned about Constance.

At the door, he wished her good night and turned to leave.

"Andrew?"

He paused and glanced back at her. "Yes?"

"If you'd like to come back, I have a door off the piazza to my room."

Chapter 23

"I don't think that would be a good idea." He tried to smile, but knew he didn't fool her. He had learned his lesson about being alone with Constance. She had managed to get him off in a private room at a ball. Although, he would admit it hadn't taken too much coaxing—nothing wrong with a few stolen kisses. But much to his despair, it seemed half the people at the ball noticed them missing and when a certain gossipmonger saw them leave the private room together he felt certain much was surmised.

It wasn't long afterwards that she'd tried to seduce him and then he found out she was with child. He supposed that she'd planned the whole thing, knowing full well the state of her condition. He'd forgiven her, but he wasn't about to make the same mistake twice.

She gave him a sad smile. "No, I suppose it isn't. Good night." With that she crossed the threshold and disappeared.

Averting another mistake in his life, Drew continued down to where he'd planned to go when he'd run into Constance, Evan Frasier's. Hopefully the man would have good news for him.

Taking the single step onto the stoop, he knocked on the wooden door and waited. Untrimmed bushes nearly as tall as him framed the small porch. Darkness had set upon the fair city of Charleston. Footfalls sounded from behind the door. Then whispering. The door opened not much more than a crack and an oil lamp was thrust up to it, sending a spear of light out and onto him.

"Good evening. I must apologize for coming by so late." Drew really didn't feel it was that late, but by the way they were acting he didn't know what else to say.

The door swung open and he was briskly ushered in. "Mr. Warwick. Please, come in and have a seat."

Drew swiped the bowler from his head. Evan Frasier had turned away before Drew had gotten a good look, but the man looked to have a black eye. Drew followed the investigator to the living room where he could see the man across from him. He'd had an unpleasant encounter with someone or something.

As Drew's gaze drifted around the room he noticed little earthquake damage to the wooden structure. Two small children played on the rug with a wooden puzzle while a woman sat nearby knitting.

"Mr. Warwick, I'd like you to meet my wife, Jennifer, and my two children, Cynthia and Carl."

The woman glanced up from her knitting. "It's nice to meet you."

Drew nodded. "It's my pleasure, ma'am."

Taking a seat, Evan spoke to his wife. "Will you take the children and get them ready for bed?" He turned his attention back to Drew. "Have a seat."

Drew sank into a chair as the wife gathered up the two young children with not so much as a word.

"Are they twins?"

Evan smiled, half of his swollen lip not turning upward. "No, however, I get asked that question frequently. Cynthia is six and Carl is five."

"They're nice looking children."

"Thank you. But I'm sure that isn't why you came to visit me."

Drew took in the investigator's injuries—not one black eye but two, swollen lips, the lower one split, cuts and bruising on his face. "What happened to you?"

He glanced toward the door where his family had exited. "It appears I have angered someone with my questions."

"Questions about the embezzlement?"

"That would be the ones. I was told in no uncertain terms to drop the case if I cared about my family. I'm sorry Mr. Warwick, but I cannot continue working for you. I have—"

Drew raised his hand to stop him. "Say no more. I wouldn't expect you to. Family always comes first. Can you tell me what you have uncovered thus far?"

Evan's eyes shifted from the door to the window. "I think it is important that you know." He lowered his voice. "These men mean business. They want this inquiry stopped."

"I appreciate your concern, but I have to follow through on this. Not for me, but for someone I care about." And he realized he meant it. This was no longer about him. As he took in the injuries on this man, he knew that he couldn't take a chance that Olivia would fall prey to whoever could be so cruel.

"You don't understand, Mr. Warwick, this is bigger than Lloyd Pratt. He's only one of the minions that got sucked into this racket. Lloyd isn't the one who did this." He pointed to his face.

Lloyd may not have been the one who threw the punches, but he knew from experience with Olivia's injuries over a year ago that he was more than capable. "Can you tell me anything? Where do I start?"

Evan got up and strode across the room, his gait giving hint of a new limp. He pulled a piece of paper from the top of a desk in the corner then dug in the drawer for something. Returning to Drew he handed him the paper. "He might talk to you, but it will cost you. He won't risk his life for free."

Drew took the paper and stood. "Thank you. I won't

trouble you anymore. It's probably better if you aren't seen with me." He stuck out his hand.

Evan clasped Drew's hand. But instead of flesh, cold metal met his palm.

Drew searched his face. "A gun?"

"You may need it."

"I think a gun is being a little overly cautious." He handed the gun back to him. "I really appreciate your concern, but I can take care of myself."

Evan spun around and went back to his desk and dug in the drawer before returning. "Take this then." He held out a knife. "Take it. Even if you don't use it, maybe it will scare them off should they approach you."

Drew took the knife and thanked him. Evan led him to the back, opening the door enough to stick his head out and look both ways.

"I don't see anyone. You should walk through the back yards of a few houses before you cut to the street—just in case they're watching my house."

Moving past Evan, Drew stepped down to the grass. "Thank you. And I am terribly sorry I brought all this on you. Can I send someone from my family with medicine?"

"No, no. My wife will tend to me. I would say it comes with the job, but this is the first time I ever thought I was going to die." Evan held the door open with one hand as he stood on the step, favoring his left leg.

"I will pray they bother you no more." Drew moved a few strides toward the neighbor's yard.

"Mr. Warwick." Evan called out in a low whisper that barely reached his ears. "Where is the knife?"

"In my pocket."

"Keep it out. It will do you no good there."

Drew took it out of his pocket to satisfy the man. He could understand the man being skittish after what he went through. "I will get your pay to you this week along with your knife."

The door clicked shut as Drew waded through the grass, leaves crunching beneath his feet. The poor man was quite shaken up. Not that he blamed Evan after what he'd endured, but Drew felt a little foolish sneaking through backyards.

Three houses down, he cut back onto the street, the knife still in his hand. A quick glance around him assured him that he walked the street alone. He slipped the knife into his pocket. Evan's suspicions had him on edge. A snort escaped his lips. Lloyd lacked scruples, and Drew knew that Lloyd could be violent. But murder—as Evan had suggested? Drew highly doubted it. Lloyd wouldn't get himself involved with murder.

The uneasiness that plagued him started to lift as he thought through the idea of what kind of person Lloyd was. And that took his thoughts to Olivia's rebuffing him earlier in the day. And of course Lloyd would have walked her home just like he had walked Constance to her sister's place. He couldn't help but wonder if Lloyd would leave her with a kiss.

Drew let out another snort. Of course Lloyd would. Hadn't he already proved that? He wished it was easier to trust God with not only his life but Olivia's, too. Maybe losing Olivia was all his doing—a lesson he wasn't learning.

He turned down the next street, suddenly anxious to be home and know that Livvy had returned. The crisp, still air carried distant sounds—dogs barking, cicadas chirping. He breathed in the smell of smoke from either outdoor camp fires or indoor fireplaces.

Something, he wasn't sure what—the crack of a twig, the thud of a footfall, caught his attention. He spun around, but nothing was there. Continuing on his way, he laughed at himself. Evan had him spooked. But as he resumed his pace an eerie feeling descended on him, causing his skin to prickle.

He slipped his hand into his pocket and retrieved the knife, sliding open the blade. A twig snapped. This time he knew he didn't imagine it. He glanced over his shoulder in the direction he thought he'd heard the sound, but saw nothing. Lengthening his strides, he picked up his pace. His heart thudded—not really from fear so much as anticipation.

Footfalls sounded on the pavement a distance behind him. It had to be two…or more. Perhaps the same two who'd visited Evan.

Drew tried to think. He was being irrational. Just because Evan had suggested that someone would be waiting to ambush him didn't mean that it was true. Evan was overly cautious after what had happened to him. For Pete's sake, this was the City of Charleston, and it wasn't that terribly late. People had a right to walk the streets. They were probably getting out of work late and, like him, anxious to get home.

As much as he tried to convince himself that all was well, his gut still knotted and warned him to beware. The footfalls grew louder. And suddenly he realized what troubled him. They weren't talking. Most men chatted casually as they walked together. But whoever was behind him strode as if on a mission.

A chill swept down his spine. A mission to keep him quiet.

The pounding of their shoes on the pavement matched his heartbeat—quick and hard. He tightened his grip on the knife, wishing he'd taken the gun Evan had offered him. One look at that and they would have went on their merry way.

He sent up a prayer. *Lord, please protect me.* He was never one for long fancy prayers, always keeping his short and to the point. Glancing around for the nearest occupied house, Drew wished he'd have taken a different route. Most of the houses on this street had been abandoned. Going to someone's door to elicit help wasn't going to be an option, as he could practically feel them behind him.

A hand clamped down on his shoulder and swung him around. "You Warwick?"

Drew steadied himself and planted his feet. "Who wants to know?"

"Wrong answer."

Drew sensed more than saw a fist coming for his face and leaned to the side. A breeze hit his cheek as the fist sailed past. The man growled.

"Look, I don't want any trouble." Drew clenched the knife, hoping the full moon allowed enough light for them to see he had a weapon.

"Yeah? Well, you should have thought about that before you started snooping around." The second guy spat out.

The pounding in his chest stopped. It was as if he knew God watched him and would keep him safe. "It's my business when it involves my fiancé and her family."

The second guy stepped forward and Drew could see the man was twice his width. He pulled his hand up with the sharp blade in it, drawing their attention to it.

"Oh look, Luddy, he has a knife. Do you think we should be scared?" The brute laughed at his sarcasm and his friend joined in.

"I'm shaking in my boots. Maybe we should leave him alone." The smaller of the two, called Luddy, let out a loud guffaw.

Drew turned to walk away. A hand slammed down on his shoulder again.

"Where do you think you're goin'? I didn't—"

They were obviously toying with him and enjoying it. He'd rather not use the knife, but he'd had enough. There was no way out of this except to fight. When he ordinarily had a knife in hand, it was for an operation. The good thing about that was he knew where to place the blade to stop a person. He tightened his fingers around the steel handle.

"I have nothing to discuss with either of you. I don't want any trouble with you and I don't want to hurt you." Drew jerked out of the beefy grasp and started to turn.

"Well, we have a little message for you." The words rolled off Luddy's tongue as his punch grazed Drew's cheek and sent his hat flying from his head.

Without thinking about the knife in his hand, Drew swung his fist and caught Luddy under the chin sending him back several steps, but that only opened the way for Goliath.

The first blow caught him in the stomach. He bent over trying to catch his breath, but the giant's hand smashed down on the back of his neck sending Drew to his knees. *Lord, I thought you were going to protect me?*

A foot connected with his ribs. His breath whooshed out and the knife went flying. He started to stand and Goliath brought his knee up into his chest. For a minute he thought he might die from lack of air.

And then he realized they'd stopped. He braced his hands on his thighs, bent over trying to draw in a breath, wondering why they weren't still pounding on him. Drew continued to attempt to draw in a breath. If he could charge the giant and get one good swing in that could knock him off balance perhaps he'd have enough time to get to his knife.

"Is there a problem here?"

Staring at the ground, Drew recognized the voice and smiled.

"No problem, mister. Just taking care of some business. You best just go on your way." Luddy answered.

"That so? Well, I'd like to hear that from him." The newcomer didn't seem fazed by the threat.

Drew straightened and a groan slipped from his throat. He wouldn't be surprised if he had a broken rib. "Evening, Captain."

Gideon Sharpe sat tall in his saddle, no longer in his dragoon uniform. "Drew?"

"Old man, if you don't want no trouble I'd get that horse of yours movin'." This time it was Goliath sending the threat.

"Looks to me like this is a bit unfair." Gideon swung out of his saddle and Drew could see he was dressed in evening wear. "I'll just even it up." He reached up and pulled a pistol from the saddle. "Now what were you boys saying about me being old?"

At the sight of the gun, the two thugs turned and disappeared into the night.

"I've never been so happy to see someone." Drew scooped up his hat from the ground, took a couple more steps and snatched Evan's knife.

"Glad to be of service. I'll walk with you home to make sure they don't come back." He grasped his horse's reins and put his gun back in the holster before they started out.

Drew gasped for air as he gave Gideon a head to toe inspection. "What brought you here?"

Gideon chuckled. "I had a meeting with the mayor."

Drew glanced around as he caught his breath. "This isn't close to your place—why are you here?"

The light of the moon shone on Gideon's face, his cropped goatee followed the slender lines of his face. His features softened as if in thought. "Don't rightly know, Drew. I guess I'd have to say it was the Lord."

The Lord had answered his prayer. Oh, he'd be sore for a few days or weeks, but God had kept him safe. He pressed on the sore ribs, hoping none were broken. "'Amen' to that."

"You didn't tell me what those two boys wanted with you."

Drew snorted and then flinched, wrapping his arm around his tender ribs. "They didn't want me asking around about Lloyd Pratt."

Gideon nodded. "The fellow I saw over at the Macqueen's place."

"He has some pretty unsavory friends."

"You know what they say, birds of a feather."

Indeed. His opinion of what Lloyd was capable of went up several notches. "How true that is."

When they reached his home, Drew thanked Gideon, seeing him in a whole new light. Though the Fourreauxs and the Warwicks went way back, Drew didn't know Gideon much beyond seeing him in his office. He never realized until now that Gideon had chosen him as his personal physician. After all, up until Drew had gotten his license to practice, Gideon had been seeing his father. Gideon had become his patient to help get him established. Oh, the Warwick name carried influence, but for Gideon Sharpe, a Fourreaux on his mother's side, to choose Drew as his physician spoke volumes to the community. Their family owned one of the largest and most prosperous rice plantations in Charleston.

They said their goodnights and Drew snuck around to the back door where he could slip up the servant staircase from the kitchen and avoid being seen. He needed to clean up and assess the damage.

He crested the top of the staircase, his eyes drawn to *his* bedroom entry and took note of the closed door. He stumbled into the room he shared with William, going directly to the large mirror. He turned his head to the right and then to the left. He didn't look too bad.

His right cheek—where the one called Luddy had grazed him—was a bit red, but hopefully no one would notice. He stripped off his shirt and looked in the mirror, prodding around the area. Drawing in a deep breath, he winced. Not good. But he'd be able to tell a little more in a day or two if it was bruising or an actual fracture.

After cleaning up and putting on some fresh clothes, Drew made his way down to the great room where he found most of the family. Gingerly sitting down in the chair, his eyes sought out Olivia. A piece of fabric in one hand and a needle and thread in the other, she worked on her embroidery without looking up.

"Where have you been?" JoAnna eyed him suspiciously.

"Taking care of some business, sis."

"Did you get bit by something? Your cheek looks red and a little swollen." She leaned forward in her chair to get a better look.

Drew frowned. Of course if anyone would notice, it would be JoAnna. Olivia raised her head and looked his way. Their eyes met and she quickly lowered her gaze back to her handwork.

"Nothing itches. Perhaps you need glasses." He smiled at her. What she really needed was to mind her own business. Didn't that girl ever miss anything?

She scowled at him and sat back in her chair as a cough escaped. William sat in quiet conversation with their father while mother sat near Olivia, working on her own handwork.

Olivia seemed to intentionally avoid looking at him. He let his eyes drink her in, remembering the softness of her skin and silkiness of her long hair. She stuck her finger with her needle and a quiet gasp escaped. Her thumb went to her mouth. He swallowed, calming the fire going through his veins.

How he wished those lips were his to kiss. No one would ever be able to take her place. Drew turned his attention back to JoAnna. "Where's Christian?"

"Out checking on his animals." She gave a wavering smile and glanced toward Olivia.

The whole evening seemed subdued, almost as if they were privy to what had happened to him tonight. His side aching, Drew excused himself and headed toward the stairs. He made it up to the fourth step when JoAnna sped around the corner, grasping the banister to stop herself.

"Drew." She called in a loud whisper.

He paused on the step and turned. "What, Jo?"

She coughed again and took the steps up to stand near him, leaning in as if she had a secret. "Something's wrong."

How did she read him so well? He had stood in front of the mirror for five minutes and felt certain no one would really notice. "Everything is fine. I promise."

JoAnna turned her head, giving in to a short coughing fit.

"That cough doesn't sound good. Are you taking care of it?"

She narrowed her eyes. "Don't worry about me. It is Olivia you need to concern yourself with. I saw her when she came home and rushed up to her room. And I'm telling you something happened. She looked disheveled."

Drew started, his heart leaping into his throat nearly

choking out the words. "What do you mean disheveled?"

♥♥♥

He settled into a restless sleep, thinking about what could have caused Olivia to come home looking as Jo described—hair falling and hat missing. He woke frequently, always from a bad dream. By sunrise he was ready to get up. Leaning over the bowl, he splashed water on his face and then blotted his skin with the towel. He was a little sore when he moved and his ribs felt only bruised, thankfully. He slipped his clothes on then sat on the cot they had set up for him. He reached under and pulled out his shoes and began putting them on.

William rolled over, his eyes barely half open. "Where are you off to so early?"

Drew shoved his foot into his shoe and began to tie it. "I am going to make a call on the man Evan said has information about the embezzlement. Want to join me?"

William rubbed his eyes. "What time is it?"

Drew pulled out his gold pocket watch from his jacket. "Six."

"You can't call on someone this early."

"By the time I eat and ride over, it will be a suitable time."

Lying on his back, William pushed up onto his elbows in his bed. "Do you think you will need me?"

"It's daylight. I think I'll be safe." Drew stood and picked up the comb and ran it through his hair.

"If you do, I'll go. But if not, I do have some other business to see to."

Drew grinned. "It wouldn't have anything to do with a lady would it?"

William returned the smile. "Could be."

Even if he couldn't find happiness, Drew was glad that William had. He deserved a good woman. "I am certain.

Just go and enjoy your day. Say a prayer for me."

Wasting time, Drew read the paper, catching up on the latest progress in the clean-up. Mayor Courtenay seemed determined to bring Charleston back to its former glory and to give the citizens confidence to move back into their homes. For the most part, the tremors had stopped. Although, occasionally there were reports of small rumblings.

When Drew climbed on Stitches, it neared seven thirty. Before moving out, he reached into his pocket and pulled out the paper with the address that Evan had given him. The streets were starting to bustle as construction workers were already hard at work. Hammers pounded and saws whined as their teeth cut into fresh wood.

He couldn't help but wonder how many of these workers he would see at the office before the rebuilding was over. With the onslaught of actual earthquake victims behind them, their practice mostly consisted of injured workers. The ones that fell off ladders or were caught under collapsed walls.

The small white home with black shutters stood virtually unscathed between two larger homes with excessive damage. Drew swung his leg over the saddle and hopped down, ground-tying his horse. He assessed the house. No smoke poured from the chimney. With foreboding, he strode up the narrow sidewalk to the front door and knocked. He waited and knocked again. No one came to the door.

He moved to the window and peered inside. Empty. His stomach sank along with his hopes.

"Hey, buddy."

Drew swung around to see if the person was talking to him. "Yes?"

"You lookin' for the people that lived here?" The man

looked to be in his late thirties, thin and short.

"I am. Do you know where they went?"

"Nope. They loaded up everything a couple days ago. Tried to talk to them and they wouldn't say a thing. Just carted off everything they owned and left without as so much as a see-ya-later."

That was it then. He had exhausted everything he knew to do. His only chance was to find the account book, and now he doubted that Lloyd had it if there were others involved who pulled the strings. But if these criminals were forcing people from their homes, beating investigators and doctors, no telling how dangerous they could be. And with Lloyd involved, that put Olivia in danger.

Chapter 24

Olivia strolled out to the stable to see Fang. Shaking her head as she thought about Drew, Olivia didn't know who Drew thought he fooled with the way he avoided answering JoAnna when she asked if he had a bug bite on his cheek. The redness and slight swelling looked like more than the doings of an insect.

It shouldn't matter to her. Not when Drew would never be hers again. But somehow everything about Drew mattered. She needed a solid plan for what she was going to do and where she was going to go. As much as she loved every one of the Warwicks, she couldn't stay any longer. They didn't need her, and she was well enough to move on.

That meant that she needed to find the account book. Spears of fear shot through her chest. She swallowed. She had to go to Lloyd's one more time. But this time she would make sure he wasn't home—somehow. Her escape last time had to have been the Lord. What was the chance of her getting free from his stronghold? Since he did not chase her down, it had to have been intervention by God. Maybe He did care about her. One thing she knew for certain was that she hoped to never see Lloyd Pratt again.

Pushing open the door to the small stable room, Olivia made her way across the straw-strewn floor, sending up its fresh-cut fragrance. The overturned barrel awaited her and she took a seat as Fang pranced toward her with Spotless pouncing on him, biting the back of his neck in puppy play.

Scooping Spotless up first to free Fang, she gathered them both in her lap and stroked their silky fur. Just holding the little puppies calmed her spirit. She had hardly slept all night—every time she dozed, she was awakened by memories of the night and horrors of what could have been.

How had she ever cared for Lloyd? She knew very well what kind of a man he was, now that her memory had returned. It was her stubbornness not to let go of Lloyd in the first place that gave her father apoplexy, nearly killing him. When she had lost the year of her life, at least she didn't remember the guilt she'd carried with her the past two years. But now it was all too clear.

Lifting the puppy to her lips, she kissed his wrinkled forehead.

"Wish I could have one of those."

Olivia jumped, thinking she was alone. She placed the puppy back in her lap.

"A puppy?" She'd certainly let him hold one.

"No. A kiss." Drew leaned his shoulder against the doorframe.

Heat shot up her neck and into her face. And by the grin on Drew's face, her cheeks were as red as they were hot. The desire to turn away tempted her, but instead she lifted her chin and met his eyes—his tender eyes that spoke of love—love that would never be hers. "I don't think so, sir. But you may have a puppy if you'd like."

His grin didn't falter and he pushed away from the doorframe. "No thanks. I'll wait and hope for better."

She ignored him and instead thought to turn the tables. "So why is your cheek swollen? And don't tell me a mosquito bite. I won't believe it."

"It wasn't me that suggested an insect bite, if you remember, but my sister." He glanced over his shoulder. "Looks like William and Christian have the horses ready to go. Have a good day, Olivia."

She sprang up from her seat, grabbing the puppies just before they went sprawling to the floor. "You didn't answer my question. And where are you going?"

"To Ebenezer's place to finish up the wall." He took two steps and stopped, worry lines suddenly appearing on his brow. "Would you keep an eye on Jo? I'm a little worried about her. I could hear her coughing all night."

"Of course. Don't worry yourself about her. I will go right now." She put Fang and Spotless on the floor and they immediately got into a wrestling match. She'd heard JoAnna too, every time she woke up throughout the night.

White dust and small pieces of straw clung to the black fabric of her gown as she stood. She brushed them off with her hands, picking the stubborn pieces of straw off with her fingers. Taking extra time to allow Drew to leave, she waited until she heard the horses' hooves clopping on the paved road before making her exit and heading to the house.

JoAnna was lying in bed with a tray of breakfast food on the table beside her.

Mrs. Warwick, sitting in a chair beside her, stood when Olivia entered the room. "I'm so glad you stopped in here, Olivia. I promised to head up a meeting on helping the families who have lost everything, but I don't want to leave JoAnna alone."

"Mother—" JoAnna broke out in a coughing spell. "I'll be fine. It is just a cold."

Olivia put her hand on the worried mother's arm. "I'll be happy to stay with her, Mrs. Warwick. I'll make sure she gets lots of rest and has everything she needs."

"Bless you, Olivia. If you need me, have Mrs. Benninger send one of the new boys Dr. Warwick hired to come get me."

Olivia assured her that she would and went to sit with her old friend. How she wished she could tell her she remembered some of their times together, but she couldn't take a chance that she'd tell Drew. Instead, she stroked

JoAnna's hand. "How are you feeling?"

JoAnna gave her a wavering smile. "I would say I'm feeling well, but then if I died, I would have that lie on my soul."

"JoAnna, what a terrible thing to say. You aren't going to die. You will probably be fit as a fiddle by supper time."

"Come now. You know I jest." She leaned up to cough. "Don't tell Mother, but I do feel rather bad."

"I won't tell her. But you need to rest." She wouldn't tell her mother, but she would tell one of the doctor Warwicks first chance she got.

JoAnna drifted off into a restless sleep. After a while, Mrs. Warwick returned and relieved Olivia. Taking the untouched tray with her, she went to eat her noon meal. She returned from her lunch with a bowl of food for JoAnna and insisted on staying with her friend. Mrs. Warwick reluctantly left to oversee some household responsibilities and confer with Mrs. Benninger on the evening meal.

JoAnna's eyes fluttered then opened. "Are you still here? Don't you have something better to do than watch me sleep?" She laughed and broke into a coughing spell.

Olivia's brows drew down in concern. She seized the glass of water off the table and pressed it to JoAnna's lips as she supported her head. "I brought you some warm onion soup to help with the cough. Mrs. Benninger said she made it special for you."

JoAnna lowered herself back down after drinking the water. "Would you prop some pillows behind me so I can sit up?"

Olivia tucked some spare pillows behind JoAnna and placed the tray with soup on it in JoAnna's lap. "Eat something. You can't get well if you starve yourself."

"I needed to take off a few pounds, anyway." A glimmer of humor danced in JoAnna's glassy eyes.

"I have never known what to expect from you, JoAnna. You are always full of yourself." Olivia nearly choked on the words. How many times in the past had she told JoAnna those same words? She hoped and prayed JoAnna would not read anything into her words as it was obvious by them that she remembered more than the last month and a half.

JoAnna eyed her. Olivia held her breath. JoAnna nodded. "So I've been told."

She seemed to search Olivia's face. Olivia tried desperately to school her features, though beads of sweat broke through her skin. "Have you now? So it must be true." She gave a forced laugh.

JoAnna sipped at her soup, grimacing as she swallowed each bite. "I detest onions. Even when they are masked with lots of chicken broth." JoAnna took the last bite and laid the spoon down on the tray next to the bowl.

"Maybe that will calm your cough." Olivia began to relax as the conversation took a safe direction.

"What happened last night?" JoAnna handed her the tray, but grasped Olivia's hand when she went to retrieve it.

"Whatever do you mean?" Olivia laid the server on the table.

"You know *exactly* what I'm talking about."

She wanted to deny the truth, but decided to play as if she misunderstood. "I have no idea what happened to Drew. I'm sure you've noticed there is a strain between us. He isn't going to share with me anything he hasn't shared with you." She swallowed before continuing. "But frankly, I tend to agree with you. That was no bite that caused the swelling on his cheek."

JoAnna rolled her eyes and then settled her head into the pillow before closing her droopy lids. For an instant Olivia thought she may have passed out. She scooted forward, ready to run for help.

"And what about *you*?" JoAnna spoke without opening her eyes. "I saw you when you returned home that same night. And might I say it didn't look good. Not that I think you did anything wrong."

The sinking of her stomach didn't stop there, as trembling filled her limbs. Olivia was glad she was sitting down. She'd concocted stories the whole way home while fleeing Lloyd's place. The most plausible was that she'd been assaulted by a stranger, but had managed to get away. But senior Dr. Warwick would want to call in the police, so she couldn't say that. And Drew would definitely put two and two together if she mentioned an attack. So she gave JoAnna the only other story she'd come up with, telling herself that it was and she was giving a simplified version to protect Drew. She would tell the whole story when Lloyd was arrested.

"As you know, it had gotten rather late when I got home. I hadn't realized the time." That was all true. "I was in such a hurry to return that I wasn't paying attention and tripped." She'd told all truths. She fervently hoped that JoAnna would leave it at that.

But she didn't. Before she opened her mouth, Olivia knew she was going to question her more and make her either lie or put Drew's well-being in jeopardy.

"It took more than tripping to bring your hair tumbling down." She opened her eyes and rolled her head toward Olivia.

Uneasiness crawled through her body. She valued honesty but now was forced to tell an untruth. "I think it caught on a tree branch which pulled it out."

JoAnna raised her brows. "You think?"

"It was dark out."

"You looked terribly distraught."

Sliding her tongue over her lips, Olivia steeled her

resolve. The lie on her tongue tasted like a bitter herb. "I was upset that I fell. I have precious few dresses as it is, and I can't afford to tear any."

JoAnna mumbled something about her and Drew deserving each other with their tall tales. The longer Olivia sat there, the more she thought she might be sick. She didn't like to tell the lie, but then by concealing the truth, she *lived* a lie.

She wasn't really sure how much time had passed, but JoAnna seemed either offended with Olivia's answer or extremely tired because she quit talking.

After a lengthy silence, JoAnna let out a huff that startled Olivia.

"Is something wrong?" Olivia scooted to the edge of her chair to look into JoAnna's face.

"Just that you find it acceptable to lie to me."

Guilt pricked at Olivia's conscience—the weight of her heavy heart breaking down her resolve. She swallowed. "I will tell you, but you must promise to keep this a secret."

JoAnna folded her arms, bringing to Olivia the memory of herself sticking her hand behind her back and crossing her fingers when Simon would make her promise something she didn't want to.

"Ah. So you admit that you did not tell me the truth."

"I would prefer not to tell you *period*, but since you won't talk to me…"

"I'm waiting for the truth, Olivia."

"Do you promise to keep this between us?"

JoAnna let out another loud huff. "Yes, yes, go on."

"Before I start, I just want to say you have put me in a very difficult situation here by your insistence." Olivia took a deep breath and waited, hoping that JoAnna would release her from explaining what happened, but she just stared at her…waiting.

Olivia blew out the breath she held and started at the beginning when Lloyd had seen her walking past his house. She skipped the part where she had planned on going to look for the account book and went to the part where Lloyd had nearly forced her inside and pulled out a handful of her hair. JoAnna asked questions throughout, but thankfully she'd not asked why Olivia had ended up near Lloyd's house to begin with.

JoAnna began coughing and gasped for air. The longer she coughed, the redder her face became. Fear shot through Olivia. She stood. "Maybe I should get you some more onion soup."

JoAnna grabbed her arm, still coughing, and vigorously shook her head.

Olivia sat back down. "That bad, huh?"

JoAnna nodded and whispered. "I think talking is making my cough worse."

"Yes, you should rest. Maybe I can find some herbs in the kitchen."

"Then mother will be up here worrying about me. I won't talk."

Olivia went over to a small bookcase against the wall and pulled out a book. "I'll read something to you, then." She pulled out *Religious Poems* by Harriett Beecher Stowe and returned to her chair, tucking her gown beneath her as she sat. She opened the book and scanned the contents, finding her favorite of Harriett's poems and began to read.

A sigh escaped JoAnna, making Olivia smile at the peacefulness covering her friend's face. She'd only made it to the second page when footfalls sounded on the staircase. Her stomach fluttered as she wondered if Drew had returned home. She found herself hoping he had, simultaneously reminding herself she needed to stay as far from him as possible.

When the door creaked, she refused to give in to the pounding in her chest to see if it was him. She continued to read, now halfway down the second page of the poem.

"*There were violet banks in the shadows, violets white and blue; And a world of bright Anemones, that over the terrace grew.*" Drew's baritone voice cut in sending quivers up her spine. "*A Day in the Pamfili Dora,* my favorite of Harriett Beecher Stowe's poems."

He sat down on the bottom corner of JoAnna's bed. His camel pants were dusty and he'd unbuttoned the top two buttons of his blue cotton shirt. The color was so deep it reminded her of a summer sky in Charleston.

"It is mine, also."

"I know it is." One corner of his mouth curved up into a half smile tipping his thin mustache into a slanted line.

"You do?"

"It's both of ours. One of the many things we have in common."

She searched his face for answers. That bit of information she didn't remember. Although many memories had returned, there were some that she still could not pull to the forefront of her mind. "Did you wish to be alone with your sister?" Olivia began to close the book.

"No. Please stay," he said, and then turned his attention to JoAnna. "How are you feeling?"

"Ask Olivia," JoAnna whispered.

Drew turned to Olivia, causing her words to catch in her throat momentarily. "Sh-she is feeling rather poorly and her cough is relentless. The onion soup helped some, but JoAnna would rather cough than eat it I'm afraid."

"Has anyone given her any licorice or horehound for the cough?" He leaned over and placed his hand on her forehead, then frowned.

"She would not let me get her anything because she

didn't want your mother to worry."

"You need to stop worrying about Mother, Jo, and start worrying about getting well." He got up and brought over the wash basin with a cloth. Wringing out the cloth, he placed it on her forehead.

She broke into a cough and Drew's brows furrowed. "I'll be back in just a moment."

He returned with the horehound drop before Olivia could decide if she wanted to slip out while he was gone. As JoAnna sucked on the hard lozenge, it calmed her cough. Drew settled back on the bed, cooling the cloth and reapplying it to JoAnna's forehead until she appeared to drift off to sleep.

"How have you been feeling, Olivia?" Drew kept his voice low.

"I've been fine. Why do you ask?" She lifted her hand to her cheek, wondering if she looked peaked.

"I wondered if Lloyd walked you home and if all went well last night?" His gaze caught hers and dared her to look away.

But look away she did. Right to JoAnna whose eyes were now wide open. Drew turned his head and JoAnna quickly closed her eyes. Olivia hoped Drew had not seen it. Even with her glassy eyes, it was obvious to Olivia that JoAnna *knew* something. And she suddenly wasn't so sure that her friend would keep her confidence. She wished she'd not said anything, but there was nothing to do about it now.

"Well?" He cocked his head.

JoAnna began to cough, drawing Drew's attention once again. The cough seemed a bit forced. Once she settled back again, JoAnna turned her head toward Olivia. "Could you read to me again?"

"I would love to." Olivia wanted to give her a big hug.

As sick as JoAnna was, she kept Olivia from having to tell Drew.

Olivia returned to reading and before long, JoAnna truly had fallen asleep. Her breathing was heavy and rattled at intervals. Olivia lowered the book and turned to Drew, wide-eyed.

"What is wrong with her?"

"I think she has pneumonia."

"Will she die?"

"Not if I can help it."

Olivia searched his face intently, his confidence calming her.

"Please, continue. I love listening to you read." His black-brown eyes turned smoky.

And then the memory was there—why they both loved the poem. And why he looked at her with those *I-adore-you* eyes that bore into her soul.

The Ashley River flowed before her. Damp ground and fragrant air from the recent rain surrounded her. Drew laid down three thick blankets to keep the wet ground from reaching them. She had stood there with arms crossed tapping her foot because she didn't want to sit on the damp blankets. But he insisted. And once he'd gotten her settled, he'd gone back to the carriage and pulled out a basket and placed it beside them.

They ate a noon meal of cheese, bread, and fried chicken before Drew handed her a bag of chocolates and a bouquet of white asters and black-eyed susans.

"What is all this about?" Olivia remembered her confusion.

"Six months ago today you agreed to allow me to court you." His eyes looked then as they did now—smoldering.

Then he'd pulled out a poetry book, opened it, and read to her. He recited every word with deep passion. That was the moment she knew that she truly loved him. He had ignored her silly mood and brought them out on a damp day because he wanted to celebrate their love.

Olivia looked down and flipped to the front of the book, hands trembling as her eyes drank in the words Drew had penned over a year ago.

To Olivia,

May our feelings grow so that the words of this book are but a spark in comparison to the love we have for each other.

Forever Yours,
Drew

Lifting her eyes, she met his gaze. He'd seen her turn to the inscription, and he watched her with hunger. He knew…he knew she remembered.

Chapter 25

Panic suffocated her. The air wouldn't enter her lungs. The room swirled around her. What was she going to do? She couldn't talk to him. Jerking her eyes away, she stood and rushed from the room.

"Olivia." Drew's voice followed her out of the room. "Olivia!"

She ran down the steps, through the house, and out the back door to the stable to see Fang. She closed the door behind her and settled on the stool, panting. Spotless lifted his head at her entry and then laid it down, closing his eyes. But Fang pounced around her feet, just out of her reach before finally edging close enough for her to scoop him up.

"Oh, Fang. What am I going to do?" Frightened at facing the truth, but relieved she could stop living a lie, she trembled.

She sniffed and pulled her handkerchief from her pocket to dab at her eyes. The air was crisp and she was thankful for the little bit of warmth that sweet little Fang brought. He nestled into a ball and his eyes fluttered shut. The silky-soft puppy fur glided under her hand. Life had gotten so complicated once Mama and Papa had died and Simon disappeared. How she wished she could have gone to one of them for wise counsel.

Just as her emotions calmed, the door creaked. Olivia didn't lift her head. She could see Drew's brown boots move into the room and across the straw-strewn floor. Her heart picked up its pace. Breathing deeply, she tried to keep her composure.

"Olivia, will you look at me?"

She raised her head, eyes locking with his.

"Will you tell me what just happened?" His voice was so tender her heart ached.

She licked her dry lips. "I ran out. I needed time to think."

"But you remember." He took a step toward her. "You knew where to look in that book for the inscription."

"Yes."

He knelt before her and reclaimed her hand. "Then you know that we were courting, that I love you."

She drew in a deep breath. "Memories have been returning. I've recalled different times and places we've been together, but yes, I'm aware we were courting."

He jerked back, letting go of her hand, stunned. "You knew all this and kept it a secret?"

"It's complicated, Drew. My life has been thrown into turmoil. I am managing it the only way I know how."

"But this means you know the truth about Lloyd. And you know the truth about me. We can be together again."

Olivia pulled her hand from his grasp and set the puppy down. Rising from the stool she swiped off the dirt from her dress then put distance between her and Drew. She was suddenly angry. "Us? Together? Surely you jest?"

His brows knitted together. "You remember. There is nothing to keep us apart."

"How dare you." The lump rose in her throat, but she would not cry.

"I don't understand. We love each other. You said you remember."

She calmed herself. "I said I have some memories, they are still returning."

"We can face them together. I'll help you remember. Olivia, darling, I'll do anything for you." Drew edged closer.

"No. Stop." She raised her hand. "I'll face them alone."

She'd face the rest of her life alone. No one could take Drew's place.

"Why? When you know I love you. When you love me? I know you do."

The calm fled and all the anger that she held inside exploded. "Why? How dare you. *How dare you.* You and Lloyd are both cut from the same cloth." Did she just see him wince? She didn't care. "Did you really think I'd never find out that you had a child? And that child has a mother who has every right to feel you should marry her."

He blinked, then smiled and reached out to her. "Olivia, sweetheart, I don't have a child."

She backed away. "Don't lie to me, I heard Constance. She even named the boy after you, *Andrew.*"

"He's not mine, Olivia, I promise."

She gave an unladylike snort. "Because I can trust your promises."

He raked his hand through his hair. "It was for your own good that I kept the truth of your parents' death from you."

She shook her head. "I'm sorry Drew, you have lost my trust."

"What can I do to prove to you my words are true?"

"You can't. There can never be anything between us. Not ever. Do you hear me? You lied by omission. How could I ever trust you? And I would never take a father from a child, no matter how much I loved him."

"By omission?" Drew's brows rose.

She could almost hear his unspoken words. *You speak of lies by omission? You, who have lived in my house, ate my food, slept in my bed, accepted my family's hospitality, yet pretended you still didn't remember.* She lifted her chin. "When were you going to tell me? After we married?" And yet he hadn't even proposed to her. Maybe he never planned to.

"Olivia, darling." His voice softened. "You aren't hearing me. That little boy is not mine. I know he isn't mine. There is no way he can be mine. Do you understand?"

"Why would a woman name her child after another man? What could she possibly have to gain from it?"

"Why indeed?" His eyes clouded.

All this time she kept telling herself she couldn't love Drew because his little boy deserved to grow up with his father, but the anger she was feeling was not for the little boy. It was for her—for what she had lost. She swallowed, trying to calm the spasm from unshed tears in her throat. "I'm sorry Drew. I'm sorry for everything. If you can just give me a couple days—I will be leaving." Where and how she didn't know. She'd have to find her grandparents—the only family she had left.

♥♥♥

Drew approached Olivia, dropped down on one knee, his hand immediately going to his chest pocket. The ring remained over his heart. If only he could propose. He'd waited, dreamed, planned for this moment when Olivia would regain her memories, but it wasn't turning out how he had planned. It was supposed to be a joyous occasion, not a goodbye.

"I don't want you to leave." He again grasped her hand. "My family doesn't want you to leave. You need time to process all of this. Don't make any rash decisions." *Lord, please don't let her make any rash decisions.*

She slowly, almost reluctantly, pulled her hand from his. Tears glistened on her brown lashes. She turned, giving him one last look and walked toward the door. If words could have stopped her, he'd have said anything, even begged. With every step and every swish of her black gown, pain twisted in his chest as his heart was wrenched from within him. *God if you have any mercy at all, either give Olivia back to me or take this pain from me.*

He didn't follow her. He wanted to, but he could see she needed time. What she was experiencing had to be not only confusing, but also frustrating. Putting himself in her shoes was what he needed to do. He sat there processing everything, unaware of the passing of time.

"Drew!" Olivia burst back into the barn.

He stood. "What is it?"

"It's JoAnna. Something is terribly wrong, Drew."

He was by her side and heading out the door, his hand on her waist guiding her. "Tell me what is happening."

"She's having a hard time breathing. I'm scared, Drew."

"Where is Father?"

"He left about an hour ago for a house call. Your mother sent Christian after him."

An hour ago? He'd been sitting out there for over an hour? Drew bounded through the house and up to JoAnna's room. She was propped up against pillows on the bed, gasping each breath into her lungs.

William sat beside her, eyes worried. "You know father is going to want to bleed her."

"We can't let him do that. There is mounting evidence that bleeding does not help pneumonia." Drew placed the back of his hand on her forehead.

"You don't have to convince me. I am just telling you what we are up against." William answered.

"I don't want to be bled." JoAnna whispered.

Drew leaned down and kissed the top of her head. "Don't worry, JoAnna, you have three brothers who are every bit as big as your father." He winked. But deep down, he hoped that they could make their father believe these new studies.

After taking her temperature and finding it at over one hundred and four degrees and her pulse at one hundred and twenty, he and William conferred and decided to move forward with what they'd read out of the medical guide *The Practitioner.* Drew quickly put Olivia to work sponging JoAnna down with cool water as he prepared tartar emetic.

Before long, Father and Christian entered the room. Drew noticed his mother hovering nervously at the door. Olivia stepped out, wrapping her arms around his mother. He turned back to JoAnna, heart cinching.

Father moved to Drew's side and grasped JoAnna's hand. "Not feeling well, my little princess?"

A smile spread across JoAnna's lips. "I have been better, Papa."

He stepped away from the bed, motioning for his sons to follow. "What do you know?"

Drew filled him in on JoAnna's temperature and heart rate along with what they had done to combat the pneumonia.

"We need to bleed her." Father glanced over his shoulder at JoAnna.

"No." William and Drew answered in unison.

Christian's eyes rounded.

Deep lines dug into the skin between Father's eyes. "It's a sound treatment which has been used for hundreds of years."

Drew swallowed. They'd been in this debate with their father before. "There is mounting evidence that bleeding is not beneficial to pneumonia."

"I can show you more instances that say it does help." Father argued. "Christian, what is your opinion? I know William agrees with Drew."

Christian glanced at his brothers and shuffled his feet.

"I tend to agree with Drew and William. Bleeding seems to cause patients to lose strength which they need to fight the sickness."

Father turned and stared toward the bed where JoAnna lay. Drew held his breath.

Father sighed. "I hope you boys know what you're doing. That is my daughter I'm putting in your hands."

"She's our sister and we love her. We wouldn't do anything that we did not believe in," Drew said.

Drew sat with JoAnna through the night. His brothers and father took turns joining him, trying to convince him to get some rest, but he couldn't. He had taken on the responsibility of her treatment and he would stay with her until she improved.

By morning, her fever had increased, as had the pain in her chest. The pneumonia seemed to have consumed both lungs.

Again, Drew consulted with his father and brothers, this time adding quinine and digitalis. Drew stayed with JoAnna as Father and William went to work and Christian went to school. He could not leave her even though Father insisted Mother and Olivia could see to her. He sponged his sister's forehead and arms with the cool water. Delirium had set in and her head thrashed from side to side.

She had to respond to this treatment. It was all he knew to do. A small niggling of doubt crept in. If she died, would Father blame him because he forbade the bleeding? He pushed the thought away. He would not let her die.

A knock sounded on the door frame. Olivia stood in the hall, worry lines creasing her brow. "Can I come in and relieve you? You need to get something to eat and some rest."

"No, I want to be here if she needs me."

"You will be of no good to her if you make yourself

sick. I can call you should anything change, and I am very capable of sponging her down."

He smiled. "Thank you, Olivia. I appreciate your concern, but I'm fine."

She walked away, leaving Drew disappointed that she didn't come in and sit with him.

♥♥♥

Olivia longed to be in with JoAnna, but she couldn't as long as Drew remained beside her. She would not give him the opportunity to soften her resolve. The anger that tore at her inside over his fathering a child out of wedlock only added to the guilt. But perhaps that was best, it should help her keep her certitude that Drew needed to marry the mother of his child—the child needed a papa.

Three days had passed, and the Warwick men all huddled together in the small bedroom. Mrs. Warwick sat beside her daughter as hushed tones escaped the circle of doctors. Olivia slipped in beside Mrs. Warwick, taking advantage of the opportunity of spending time with JoAnna. The last few days she'd only managed to steal short periods of time with her old friend, when someone accompanied Drew on the vigil, if he left to get JoAnna's medicines, or if he went downstairs to eat.

Olivia clasped Mrs. Warwick's hand. "Has something happened?"

"JoAnna is not responding to the medicines given to her." Mrs. Warwick glanced over her shoulder at the men. "They are discussing other options."

"We all still stand in agreement that bleeding is not the answer." Drew's voice lifted above the mumbling conference.

Olivia's stomach churned as she looked at her friend whose color looked almost gray and her eyes hallowed. She sent up a prayer for wisdom for the Warwick men as they had to make decisions that would either save JoAnna or cause her to lose her life. She prayed that everything they did would be orchestrated by God and JoAnna would regain her strength and her health.

Another stab of fear surged through her. What if God was so angry with her that He not only ignored her prayers, but kept them from being answered? JoAnna's ashen face reminded her much of Papa's in the days following his apoplexy.

Mrs. Warwick's hand covered Olivia's. "Don't worry my dear. God is in control. My prayer is that He guides my husband and sons to find something that will heal her body."

"But what if they can't?" The words that she had been asking herself were out before she could stop them. "I'm so sorry. I did not mean to ask that."

Mrs. Warwick squeezed Olivia's hand. "The question won't change anything, dear. You can ask." Mrs. Warwick paused and seemed to give deep thought to the question. "The Bible says, '*All things work together for good for them who love God, and for them who are called according to His purpose.*' I have to believe that everything that happens in my life—, no matter how grim it looks, no matter how much pain it causes—will somehow work together for good. I have to trust Him in that. It's all I have."

Olivia paused before slowly asking. "Do you think my loss of memory can work for good?"

The older woman's eyes warmed. "I know it can. It already has. Your presence here has given me strength through all of this, whether you realize it or not."

Tears broke loose and streamed down Olivia's face. The woman was so kind even after her deception, which she felt certain Drew had shared. If she could hope to believe that Mrs. Warwick's words were true, then even her sin against her father could be forgiven. Olivia sniffed and a handkerchief appeared over her shoulder. Looking up, her eyes met Drew's. The lump in her throat enlarged. Before she could retrieve the cloth, he squatted and dabbed the tears staining her face, then gingerly closed her fingers around the handkerchief.

"Don't cry." He didn't let go of the cloth or her hand. "Everything will work out."

His words were so close to his mother's, yet he couldn't have heard them talking. Olivia knew he spoke in far more reaching areas of her life than his mother's, but maybe it was God who really spoke. Why couldn't God be clearer? She just wanted to do His will. If He would only show her the path He desired her to take, she would walk down it.

But then you would need no faith.

Her insides twisted. She wanted faith. But there were so many doubts that bombarded her mind. Thoughts of failure, inadequacy, and unworthiness. How could she have faith?

You are mine whom I have chosen. Your faith will strengthen you.

Drew's brown eyes held hers. She looked down. She didn't even have faith in what she could see, so how could she have faith that God could forgive her? There was so much to forgive.

"Olivia? Are you feeling ill?" Alarm shone in Drew's eyes.

Pulled from her daze, she hurried to relieve him. "I'm fine, truly. I believe I'm just weary."

"Go get some rest, dear. We will keep you informed if anything changes."

Olivia left the room, her heart in more turmoil than

before. Could she really believe that God cared if He took all the people she loved from her?

♥♥♥

She had to do this. Olivia winced as she twisted the back of her hair up and pinned the tresses. The back of her head remained tender where Lloyd had yanked her hair—a good reminder of what he was capable of and why she needed to be careful. This time she left nothing to chance. Instead, she sent a missive to Lloyd, asking him to meet her at the Battery. That was a far enough ride to keep him busy. She'd told him to meet her there at nine, and if she was late, to wait for her.

But still her stomach churned and her knees weakened. She lifted her chin as she stared in the mirror. She could do this. For Papa, Simon, and their family name and business. All was left up to her, and she wouldn't let them down.

Chapter 26

Elbows propped on his legs, Drew rubbed his face. The week had passed with no glimpse of improvement. If anything, JoAnna seemed to weaken. He had done everything he could possibly think of, so why wasn't she getting well?

He lifted her limp body at the shoulders, supporting her head, and pressed a glass of water to her lips. The fluid in her lungs hadn't lessened. Truly, he wasn't sure how she hung on as long as she had. It was as if she lingered at death's door. He knew Father wanted to overrule his decision on bleeding her, but even as his father looked down on his youngest child and pain etched every feature in his father's face, he never said a word.

Though she hadn't died, Drew had wondered what really went through his father's mind. He probably felt that it was too late to bleed her. Every nerve in Drew's body twisted in frustration. He'd done everything, so why didn't she get better? It was as if God had taken the ability to heal out of Drew's hands. He wanted to scream in anger at God.

Father came in and stood next to Drew. "Still no improvement?"

"No, sir. I just don't understand. I've done everything I possibly could. I've scoured medical journals and books on pneumonia and yet she still lies here near death."

"Life and death are not yours to choose, Drew. We use the medicine we've learned, but ultimately it's God who decides our fate."

"But I—"

"But you want to be in control." His father cut him off.

"Don't you?" Drew searched his father's face for the

truth.

"I did once. But when I wasn't much older than you I realized that God does know best. When your mother lost the baby she was carrying, I questioned God. But then you were born and when I held you in my arms and looked down into your face I knew that though I would have loved that other child every bit as much, I could not question God for taking the child home to heaven and giving me you. Because had our other child lived, you wouldn't be standing here today."

"So you can accept JoAnna's death should it come?"

"I will. It won't be easy, but I trust my Savior and His promises."

A soft knock sounded on the door frame. "I don't mean to interrupt." William stepped in, holding out a missive with Lloyd's name on it. "This was just returned to Olivia, and I thought you should see it, Drew."

William handed a missive with Lloyd's name on it to Drew.

Drew frowned. "I'm not opening something she sent to him."

William's gaze went to the missive. "I didn't have any qualms."

Drew flipped the envelope over to see the seal broken. He shot a glare at his brother. "Since when do you open other peoples' mail?"

"Since the delivery boy told me that he was terribly sorry that he couldn't deliver it and to be sure and tell Miss Macqueen so. It seems she told the lad that it was urgent that Lloyd receive it before she visited. He seemed extremely upset that he had not been able to do Olivia's bidding. Said she made it sound imperative. And I thought I'd save you the trouble of having to decide on what was the *right* thing to do. I was concerned you'd choose the wrong answer."

William knew him too well. Drew pulled out the note and read.

Dear Lloyd,

I wish to talk with you about our last encounter. I will not come to your house after what happened and I do not think the Warwicks is an appropriate place either. I thought the east side of the Battery would be suitable. Please be there at four this afternoon. If I am late please wait.

Sincerely,

Olivia

Drew read through the words twice. What did she allude to? His gut churned and bile rose in his throat. Had Lloyd dishonored her? He stood. The letter trembled in his hand as he glanced toward JoAnna. They both needed him.

"You've done all you can do, Drew. Go. Olivia needs you." William seemed to understand his struggle.

William was right. He didn't know what else to do for JoAnna, and his father and William were both as capable as he. His eyes searched out the one line again. *I will not come to your house after what happened.* He had put Olivia in God's hands, as father had suggested, and what good did it do? God had let him down. If he left JoAnna in God's hands would God allow her to die?

William placed his hand on Drew's shoulder and propelled him toward the door. "You need to go and see her. What if when Lloyd doesn't show, she ends up going to his house?"

That took Drew's breath away. He rushed out the back door and saddled Stitches. How did his life get so out of control? He shoved the missive into his pocket and dug his heals into his horse's sides. Not used to the rough handling, Stitches took off at a run. Taking the shortest route, Drew headed for the Battery.

♥♥♥

Olivia stood before Lloyd's house, trembling and telling herself that he was not here, he was at the Battery. Forcing one foot in front of the other, she reached the door and knocked—just to be sure. With no answer, she rushed through the door only to feel a tug of her skirt and hear the sound of ripping fabric. She peered down at her gown to see a three-inch tear in the fabric from catching it on a nail protruding from the doorframe.

There was no time to fret. She hurried forward and gazed around, interested in what might hold the valued item she sought.

She glanced across the room to one of two smallish tables sitting on either side of the sofa. She rushed to the first one. Pulling the drawer open, she peered in at a few scraps of paper before closing it. She scuttled to its mate and tugged on the handle. The drawer was empty. Turning around, she perused the entire room.

Olivia cast an eye over the room turning slowly, taking in each piece of furniture. A mahogany drum table accompanied two chairs on either side of it. What looked to be two small doors were in place of the drawer. She crossed the room. Instead of swinging out, the doors of the table slid along a small track, revealing storage. She bent over to take a closer look inside. Nothing big enough to be the account book. She quickly shut the opening and made her way around the room, lifting cushions, checking behind and under pieces of furniture until she'd exhausted all possibilities in the room.

On her way to the next room, she glanced across the hall to a study. She tiptoed to the archway and darted to the room on the other side of the hall. Foolish of her. Trying to calm her nerves, she reminded herself that no one was here except for her. She skimmed the room. What better place to put an account book? He wouldn't hide it because he'd have no reason to.

Slipping behind the plain pine desk, she opened the middle drawer, flipped through the papers and shut it before moving on to the next. She'd made it through all five drawers, rummaging through stacks of papers and making sure it wasn't lost among them. Built-in shelves decorated one wall, and she meticulously went through each book to be certain she didn't miss it, even though she felt confident she remembered what it looked like.

The clock's pendulum swung back and forth counting off the time. She'd already been there well over half an hour. Down the hall, she entered the dining room. Not many places to hide a book in there. She went to the side table, opened the doors, and began her search.

Despair began to fill her. What if it wasn't Lloyd who had stolen the book? She might never find it and might never be able to do what her father and brother where now unable to do. She walked into the kitchen going through every bin and drawer in hopes of discovering its hiding place. She moved on to the small storage room where linens, food, and other necessities were kept, but she came up with nothing.

If she didn't find any evidence to prove Lloyd's guilt, how would she continue to put him off from marriage while she sought other methods of clearing her family name and seeing justice served? A cold shiver ran down her spine. Could she continue to see him knowing full well she could face beatings, all for the honor of her name? She swallowed, trying to push down her fear.

She loved her father and brother, and if she couldn't

discover proof this way, she would manage to find the courage to do what she must do. Would God help her through anything she could not bear on her own? Did He care for her enough, knowing how she'd gone against her father's wishes, knowing she'd not been honest with the Warwicks about her memory returning, and knowing the person she truly was. She didn't know. She could only hope that the book would surface.

Just as she finished, the clocked chimed. She had to hurry.

Olivia glanced around the rest of the storage room looking for any other place where one might put the book. Satisfied it hadn't been left in the room, she entered the last of the rooms on the main floor—a parlor. The fire still burned in the fireplace and the sweet odor from a pipe filled the air, making her stomach want to rebel. Flashes of memories with Lloyd raced through her mind. She needed to finish looking and get out of the house.

Scanning the room, her gaze landed on a book sitting on the end table. She rushed over, giddy with excitement. It looked to be the account book.

What was that? Pausing and heart racing, she listened for the sound that had caught her attention. A nervous squeal escaped. Her nerves were getting the best of her.

She clasped the book in her hands, drawing it to her chest. She'd found it. Flipping through it, she searched for missing pages. Anything that would tell her that Lloyd had covered his tracks. But it all seemed to be there. She had the proof she needed. Her father, Simon, their business, and the family name could now be vindicated. Lloyd would go to jail. She smiled and turned.

"Ah, you've come to see me, my dear." Lloyd stood in between her and her escape.

"Lloyd." Her heart bucked like a spring foal. She

thought she might swoon.

"So, the ruse is up."

She swallowed—sure her voice would fail her. "Ruse?"

He swept into the room with confidence. "How long have you known?"

"I-I'm sure I don't know what you mean."

He snickered and mocked her. "I'm sure I don't know what you mean." He plucked the book from her hands. "Let me explain then, my dear. You don't have amnesia."

How would she ever talk her way out of this? "I did…and I still don't have all my memories."

"Then why are you here at my home? Did you come to see me?"

Her mouth went dry.

"Ah, I see you are at a loss for words. Well, if you didn't come for this." He tossed the account book into the flames of the fireplace. "Then you must have come for me."

"No!" She ran after the evidence, but he clutched her wrist, jerking her back.

"No, you didn't come to see me? I'm crushed." He grabbed the chest of his shirt in dramatic play, wrinkling the fabric.

Dragging her across the room to the settee he released her hand and swept out his arm in a welcome gesture. "Have a seat, my dear."

Olivia wasn't sure her legs would hold her up much longer, but didn't wish to sit where he could join her. She moved toward the chair. The look in his eyes made the hair on the back of her neck stand up. "Not there. Here." He pointed to the settee.

Next to a table, her hands went behind her to grasp the top and keep her weak knees from buckling.

Lloyd's gaze pinned her where she stood. He prowled

toward her reminding her of a cat stalking its prey. "I said, have a seat."

She couldn't move. Her feet seemed stuck to the floor. If she could just run past him and make it out of the room, maybe she could get to the outside door. Darting to his left, her feet obeyed and raced for freedom. But before she could make her escape, Lloyd towered in front of her. She backed up, hitting the wall.

He leaned in, his hands caging her in. His lips covered hers. She tried to push him away, but he wrapped his arms behind her back and shoulder, pulling her close as he lowered his head again.

His kiss suffocated her. She turned her head, breaking the contact long enough to gasp a breath.

He squeezed her jaw in his powerful hand, locking her where he wanted her. "Oh don't play the shy one now. Any woman who walks into a man's home alone is not so naive. You either wanted me or the book. And since the book is gone, that leaves one option." He laughed and raked his gaze over her with the desire of a starving man.

Her heartbeat thudded so loud in her ears, she had to read his lips. And she knew exactly what he meant.

"Cat got your tongue?" He stroked her arm with the back of his finger. "Let me help you out. It was me you wanted all along—you only played hard to get. You know that's why I stayed away the last few days. I knew it would draw you to me. I knew you would come back to my house." His hot breath brushed over the skin of her neck and she thought she might be sick.

She tried to twist away. "No, you misunderstand."

He tightened his hold and laughed as he dragged her toward the settee. "I understand you, Olivia. You're a woman who needs a real man."

She pawed at his hands, now on her waist. If she could

just get to the door and yell, surely someone would hear her. She pried off his one hand and yanked herself free. He shoved her down. The air whizzed past her. Her back hit the settee cushions. He pinned her with his hands before she could catch her breath. *God, please save me.* It was as much a silent prayer as it was a plea. As she felt the first button rip from her dress, she knew God indeed did not hear or care.

♥♥♥

The Battery showed no sign of Olivia. The chill that swept his body had nothing to do with the crisp air. Lloyd had no way of knowing Olivia wanted to meet him here. So did she go to his house to find him? Sweet merciful heavens, he prayed she would know better.

Turning his mount, he headed to Lloyd's place. Over and over again he told himself that Olivia would not go to Lloyd's if the letter in his pocket implied what he thought it did. But he had to go and check. He loped his horse through the streets as the afternoon sun beat down, praying all would be well.

Stitches' hooves echoed on the street as they devoured the distance between him and his destination. Drew pulled his gelding to a stop, jumped out of his saddle, throwing the reins to the ground, and dashed to the door. *Bang- Bang- Bang.* He pounded on the door—and waited. Seconds felt like minutes. *Bang-Bang-Bang.* He pounded again. Still no answer.

Glancing around, he didn't see anyone around to ask if they'd seen Olivia. He knocked one more time. No one was home. He let out a pent-up breath he didn't even realize he held. Olivia was probably home by now having thought she'd missed Lloyd at the Battery. With relief, he strode back to his horse for the ride home.

She was probably safe at his house and upstairs sitting

with JoAnna. *JoAnna*, he hadn't even thought about her. He needed to get home. Climbing on Stitches, he nudged him into a canter.

Chapter 27

The farther he got from Lloyd's, the more his stomach knotted. Slowing his horse, he glanced back from where he'd come. *God, is that you?* He waited, but there was no writing on the ground, no burning bush, no audible voice. He continued home. A wild imagination that was all it was. Olivia was safe at his house. The only thing he needed to do was get there to see.

Finding peace in his decision wouldn't come. Something in his soul stirred…just like after the earthquake and he knew Olivia was somewhere close. The drive that was in him to find her in the devastation of her home burned within him again. Pulling the reins sharply to the right, he headed back to Lloyd's.

Drew pounded on the door, knowing no one would answer. No one had moments ago, so why did he think that would change? Drew stared at the door handle. Should he enter? If he were to be found inside the house, Lloyd could claim self-defense and do as he wished to him. And Drew no longer believed he was harmless.

Something dark fluttered like a small black flag on the door frame. Drew plucked it off the nail that held it. He lifted it close to his eyes and ran the piece between his thumb and finger. Black silk brocade fabric. Just like the mourning dress Olivia always wore. Was this God's whisper?

♥♥♥

Lloyd seemed to be enjoying his game of cat and mouse—he seemed in no hurry. She would be thankful for every distraction she could find. *There had to be a way to free herself.* The burning book threw heat into the small room. She tried to look for something to grab that she could hit him with.

Olivia heard the knock again. Someone had returned. She tried to scream when she first heard the knocking, but Lloyd had covered her mouth with his hand. She'd bit him with everything she had in her, and he'd hit her so hard across the face that she'd been dazed for a moment. But it hadn't mattered, because whoever had been at the door had left. But now they were back, and she wasn't about to let them leave again.

She drew in a breath to scream but Lloyd clamped her hand over her mouth, holding it there with his beefy hand.

He chuckled. "Go ahead and bite."

She twisted and bucked trying to free herself from him, but her strength was no match. The visitor hadn't knocked again. Tears stung her eyes. "No." She sobbed into her hand pressed against her mouth.

"What's that you said, my dear? I can't seem to understand you." He ran the back of his nails down the side of her neck and looped his fingers into the neckline of her gown and pulled. She could feel the bodice give with the missing buttons. She whimpered. *God, where are you?* Tears spilt down her cheeks and into her hairline. Why would He care about her? He hadn't before. And she certainly hadn't given Him any reason to care about her.

Lloyd lowered his head and she shut her eyes, wishing she could disappear. She couldn't look at him, couldn't stop his advances. But he backed away from her. She opened her eyes and blinked. No, Lloyd was pulled from her.

"Get your hands off me." Lloyd growled the words out.

The dark figure that had freed her drew back his fist and slammed it into Lloyd's jaw. He crumpled to the floor, no longer casting a shadow on her rescuer.

"Drew." She pushed up from the couch and flew into

his open arms. A sob escaped as his arms wrapped around her. Not even a hint of fear surfaced as he held her in his arms.

He lifted her chin with his finger. "He hurt you."

"But you saved me. God sent you. I prayed. But I didn't believe He would. But he did." She hoped he understood her jumbled words. God had truly heard her even when she didn't believe He would save her. Maybe He did care about her.

He gently touched her bruised face. "Did he…hurt you anywhere else?" His eyes locked with hers, the intensity nearly taking her breath away.

"No, just this." Her eyes widened. "The book!" She pushed away and ran to the fireplace. Little remained of the account book. The tears began again. "It's gone. Without those records I'll never be able to see Lloyd jailed."

Drew took off his jacket and wrapped it around her, covering her torn gown and missing buttons. "Let's worry about that another day. We need to get you home."

A groan came from behind them as Lloyd staggered to his feet. He stepped forward putting himself almost nose to nose with Drew. "She isn't going anywhere with you, Warwick." A vein in Lloyd's forehead pulsed. The hate in his eyes prickled her skin, and she backed away.

"I am certainly not leaving her here with you." Drew pushed past him, keeping himself between her and Lloyd.

They had made it out the door when she heard the click.

"Leave her here, Warwick, or you will both be staying."

Drew didn't turn around. He kept walking, only now he had her in front of him.

Olivia glanced over her shoulder and the hairs on her neck stood up. "He has a gun."

"I know. Just stay in front of me and keep walking."
He kept his voice low.

Darkness had fallen, and had it not been for the
cloudless night and the bright moon she wouldn't have been
able to see. Still she hoped she'd not trip as he guided her
forward.

"I am not bluffing, Warwick. I will shoot you. Leave
her here." Lloyd's angry voice boomed on the evening air.

"I'll not leave her here for the likes of you." Drew
pushed her behind the horse as he grabbed for the reins.

"I won't lose her to you again, you hear me?"

A loud bang split the air like the Fourth of July. Drew
held tight to the halter of his horse as it tried to rear. A
second shot boomed and Drew flinched. The horse fought
to get away.

"Let's go. Keep the horse between you and Lloyd." He
pulled the horse forward, and she knew full well he was still
within range of Lloyd's gun.

"You are shot?"

The gun clicked. Lloyd mumbled something.

"No. And I'd like to keep it that way. Hold on to the
saddle as we walk to make sure you keep Stitches between
you and the gun."

"What about you? You're the one he wants to shoot."
Her terror filled voice rose in urgency.

"That's why we need to get out of—"

The blast drowned out the last of his words. Stitches
reared.

♥♥♥

Pain shot through Drew's chest. He tried to stop his
fall, but the ground seemed to rush up to him. As his body
met the pavement, splinters of colors streaked before his
eyes—and then everything went black.

When Drew came to, he was propped up on the sofa,

Olivia sat next to him, and Lloyd stood across the room talking with an unfamiliar man. He was wiry in build and a gun dangled from his fingers.

"Are you hurt?" Drew kept his words low, searching her intently.

"No," she whispered back, squeezing his hand. "But what about you?"

He shifted. "Very sore. How long have I been out?"

"Thirty minutes, maybe. I thought you'd been shot. I was so scared." Olivia's eyes searched his.

"When Stitches reared at the gunshot, he kicked me in the chest. My head hitting the ground is what knocked me out." He glanced over to the two men talking. "Who is Lloyd speaking with?"

"I don't know who he is. He came in with Constance. He was holding another man—with a flour sack over his head—at gunpoint."

"Where are Constance and the other man?"

"They went into another room. Drew, I don't think they will let us go."

The man with the gun headed straight to Drew, his eyes narrowing. "I see you woke up."

Drew stared at him. The man looked faintly familiar, but he didn't remember meeting him. Beside him, Olivia squirmed in her seat. Hoping to calm her fears, he squeezed her hand, but didn't look her way. Instead, he kept his eyes trained on the slender, hawkish man.

"Simon has refused to tell me where the account book is. Since you're here, I'm going to ask *you*—where is it?" He lifted the gun to Drew's face. Drew didn't move a muscle, but out of the corner of his eye he saw Olivia sit forward.

"Simon, my brother?" Urgency laced her voice.

The man kept his gun trained on Drew but flipped his

gaze to Olivia, slowly smirking. "Constance, bring him out." The door opened, and Constance walked out with a lean man whose hands were tied behind his back. She guided the hooded man by his arm until they both stood beside the hawkish-looking man with the gun. That was when Drew saw it—the resemblance in their eyes.

Drew gritted his teeth. "Constance, you said you didn't have any brothers."

Constance laughed. "I must have forgotten about Hal."

"Take the blindfold off Simon." Hal ordered.

Constance stood on her tiptoes and pulled the flour sack from the prisoner's head. Olivia let out a cry. A lump formed in Drew's throat.

"Simon!" Olivia sprung to her feet. She'd not made it two feet when Constance interfered, shoving Olivia back to the couch.

Drew reached out and softened her landing. "Allow her to see her brother. She's believed him dead for nearing two months." For some reason, he'd never believed Simon was dead. Probably because his body was never found, but he'd also struggled with why Simon hadn't been in contact. That wasn't like his friend. But now, seeing him standing there, alive and—for the most part—well, Drew worked hard to keep his composure.

"Hello, sis." Simon smiled bravely.

"No one is seeing anyone." Hal said. "I didn't bring Simon here for a reunion. I brought him here to find the information I'm seeking."

"I don't understand." Olivia scooted to the edge of the sofa as if she was ready to run to her brother. "Lloyd had the account book. Why would you take Simon?"

Hal and Constance both turned to face Lloyd.

Lloyd took a step back. "When Simon came after me the night of the earthquake and you took him away, Hal, I figured you killed him. I needed some insurance. Something to keep you from getting rid of me, too."

"So you have the book." Hal turned the gun toward Lloyd.

"Why did you tell me you killed Simon?" Lloyd stepped back.

"We did that to keep you in line." Constance laughed.

"Where is the book?" Hal waved the gun at Lloyd.

"I don't have it. I threw it in the fire. Ask Olivia and Drew."

"Why would you do that if you kept it for your own safety?"

"Because these two kept trying to steal it. I couldn't risk it getting to the police." Lloyd eyed the gun warily.

"You've become a liability, Lloyd. You bring more problems than you do money. You can't go around shooting at doctors. And now we have a room full of witnesses, thanks to you." Hal squeezed the trigger.

The gun shot boomed. Olivia screamed and Drew sprung off the sofa and flew head first into Hal's belly, knocking him off balance. A jolt of fiery pain shot through the back of Drew's head where he'd hit the road earlier. Hal staggered backwards raising the gun. With everything he had, Drew pulled back and swung his fist into Hal's jaw. His eyes went up into his head. As he fell, Drew snatched the gun from his hands and let him crumple to the floor.

He swung around as he straightened, fearful of what he would see. Lloyd was laying on the ground with blood spreading across his shirt. Olivia had rushed over to untie Simon's hands. Constance was on the floor, face down and squirming, with Simon pinning her down with his knees. When Olivia tossed the rope to Drew, he pushed the gun into his pants and bound Hal. Then he went to Lloyd. He'd been shot at close range, but the bullet had missed his heart.

He reached over and grabbed the flour sack they'd put on Simon's head and pressed the cloth against the wound, trying to stop the flow of blood. He'd more than likely fainted. He certainly hadn't lost enough blood. He turned to Olivia.

"He should recover as long as infection doesn't set in. He's lucky that his friend was a bad shot, because as close as he was, he missed his heart and both the subclavian vein and artery."

Tears glistened in Olivia's eyes, causing Drew's chest to cinch. Did she still care for Lloyd after all he had done? Suddenly proving what a terrible person Lloyd was didn't seem so important. Not when it ended like this. Not when it hurt Olivia. "I'm sorry, Olivia."

A sad smile played on her lips. "Me too. He was a ruthless person, but I am sad to see that he has come to this."

They turned as Simon pulled Constance from the floor and sat her in the chair. He had bound her arms with his belt.

Olivia turned to her. "I don't understand how you could do such terrible things. Don't you care anything about your little boy?"

Constance gave an unladylike snort. "The brat's not mine. I don't ever plan to have kids." Her eyes went to Drew.

"Where you're going I don't think that will be a problem." Drew answered.

Boots pounded down the hall coming from the front of the house. Drew spun around, tightening his grip on the gun and thrusting Olivia behind him. He prayed Hal didn't have more thugs coming in to help.

But instead of more trouble, four police officers and one off-duty dragoon burst into the room.

Chapter 28

It thrilled Drew to have Simon come home with them. God had certainly been looking out for his friend. He'd endured plenty of torture at his captor's hands as they tried to get information out of him. The only thing that truly kept him alive was his insistence that he had hidden evidence that tied them to the embezzlement. They needed him alive to reveal where they could find the incriminating evidence.

But all had ended well, and even if Constance and her brother were never brought to trial for other crimes, they would both be charged with kidnapping, and Hal would face attempted murder. Lloyd would recover, but he probably wouldn't be seeing the outside of jail for a long time. His connection with Hal and Constance would make his sentence harsher as they were suspects in other crimes around the Charleston area. Justice would still be served.

Drew, Olivia, and Simon rode away in a carriage borrowed from Lloyd. As the wheels rolled toward home, Drew's stomach knotted tighter and tighter. He'd been gone from Jo for hours. His heart ached. Her steady decline of the last two days did not bode well for her. He'd done all he could. The feeling of helplessness was the most frustrating feeling he'd ever experienced. But it seemed he'd been facing it a lot lately, first with Olivia, then Simon, and now with Jo.

When they reached the house, Drew had to keep himself from hurrying Olivia along, as anxious as he was to get up to Jo's room. Once inside, Drew took long strides and headed for the stairs, noticing on the way that no one was in the parlor or the great room. He swallowed down the apprehension, forcing himself forward.

Father met him outside the door. He tried to read his father's face.

Father put his hand on his shoulder. "I'm sorry, Drew."

Could she have died while he was gone? He was going to be sick. "I want to see her."

"Of course." Father pushed open the door.

The family had gathered around the bed, cutting off his view of Jo.

"As I was saying, Drew. I'm sorry to break this to you, but God was able to heal JoAnna without you."

"What?" His heart leaped.

Christian turned and smiled, exposing Jo propped up in bed.

"After you left this morning, JoAnna's temperature started to come down. She's improving."

"Then the medicine worked?" Drew had never been so happy to see Jo scowling at all the attention she received as she combed her fingers through her tangled hair.

"I guess you could say that. But I like to think God worked. I hope this makes you see that God doesn't have to have you sitting vigil day and night to heal someone. He did just fine by using your brothers and me to see to her care."

"It seems He's been trying to teach me that lesson a lot lately." Drew had felt so helpless when they were being held by Hal and Lloyd. He worried they wouldn't leave alive. And he was no longer disillusioned enough to believe he did it all himself. God had made the opportunity and Drew had acted on it.

Father grinned. "I hope you are learning and taking notes."

"Oh, I am, Father, I am." And he was. Trusting God with his prayers, problems, and the people he loved would be on the top of his priority list.

A light tapping caught his attention.

"Come in" Mother prompted. Olivia came through the door with Simon behind her. Gasps sounded all over the room.

Drew laughed. "Did I forget to mention that we brought Simon with us? God is still in the miracle business."

Silence reigned over the house except for the ticking of the clock. Olivia sat next to Drew, staring with great interest at her hands. No words would come to her. Simon had given his blessing for the two of them to have some time alone to talk after everyone had headed to bed. Olivia smiled inwardly. Drew seemed as uncomfortable as she did. He looked like a young kid on his first date, awkward and tongue-tied.

"Do you have any questions for me?" Drew turned to her, his brown eyes melting her heart.

There were lots of things she wanted to hear from his lips, even though she felt she knew the answers. "Do you have any feelings for Constance?"

"No."

She frowned. "Just no? You don't have anything else to add?"

"I believe that was a yes or no question." He shrugged. "The answer is no."

"But I saw from my window you embracing her in the back yard."

"Olivia, what you saw was a manipulative woman who told me her child was sick and then threw herself against me. I didn't know what else to do. Now, can I ask you something?"

She frowned, but nodded.

"Why wouldn't you believe me after you started remembering?"

Olivia looked back down at her hands. "I was so confused, Drew. I felt like I had brought all this on by my disobedience with my father. You know I almost killed him before we had ever started courting."

"You, Olivia? You've never told me that? Are you sure that maybe your mind isn't playing tricks on you?"

"I'm sure. I could never talk about it. I felt so guilty. Papa saw something bad in Lloyd that I couldn't see. He told me he wanted me to stop seeing him, but I refused. One night Papa ended up in the hospital and nearly died because of me. We'd gotten into the same argument that we'd been getting in—, that I needed to stop seeing Lloyd. He got so upset his heart nearly gave out. If he'd have died, it would have been my fault."

"But he didn't die and you changed. You obeyed in the end."

"Only because Lloyd had been unfaithful and I found out."

♥♥♥

Drew decided not to tell Olivia what Constance had confided in him after they'd taken Lloyd off to the hospital. He supposed Constance shared it with him to relieve her conscience. Lloyd had been the father of her unborn child and he had shunned her when he found out she was pregnant. The man deserved as many years as the judge threw at him. But Livvy didn't need to know about Lloyd and Constance. It would serve no purpose to tell her. Drew shook his head, amazed at how God had brought them together after they'd both been hurt by someone they were seeing.

He gazed at his Livvy, compassion weighing heavy in his heart, seeing she still carried the burden of her father. "But you still repented and God forgave you."

"You don't know what it's like living with that guilt.

You know even when I couldn't remember anything, I had this heavy burden. I felt as if I had brought about my family's death." She swallowed and he could see she tried hard not to cry. But a rogue tear escaped and slid down her cheek.

Drew wrapped his arms around her. "I hope you see now that God doesn't work that way. He doesn't punish you by taking other's lives. You punished yourself. He just wanted to welcome you home like the prodigal son and forgive you."

She sniffed. "Can you forgive me?"

"For what?"

"For all the terrible things I said about you and about your family. I accused all of them of lying. I said some terrible things about you, Drew…and then when I did remember the truth, I didn't come forward with it. I lived a lie every day I was here. It was wrong of me. I didn't trust you and I didn't trust God."

"Olivia, every word you spoke against me has been forgiven and forgotten, never to be brought up again."

"I don't deserve you."

Drew laughed. "It's I that doesn't deserve you, my dear. I've had my own Goliaths to slay."

He slipped off the couch and onto one knee.

Olivia's hands went to her chest.

"I had planned a special evening for Friday, September third, but the earthquake struck and stole that from me…from us." He reached into his shirt pocket, feeling for the ring that he had held close to his heart the last two months and pulled it out. "Olivia, I love you with all my heart. Will you marry me?"

Tears streamed down her face.

He held his breath. Had he asked too soon? She still had mourning to do. He took her hand in his. "I know we will have to wait, but if I could have your promise, waiting will be a joy."

A beautiful smile spread over her face. "I hope someday to remember every moment that I lost. I may never remember fully our time together. However, I can promise you this, that even when I didn't remember you, I learned to love you all over again. It wouldn't matter wherever we met or whatever the time or place, I would always fall in love with you."

Hope took wing in his heart, rising like a majestic soaring eagle. He had to hear her say yes once and for all. "And so your answer is?"

"Unless my memory fails me…" She giggled. "The answer is *yes*."

He leaned forward and covered her lips with his. She was his. God hadn't taken her from him, it was all in His timing.

Epilogue

Ten months later

Standing beside his new bride in the study of his parent's home, Drew opened the ancestral wedding book and took out his fountain pen.

Olivia looked up at him. Soft wisps of her light brown hair escaped from her veil and framed her silky skin. "What are we doing?"

As much as he had enjoyed the wedding, Drew couldn't wait to get back to his parent's for this moment. Something that he'd looked forward to since he'd met Olivia. "Just adding our name to the family wedding book."

Olivia stepped closer to the heirloom. He waited as she inspected the pages.

She flipped the pages back to the beginning. "Who are Royce and Brithwin? Were they really married in 1398?"

"They sure were." Drew grinned with pride. "Almost 500 years ago. The book has been handed down to the eldest Warwick boy for hundreds of years now."

She gingerly touched the delicate pages. "How fascinating that it would remain intact that long and never be lost to a fire or a flood, or even just lost through time."

"Every owner of this book has realized the importance of keeping it safe. It was given to them on the day of their marriage." He pointed to an inscription at the top of the page. *So Jacob served seven years for Rachel, and they seemed only a few days to him because of the love he had for her.* Genesis 29:20

"How very beautiful. It sure makes me wonder what they were like."

"I know that Brithwin was a strong woman." Drew

paused and smiled at his new wife. "Much like you."

A pink hue rushed to her cheeks. "I'm not that strong."

Drew brushed the back of his hand against her cheek. "My love, you are stronger than any woman I know."

Olivia dropped her head, but not before the pink hue had turned to a deep red. She peeked up from under her brows. "I'm glad you think so."

"You are a woman much like Lady Brithwin, me thinks."

"And how would you know so much about your ancestor?" She gave him a challenging look.

He grinned. "They had such a deep love that they tucked letters and love notes in the book for safekeeping. Those letters gave me a glimpse into Royce and Brithwin's lives."

"It sounds so romantic. They must have had a special love."

Drew put his arms around his new bride. She tipped her head up and he gazed into the eyes that could steal his breath away. "No more special than ours."

A Note from the author.

I spent many enjoyable weeks researching the Charleston earthquake of 1886. While doing my research I came across some wonderful eye witness reports. I've tried to bring these to life in Shattered Memories so you can experience what the people of Charleston suffered. Everything you read about the earthquake is from people who lived through this terrible disaster, from the sounds they heard, to the reactions of the people. I think one of the things that touched me the most when reading about this catastrophe was the way the people of Charleston sang in the midst of the chaos to calm and comfort one another.

Debbie Lynne Costello has been writing since the young age of eight. She went to college for journalism. She enjoys medieval settings and settings set in ninteenth century Charleston, South Carolina. She loves the Lord and hopes to touch people's lives through her stories. Debbie Lynne lives in the beautiful state of South Carolina with her husband of 35 years, their 4 children, Tennessee Walking horses, Arabians, miniature donkey, four dogs, and cat.

If you enjoyed reading Shattered Memories, one of the best ways to let me know and say "thank you" is to write a favorable review on Amazon as well as other sites. Thank you so much!

I love hearing from my readers. If you have any comments or questions please feel free to contact me at debbielynnecostello@hotmail.com.

Catch me online at:
My website: DebbieLynneCostello.com
Facebook: https://www.facebook.com/debbielynnecostello
Twitter: https://twitter.com/DebiLynCostello